BULL STREET

DAVID LENDER

BRINDLE
PUBLISHING
BP

Published by Brindle Publishing

ISBN: 978-0-615-49244-5

For Mom and Dad

Also by David Lender

Trojan Horse
The Gravy Train

About the Author

David Lender is the bestselling author of the thrillers, Trojan Horse and The Gravy Train. He writes thrillers set in the financial sector based on his over 25-year career as a Wall Street investment banker. He draws on an insider's knowledge from his career in mergers and acquisitions with Merrill Lynch, Rothschild and Bank of America for the international settings, obsessively driven personalities and real-world financial intrigues of his novels. His characters range from David Baldacci-like corporate power brokers to Elmore Leonard-esque misfits and scam artists. His plots reveal the egos and ruthlessness that motivate the players in the financial sector, as well as the inner workings of the most powerful of our financial institutions. More background on David and his writing can be found at www.davidlender.net.

Excerpt from *Vaccine Nation*

An excerpt from *Vaccine Nation*, David Lender's new thriller, follows the text of *Bull Street*. *Vaccine Nation* is the story of an award-winning documentary filmmaker who uncovers evidence linking the US vaccination program with the autism epidemic, and then races to expose it before a megalomaniacal pharmaceutical company CEO can have her killed.

Acknowledgements

Thank you to all who read and commented on the manuscript and drafts of individual scenes: Terry Collins, Cindy Begin, Lisa Begin-Kruysman, Rich Kruysman, Tina Bachetti, Jon Lender, Paul Lender, Mark Lender, Penny Page, Manette Loudon, Shaun Strub, John Short, Russ Deihl, Michele Young and Frances Jalet-Miller.

Thank you again to those who transcribed and typed the early drafts: Julie Widmer, Madelynne Sansevere and Marcie Herkner.

Thank you to the team at Createspace.

Thank you to Cheryl Bradshaw for your copy editing.

And thank you again to Dad for the photo on the cover. I wish you could see it.

CHAPTER ONE

New York City. Before the global financial crisis.

"If I don't have a job by April, I'm not getting one," Richard said. "At least that's the adage at B-school."

"And this the Ides of March," Dad said.

That ominous reference hit home. Richard's guts rumbled.

Richard Blum and his dad, Hank, sat in a Greek diner in downtown Manhattan near Wall Street. It was two blocks from Walker & Company, Richard's first interview of the day, and four blocks from Dad's insurance convention. Richard played with the tag on his teabag, preoccupied; this five-day trip to New York was his last chance to salvage a job on Wall Street from an otherwise failed recruiting season. It was opportune that Dad and he could squeeze in breakfast together while Dad was in town from St. Paul at the same time for his convention. They sat at a booth across from the counter, leaning in toward each other so they could hear over the clink of china, barked orders, the clang of spatulas on the grill. Richard savored the clamor and aromas of the place. It had a casual comfort, a folksy smell of eggs and home fries Richard knew Dad must be enjoying. He eased up his cuff to check his watch.

"You getting concerned?" Dad asked.

"It's never over until you call it quits, I guess, but in finance parlance I'm a wasting asset."

"Not what I asked. You worried?"

"Sweating bullets."

He looked at Dad's clothes: cotton/polyester button-down, spot on his pin-dot tie, suit shiny from wear. He smiled; it made him comfortable, too, warmed him inside. He glanced down at his own clothes. He was wearing $3,500 in Polo Ralph Lauren. The topcoat he'd sprung for as part of this last-ditch effort to land the big one was dragging on the floor. A barometer for how it was going.

"You must be making progress, though."

"I've struck out in all my on-campus investment banking interviews—the few I've gotten."

Dad just nodded, taking it in, thinking. "Anything useful to you come of them?"

"Only that Michigan's a second-tier school for the Wall Street firms. The entire recruiting season of interviews only netted all our MBAs twelve investment banking second-round callbacks on campus, four trips to New York, one offer."

"That's at least one." Dad, trying to be positive. He smiled, then squinted and pursed his lips. "There must be others coming to campus."

"No. It's too late in the season for first rounds on campus." Richard resisted the urge to squirm in his seat. "So that's it for anything through the Placement Office."

Dad winced. He looked down at his plate, hesitated, then back in Richard's eyes. "Now this trip," he said, continuing to eye him. Richard first thought Dad's expression meant he realized this was Richard's last gasp. Now he had an inkling maybe there was more to Dad's look than that.

"Yeah, eleventh-hour effort. In New York to pound the pavement, follow up on cold letters attaching my resume. See if I can beat down some doors."

Dad leaned back. "So how's the trip going?" Richard felt him zeroing in, watching him.

"Four screening interviews, down to my last two." Richard started twirling the tag from his teabag again, beginning to get anxious, knowing today's interview was his only real chance.

"Remember *A Mathematician's Apology?*" Dad said. His gaze was now locked in on Richard, intent. Richard swallowed.

"How could I forget? It's been a big influence on me."

It was the book Richard and Dad had both read as he headed to college. Richard was turning the corner from defiant teenager, starting to get close with Dad again, this time man-to-man. When Richard landed the job after college writing ad copy at McAlister & Flinn, still living at home, he and Dad developed a working relationship. Dad helped out as proof-reader and critic. Richard learned Dad actually had business wisdom to impart; insurance was at least on the same hemisphere as writing copy to convince people to buy steak sauce or annuities. Business became a common language and culture that kept them up late nights, talking about interest rates, the CPI. And eventually, over a scotch now and then, they discussed the novels of Elmore Leonard or Trollope, the music of Mozart and Beethoven. Richard thought back to *A Mathemetician's Apology*, said as if reciting, "Three kinds of people. The first, I do what I do because I have an unusual talent for it. The second, I do what I do because I do lots of things pretty well and this was as good a choice as any. And the third, I don't do anything very well and I fell into this."

"I'm a good fidelity bond underwriter, and I could've done a lot of other things probably just as well. What you're going after is a world I don't understand much about. But if you think you have it, go for it." Still searching Richard's face.

"Yeah. I can do this." Telling himself, needing it for this interview.

"So don't give up. But don't compromise who you are and where you came from. Don't let Wall Street turn your head."

"Any other advice?"

"Well, since you ask," Dad said, now giving him that half-smile he wore when he launched a zinger but still wanted to show affection. "All I've heard is excuses. This isn't like you. Get primal. Think like these Wall Street guys, like a caveman who needs to win over a woman or he can't procreate. Put some oomph into it. You're on your own; nobody can do it for you."

They sat in silence a moment, Richard looking at the half-smile still on Dad's face. Dad was right. *It's all up to me.*

Dad said, "What? You think I can't still kick your butt?"

Richard felt his throat thicken. "Thanks."

"You're very welcome."

Richard looked at his watch. Dad grabbed the check, said, "Get going. Give yourself some time to collect your thoughts."

"Why don't you let me get this?"

"When you're a mogul you can buy me dinner." They both stood. Dad stuck out his hand. They shook, then hugged.

"Love to Mom," Richard said.

"Call her. Tell her yourself."

Richard nodded. "Any final thoughts?"

"If you fall flat you know you can always come home to regroup." He smiled. "But you aren't going to let that happen. Both you and I know that, don't we?"

#

Richard looked at his watch: 7:45. *He's late.* He sat in Walker & Company's reception area at 55 Water Street, waiting for his interview with François LeClaire. And he'd rushed through breakfast to get here by 7:30. He caught himself clenching and unclenching his fingers into his palms, forced himself to relax them.

Great. More time to ponder the imponderable.

Richard picked up a magazine from a Sheraton end table next to the antique Chippendale chair he sat in. *Fortune.* The current issue; Harold Milner was on the cover. He'd also graced the covers of *Forbes* and *Financier* magazines over the last decade. In the cover picture for the article, "Financial Engineering on Steroids," Milner stood in a conference room at Walker & Company. It was probably the very one Richard sat outside now. The picture showed Milner framed against the backdrop of the Brooklyn Bridge, the back door entrance to Wall Street. Inside the issue Richard knew the first page of the article showed a photograph of Jack Grass and Mickey Steinberg standing on either side of Milner. He was Walker & Company's most important and prolific client. Richard knew all about these guys. He'd been Googling them before Google was a verb.

The *Fortune* article got it mostly right, although it was obvious to Richard he'd done more research on Milner than its author. Milner, then Chief Financial Officer of Coastal+Northern Corporation, had taken his entrepreneurial leap at 40 years old. He'd cashed in his C+N stock options for $1.5 million, used them for his first deal and never looked back. Now his $7 billion private empire employed 17,000 people in 22 states. The article called him brilliant, eccentric, wildly creative, and a compulsive workaholic—one of the most powerful and wealthy entrepreneurs in the U.S.

Richard looked into the open door of the conference room at the table that was set for breakfast. He imagined Milner, Jack and Mickey discussing a deal over breakfast and felt an airiness in his stomach.

Richard saw a young guy, probably an Associate, walking toward him. He had his jacket off, a pile of papers and some presentation books in his hands, quick pace, looking tense. *Yeah, an Associate, probably first year.* He hurried past Richard and peered into the conference room. Seeing no one there, he sat down in the chair across from Richard, apparently waiting. He was twitchy and sweaty. It made Richard feel sorry for him. The guy's papers started sliding out of his lap. Richard reached out to help him but the guy shook Richard off, reined them in himself.

Richard now saw the guy checking him out, probably guessing why Richard was here.

"Who you waiting for?" he asked.

"François LeClaire." Richard saw his face show recognition, then his forehead wrinkle with tension. The guy sighed and leaned back in his chair. At that moment his Blackberry vibrated in his belt and he sat up with a start. Richard heard someone talk fast and loud on the other end of the call. The guy left in a hurry, papers rustling. Richard got the uncomfortable sense that this could be him in a few months, stealing a moment of relaxation as he waited for somebody to yell at him about a column of numbers that didn't add up.

The elevator door opened and Richard turned to see Harold Milner, the man himself, walking toward him. Milner carried himself with an understated manner that somehow magnified his power and importance. Richard instinctively stood, and then a surge of adrenaline froze him in place like a ten-year-old meeting Babe Ruth. He realized as Milner approached he was as big as the Babe up close, too. Six feet five or so, thick in the chest like a football lineman, massive hands. Trademark shaved head. He cruised up to Richard. "Harold Milner," he said, extending his hand. Just like that.

Richard felt himself starting to speak without knowing what would come out. He said something gushy after introducing himself, his voice faint as he said, "Mr. Milner."

"Call me Harold." Milner looked into the empty conference room, then sat where the Associate had moments earlier. He glanced down at the copy of *Fortune* Richard still clutched. "And I'm not as bad as they say," he said. "Or as smart."

Richard smiled, more relaxed now. His body had unfrozen and he sat back down, now sitting with Harold Milner like they were shooting the breeze. "I'm not sure I believe that."

"Which? Bad or smart?"

"Smart. I'd say you've done okay . . . Harold." 'Harold' came out haltingly, Richard trying it out.

"Yeah, well, 'with money in your pocket, you are wise and you are handsome and you sing well, too.'"

"F. Scott Fitzgerald?"

"Yiddish proverb. Don't believe everyone's press clippings."

"Hard to believe you've just been lucky."

"No, but the stuff in that article is downright silly."

Richard smiled. "You've done some interesting deals."

"Yeah, but this 'steroids' nonsense is just to sell magazines. My approach is about as low tech as they come."

"I don't know. On the Brennan deal it was pretty exotic the way you set up that special-purpose subsidiary to finance the receivables on the McGuffin division."

Miller gave him a shrug and a look that said, "So?"

"So, that extra financing gave you about a twenty percent price advantage over the other bidders. It got you the deal."

"Maybe."

"And on Dresner Steel, the way you sold off two of the divisions and merged the rest with Tilson Manufacturing and Milburg Industries within a year. How many guys could pull that off and still keep the tax-loss carryforwards intact?"

Milner looked at Richard as if pondering something for a moment. He said, "Good insights. I'm impressed. But I'll let you in on a little secret. I don't consider I've done anything particularly imaginative or creative in my life. I stick to simple, risk-averse basics. You know who Vince Lombardi was?"

"I'm from Minnesota. Our state seal has an image of the Packers kicking the Vikings' asses."

Milner smiled. "I'm like Lombardi's Green Bay Packers. We come up to the line and crouch in position for an end sweep. The defense knows it's probably an end sweep because it's second and seven, and, besides, Lombardi's only got ten plays in his playbook anyhow. Whattaya think we do?"

"Throw an eight yard pass to the opposite sideline."

"End sweep, perfectly done. Seven yards every time. Nothing exotic, just basic execution."

Richard wanted to ask him if this 'aw shucks' routine disarmed CEOs whose companies he was trying to take over, but settled for: "Good story. Works for me."

Milner put his elbow on the end table, cupped a big hand over his mouth. Richard could see him smiling with his eyes, apparently thinking. He remained silent, then: "Are you new?"

"So new I'm not even here."

Milner scrunched his eyebrows like he was puzzled.

"I'm waiting here for an interview," Richard said. Milner smiled with his eyes, his hand over his mouth again. "I think the guy who was supposed to meet you was just called away."

"Well, then you stepped in and did the job. You got my vote." He stood up and held out his hand, a big smile on his face. Richard got up and shook hands with him again. "Welcome to the firm, Richard," Milner said.

Richard laughed. Not a nervous one because he was freaked out that he was actually bullshitting with the most famous guy in finance. He just laughed because it was funny, Milner telling him to call him Harold, putting him at ease, joking around. Not some stiff, but a regular guy.

They were still shaking hands, Richard laughing, when Jack Grass and Mickey Steinberg walked up. There he was, standing among the guys who'd done 15 major deals together over the last 20 years, not including scores of financings, refinancings, divisional divestitures and add-on acquisitions; a mini industry, the three of them.

Richard heard Jack and Mickey greet Milner, saw them shake hands, exchange a few good-natured barbs. But not clearly, not like it was real, because he was now somehow out of his body watching from a distance. He zeroed in on Milner, larger than life again. The casualness that said he didn't need to make an effort to impress was still there. Now Richard took in Mickey, Walker's genius in Mergers and Acquisitions, with frizzy Jewish hair, sleepy eyes, who droned on in a monotone. Mickey was probably laying out some wisdom, because Milner gave him his complete attention, nodding as Mickey spoke. Now Richard studied Jack, the firm's Chief Executive Officer. Jack stood smoothing the peaked lapels on his European-inspired suit, looking artfully put together from his French tie and matching pocket square down to his Italian loafers. Jack's eyes moved around like a big jungle cat's. Watching Milner, taking in everything, now sizing up Richard, now back to Milner and Mickey. His athletic build showed in the close-fit suit, shirt cuffs protruding Cary Grant-like from his sleeves, hair razor-cut, Palm Beach tan standing out against his white collar and cuffs.

They walked into the conference room, Milner smiling and lifting a hand in a restrained wave goodbye to Richard. Jack Grass saw it and glanced back at Richard, seeming to make a mental note.

Richard looked into the open door of the conference room. A mahogany table was set for three, bedecked with crystal, china, formal silver and fresh linen. Its subdued sheen and worn edges showed graceful age, complemented by the oriental rug it sat on. The aroma of rosemary and eggs mixed with some other scent he couldn't identify emanated from an unseen kitchen.

Richard wished he could listen in on their meeting, be in the room with them. Hell, he wanted more than anything to *be* one of them, particularly Milner. He was a big part of why Richard was here.

Just as they sat down at the table to breakfast, a trim man in a double-breasted suit walked into the reception area with an air that he owned the place. Richard took him in: slicked-back hair, pocket square that matched his bold Hermes tie, English-striped shirt with white cuffs showing below his jacket sleeves. *A Jack Grass wannabe?* He walked erect, lips pursed, projecting arrogance. *LeClaire, no doubt.* He'd be the most important person in Richard's life for the next hour.

"François LeClaire. Sorry I am late." He smiled, but modestly, as if to overdo it would wrinkle his suit. His accent had the exaggerated edge of a cartoon character, almost too pronounced to be real. "Conference call to Europe. Unavoidable," now adopting a manner like Richard, of course, knew the import of all this. He shook Richard's hand like he wanted to leave no doubt that he understood the concept of a firm American handshake. He extended his other hand in the direction of the offices with the formality of a Swiss hotelier.

Here we go. Richard resisted the urge to peek back at Milner.

#

Harold Milner looked down at the rosemary and goat cheese omelet on his plate, then at his hands; the meaty hands of a carpenter or mason. But for some turns in his life, that could've been him. It was something he tried hard never to forget. He couldn't help laughing at himself now: he was uneasy, and trying to hide it. He'd been at the deals business a long time. Lots of tense moments, tough deals, pressure. But he rarely felt like this.

He looked over at Jack and Mickey. They sure took Milner back. Twenty years of dreaming, manipulating, trial and error, making it work. Elbow-to-elbow, the three of them. Jack, the ideas guy, sitting there now, puffing and blowing, preening himself in that $5,000 custom suit. Mickey the planner and thinker. Jack should thank God he had Mickey. He made Jack's schemes real. And it really wasn't just Mickey's brains and technical mastery; it was Jack's crazy ideas, because without Jack's dreaming Mickey wouldn't have had anything to breathe life into.

Before he met these two he was just a scrappy guy doing pint-sized deals. Then he met Jack, and a month later, this new guy he had in tow, Steinberg—Mickey, not a nickname for Michael, just Mickey—short, plump and unathletic. They both showed up at Milner's New York office in that dowdy building he'd started out in at 8th Avenue and 34th Street. Smelled like the Chinese restaurant downstairs. Jack grinning his golden-boy grin in a $2,000 English-cut suit, still only 31 years old and Walker's top producer, already running the firm's Corporate Finance Department. Mickey blinking slowly, shaking hands more firmly than Milner expected from someone with that weasely face and punch-drunk demeanor.

Jack pitched the Caldor idea almost before they sat down, itching to get at it. Jack talking nonsense about buying a billion dollars of debt owed the retailer Caldor by its credit card customers for 20 cents on the dollar. Mickey explaining that Caldor was near-bankrupt and desperate for cash. Jack saying Caldor's credit card customers would ultimately pay their bills, Milner would make a killing. Mickey laying out how to finance the deal. Back and forth, Milner's eyes shooting from one to the other like at a tennis match. Then Jack telling Milner all he had to kick in was $10 to $12 million, maybe make 20 to 30 times his investment in a few years. Milner thinking, *that* got his attention, whoever these guys were.

It had turned out to be a recipe for an incredible home run: Milner had invested $16 million of cash, almost all he had laying around, and borrowed the rest to buy Caldor's credit card receivables. After paying off his lenders in two years, Milner had netted $455 million. Jack and Mickey had propelled Milner into the big time. Within a year he bought a Learjet and apartments in New York, Palm Beach and Los Angeles. He moved his office to the penthouse of the Helmsley Building; the anchor of the 45th

Street entrance to New York's power alley business district on Park Avenue. And that had only been the beginning.

But now, this was the end.

"I wanna do a deal on Southwest Homes," Milner said.

He saw Jack perk up across the table like a dog sniffing a bone. Mickey was characteristically quiet, eyes blinking. Milner sipped his water, swallowing hard without worrying about that crinkly sound he made. One of the keys to his humble roots that Mary Claire always cast him a disapproving eye about at dinner parties. He didn't have to try to impress these guys.

Mickey said, "Mind if I ask why?"

Milner saw Jack look sideways at Mickey, as if to try to shut him up.

"I don't like the business anymore. Any schmoe who can sign an "X" on a mortgage application can buy a house he can't afford."

Jack said, "Yeah, a real bubble mentality."

Milner nodded.

Jack said, "This round of musical chairs won't last very long. Better pick your seat before the music stops. Remember when the internet stock bubble popped?"

Milner felt himself smile beneath his hand, knew it was showing in his eyes. This was Jack at his best: always selling. Milner would miss Jack and Mickey in a way, but they'd become his chaperones on a trip to the dark side. Churning out deals together that just moved pieces around on the table; they were all making piles of money but not creating anything. He'd made a commitment to himself that he'd go back to building companies again, not this "financial engineering on steroids" crap the magazines lauded him for. Even that kid in the lobby only talked about his deals that busted up instead of built things. Milner looked over at Mickey. "Mickey, whattaya think?"

"You want to sell it to a corporate buyer, or do an initial public offering?" Mickey asked.

"Take it public—the IPO."

"The IPO market's still shooting out deals like a baseball pitching machine," Jack said. "And homebuilding stocks are red hot."

"Everything's hot. Maybe too hot," Milner said.

"Yeah, white hot. All the more reason to unload a chunk of Southwest onto the public," Jack said.

Why did Jack make even the right answer sound like bullshit half the time?

Mickey said, "It's worth about $1.5 billion. How much do you want to sell?"

Milner put down his fork, rested his elbows on the table and put his hand over his mouth, taking his time. He glanced over at Jack and saw him observing. Milner said, "All of it." He saw the muscles in Jack's jaw flex. Then he saw Jack inhale, sensed the animal arise beneath that bespoke tailoring. *Okay, Jack—ready, shoot, aim.*

"We can sell 100%," Jack said. "A number of 100% IPOs have gotten done lately. And with home prices setting new records each month, and getting a mortgage as easy as eating popcorn, the public markets are bidding up homebuilders' stocks like crazy."

Milner said, "I've noticed." He looked at Mickey.

Mickey said, "In general, Jack's right. But if you sell it all in the IPO you'll take a major discount versus selling, say, half. If you sell it all, people ask: 'What's wrong with it that *he* doesn't want to keep any?'"

"I know. But I like the idea of selling it all. How big a discount would I take?" Milner felt his stomach tighten.

Milner saw Jack and Mickey take time to look at each other. Milner felt himself smiling again. He had to admit he loved watching these guys, had since the beginning. Back and forth. Jack trying to urge Mickey with a glance and body language, Mickey considering his answer, blinking, contemplating.

Mickey said, "I'd say at least 300 million dollars."

Jack didn't move.

Milner shrugged, then nodded. "Done."

Jack looked over at Milner with his best shit-eating grin.

Milner looked down, observed his hands again. In a way, he'd get to be a carpenter after all. And put in an honest day's work.

#

In LeClaire's office, Richard settled into a reproduction of the Chippendale antique chairs in the lobby. He looked around. It was a real office, not some eight-by-twelve hole. Mahogany desk and credenza, Oriental rug, textured fabric wall covering, and tasteful print curtains. LeClaire was a Senior Vice President, which had its status, but his title aside, what Richard had heard was right: Walker, privately-held, still had the appointments of an old Wall Street firm that even Goldman Sachs and Morgan Stanley had given up years ago.

Richard hoped to exchange some small talk, loosen himself and LeClaire up. He checked out LeClaire's desk. The guy was a neatnick, ordered piles of documents on either side, more on his credenza. A pencil holder with a dozen or so sharpened #2s. Pictures of his wife and it looked like three kids.

"Can we get right to it? I've got another conference call in an hour and I need to prepare before it," LeClaire said.

"Sure," Richard said. *This is it; don't blow it.*

LeClaire held up Richard's resume. "Here is what this tells me: nice middle-class kid from the Midwest; public high school, including the obligatory sports. Undistinguished undergraduate school—Michigan State was a choice I would like to understand—then on to a successful career track in advertising . . . how am I doing?" His thick French accent had a cadence that emphasized the syllables on the up-beat.

"Okay, you're getting to the part that should be more interesting to you, I . . . ."

LeClaire talked over Richard, "You say you had some successful campaigns. 'Wow! What a Whopper', 'Morton steak sauce sizzles!', and the Michelin tire 'Baby' campaign—I do not recognize any of those. And you won some award."

"A Clio isn't just 'some award.'" *That was like saying Institutional Investor's "Deal of the Year" award was like a gold star in grammar school. Who does he think he is?*

LeClaire now put Richard's resume down on the desk and looked at it. "But it was not sufficient to achieve one of the top American business schools that Wall Street gets its real talent from. Do you disagree?"

"I see a different picture. A hard-working kid with solid Midwestern values excels in public school . . . . "

LeClaire interrupted, "Have you ever met anybody from your American boarding schools?"

"A few, but . . . ."

"It is my experience that they are better educated."

The hell they are. Could this guy be more of a stiff? "Public schools teach people how to think, too. Besides I've met some boarding school types who may know how to say the right thing, but haven't had an original thought in their lives."

"Point taken. So why are we here, thinker?" He was sitting up straight in his chair, hands clasped and resting on his desk blotter.

Richard leaned in toward him for emphasis. He felt himself starting to breathe faster. "Because I gave up a promising career in advertising . . . ." He heard his voice rising.

"How much were you making?"

"A hundred and twenty thousand."

"That is considerable for advertising. They pay poorly."

"I know. I was worth more. But I still gave that up to—"

"To crunch numbers until 2 a.m. most nights, put together pitch books for people like me you will perhaps learn to hate, and if you are very, very lucky, carry bags for senior officers such as Jack Grass and Mickey Steinberg?"

"No, to learn the business. To be *like* Jack Grass or Mickey Steinberg, or if I can pull it off, like the guy they're outside having breakfast with, Harold Milner."

"That is ambitious."

"I am ambitious. And Milner's only one of the deals guys I studied, who got me interested in this business."

Richard realized he had leaned in so far forward that his hands were on the edge of the desk.

"Today it is my job to see if you are ambitious enough." LeClaire slouched in his chair and smiled for the first time.

Richard now felt perspiration on his upper lip and realized his pulse had quickened. He used the pause to settle back into his chair. He'd let this guy get under his skin right away and he was disappointed in himself. *Calm down, this isn't gonna get it done. You need to get past him.* He smiled back, then tried to lighten it up. "So did I get past the first hurdle?"

"You did that two weeks ago."

Richard raised his eyebrows as if to ask how.

"You beat down the door."

"I guess I was a little persistent. It took a few calls."

"Six. So, my young friend, let's talk."

This time he smiled like he wasn't afraid it would make him soil himself. Maybe it meant LeClaire had just been testing him. But 'my young friend?' *Gimme a break.* The guy was barely 35. *At least he didn't call me 'old sport.'*

Then he said, "You know what? I have time. Would you like something to drink?"

"Coffee would be great."

LeClaire seized the phone handset and chattered in staccato French to someone named Marcel. He turned back to Richard. "So how is it going?" Now warm, like they were colleagues. Richard couldn't figure this guy.

Richard said, "I haven't got the job offer I want and it's mid March. Two fallbacks. Corporate finance offers from BFGoodrich and Procter & Gamble. Good jobs, but backups."

"Why do you think that is?"

"You said it yourself. My resume doesn't fit the mold and I didn't go to a B-school that's a main Wall Street feeder."

"Your resume has neither a comfortable, aged patina nor crisp, institutional packaging."

Richard chuckled at that. "That's one way of putting it."

LeClaire laughed, too. "Something I wrote down from an article on recruiting. It sounds even stupider said aloud than read." Finally starting to let his hair down? LeClaire said, "You have no idea how sick I am of seeing these pretty boys come in here and fill me full of perfectly useless theories and impractical business school nonsense." His face softened, like he really was loosening up.

LeClaire continued, "But when it comes down to this business, real financiers feel something in the pits of their tummies when they think about money and bonds and stocks. That has nothing to do with business school theory."

Somebody knocked on the door. "Who is it?" he called.

"Marcel," came the answer in heavily accented English. A demure woman in a white outfit entered and served them from a tray. It was real china. Richard took a long, grateful swallow of coffee and noted that LeClaire had chosen tea. LeClaire seemed to go someplace else as he took his first sips. He turned and admired the photos on his credenza.

"Three kids?" Richard asked.

LeClaire swung back, looking like he'd been caught. "Yes. Girls. For years I did not bring any pictures of my children to the office because I was afraid I would never get any work done. I thought I would just spend all day staring at them." He seemed embarrassed, then straightened his back and went on, "When I said institutional packaging earlier, I meant, of course, the right Ivy League undergraduate school, then two to four years of an Analyst position at an investment bank, prior to attending one of the top business schools."

"Uh-huh." Richard was wondering where this was going.

"Let me tell you my primary role as head of recruiting. The elite schools are easy. The recruiting infrastructure, the inertia takes care of itself. My real job is to research people from the second-tier schools, ferret-out the good ones and convince them to join us. Are you one of the good ones?"

Of course he was. But how to convince this guy?

#

The more Jack watched Milner, the stranger he thought he was acting today. It wasn't like him to just blurt out that he wanted to IPO Southwest like he did. Milner was anything but impetuous. And if Jack didn't know better, he'd say Milner was actually nervous. He'd never sold anything on this scale before. Hell, it was 15 to 20% of his empire, and he'd sell at a discount, no less. What was up?

Yeah, Milner was acting strange today. But Jack would think about that later. Right now he was doing his own math. Walker & Company's fees were close to $100 million for selling all of Southwest. That 100 million bucks would do a lot for his budget this year. Not to mention the 5 percent of Southwest that he and Mickey got as part of the fee for helping Milner buy it years ago. They'd each make 35 million bucks on that when it went public. Jack felt his fingers tingle, then his balls.

"Might be one of the year's hottest deals if we play it right, Harold," Jack said. He looked at Mickey. "The scarcity and exclusivity value of a Harold Milner deal."

"Jack, I'm already sold. You trying to convince Mickey or yourself?"

Mickey said, "Not himself. You know Jack. He believes in everything."

"God help us all. A man who still believes his own bullshit."

Jack laughed along with them but he was thinking about the fees again. And what they would do to the bonus pool, and his bonus. And there wasn't anything Sir Reginald Schoenfeld could do about the $35 million each he and Mickey would make. Sir Reginald had put an end to taking pieces of deals instead of cash fees shortly after the foreign partners invested their $250 million into Walker & Company four years earlier. Looking over at Milner, thinking about Sir Reginald struck him: what a contrast. Milner knew how to become somebody, big time, but still be a normal guy. He was someone you could have a mano-a-mano with. But this Brit, Sir Reginald, born into it, running Schoenfeld & Co. after his old man died. He was a fourth generation idiot who inherited his living instead of hitting the streets to make one. But he walked around all haughty like he earned it and deserved it.

Milner sailed right through Jack's Peter Luger Steak House test; Sir Reginald flunked it before he even got out of the car.

A year after doing the Caldor deal with Milner, Jack and Milner drove over the Williamsburg Bridge from Manhattan into Brooklyn and up to Peter Luger in Milner's Mercedes 500 series. "They've got valet parking," Jack said, as Milner pulled up to the restaurant. Milner watched the lead kid come around to the driver's side. The kid was wearing a tan shirt, black slacks, black bow tie, same as Jack set it up when he was 16. Jack was watching Milner. Milner was looking at the kid, smiling, probably wondering is this kid even old enough to drive, and how's he gonna see over the wheel of this big Mercedes?

Milner didn't flinch, not even glancing at Jack with a questioning look like most guys. He rolled down the window. "Good evening, sir, welcome to Peter Luger," the kid said. The kid had it down: polite and respectful, in the tradition, doing Jack proud even though the kid had no idea who he was. "You gentlemen can get out and we'll take it from here."

They got out, Jack still watching Milner, Milner handing the kid a few bucks, then seeing a different kid, the car hop, jog up and get into the car. Then Milner asking the lead kid, "Don't I get a ticket?"

"No, sir, we take it to the lot and then bring your ticket back to you in the restaurant. After dinner you can pick your car up yourself or one of my boys will bring it back to you."

Milner shrugged. "Alright, my man, we'll be inside." No fuss, no attitude, not talking down. Passed.

The valet parking routine was the same as when Jack hatched the idea with Mickey "Splits" Duncan, Lionel Preston, Booker T. Wilson and Moravian White, buddies from the neighborhood in Canarsie. It took Jack three weeks to work the deal out with the maître d' at Peter Luger, selling him on the virtues of a 'seamless entry for his clients,' pitching himself as 'in the process of earning my diploma.' Then he lined up the four surrounding parking lots. What a pain in the ass, three different parking companies, days to find the managers, get them to agree. One of them even insisted he meet the Peter Luger maître d', who was off that day, and came back three more times before clinching the deal. Then Booker T.

saying, I ain't wearing no bow tie. Jack telling him, Then you aren't in the deal. Then Booker T., seeing that the other three car jockeys cleared 200 bucks between them the first weekend, even after Jack took his 25% off the top, finally joining in.

The lead kid trotted up to the front door as Milner and Jack walked toward it, held it open, Milner smiling back and thanking him. It was the same as when Jack used to hold the door and watch the mob guys pile out of their Cadillacs, the young ones flashy with gold chains and parading girls from New Jersey with big hair. The old mob bosses were quiet and classy except for their ugly ties and shirts and smelly one-dollar cigars, and sometimes those shiny sharkskin suits. And usually they had young babes on their arms chewing gum and looking cheap with their tits hanging out of skimpy dresses. Jack knew he didn't want to be like them.

He didn't want to be like the lawyers, either. The partners were abusive, never making eye contact, lousy tippers and their shoes scuffed and suits wrinkled. The young lawyers looked whipped, eyes lowered, cowed in front of the partners.

It was the Wall Street guys he liked to watch, learn from their subdued movements. Not the young ones, they were assholes— loud, like saying 'look at me, see how much money I make, how big I tip,' making a display of it. They treated Jack and his boys like pieces of car parking machinery. And they always had newspapers and sweaty workout stuff on the back seat—loose, not even stuffed in gym bags—candy wrappers on the floor, sometimes cigarette ashes and butts, real slobs. You could tell a lot from how they kept their cars.

But the older ones from Wall Street, they were established and comfortable inside their skins, walking erect but relaxed, like they didn't need to impress anybody. Suits with smooth fabrics that hung like silky elegance on their bodies: super light-weight worsteds in the spring and summer; lush, beautiful cashmere in the fall and winter. Their shoes were always shined like glass. Those were the guys he studied, went to school on. They had something to show him. They glided with the understatement of power. Sure, some of them were arrogant, barely noticed him. But the ones who did speak to him didn't try to act all friendly and chummy like the young mob kids, or disdainful like the young Wall Streeters. And every once in a while one of them would stop and strike up a conversation, shoot the shit just to pass the time without being condescending. And always, always they were good tippers. Sometimes they arrived in cabs or limos, but usually because it was Brooklyn they drove. And those cars were clean; big Mercedes, BMWs, occasionally Cadillacs or Lincolns and even sometimes Rolls-Royces, but always spotless, chrome shining and no papers or shit lying around inside. And when they brought their wives, they were classy with good perfume, tasteful jewelry, modest but elegant dresses. And polite. Even when they were tight-assed bitches they were at least polite. That's what Jack was shooting for: Wall Street.

And Sir Reginald, when they were negotiating the deal for the Brits and the Frogs to buy into Walker & Company, sitting in the passenger seat of Jack's BMW 760, name-dropping all the way out to Brooklyn. And as they pulled up in front of Peter Luger, saying, "My goodness, they're using child labor." Then when Jack stopped the car and without hesitation got out, handed the lead kid his key and five bucks, then headed for the entrance, Sir Reginald saying, "You're just going to leave the car with *him?*" Jack turning back to see Sir Reginald get out of the car, the lead kid already around to open his door, Sir Reginald looking through the kid like he didn't exist; no 'thank you,' nothing. Jack knew then that this guy Sir Reginald was a douchebag. But Sir Reginald Schoenfeld and Philippe Delecroix, Walker's other foreign partner, just happened to have $250 million they were willing to invest in Walker & Company. Sometimes you just had to suck it up and live with it.

Jack came back to the moment, how strange Milner was behaving. Leaving over a quarter of a billion of value on the table just wasn't like him. Clients acting out of character meant busted deals, usually at the eleventh hour. He looked over at Mickey, see if he noticed anything. Mickey and Harold had already started jawboning each other about stereo equipment, their perpetual argument. Solid state versus tubes. Vinyl records versus CDs. *Stereo schmereo. A couple a big kids.*

#

Richard felt as if LeClaire's question had given him his first opening, like this trip to New York hadn't been a waste of time. "I was doing great in advertising, but . . ."

"Richard, my friend, I accept that. But why are you here?"

Richard glanced at his watch. This was his shot. "I told you I've been a student of deals. And deals guys. I've read just about everything on James J. Hill, Harold Milner, Carl Icahn, Sam Zell, even J.P. Morgan and Jimmy Walker."

"What about Donald Trump?"

"A comb-over windbag who licenses his name to real developers. Are you kidding?" Richard saw LeClaire smile, a genuine smile this time that showed his teeth, his face losing its angular lines and dissolving into roundness. Richard went on, "The guys I mentioned were the ones that convinced me to go back to business school."

LeClaire said, "But I'm still waiting to be convinced." He lounged back in his chair, cradled his teacup in both hands and settled down as if to wait for Richard to make his case. "Just tell me about money."

"I see money as the true medium of the financier. It has an allure and an intrigue of its own; money begetting other money, compounding upon itself. It's a fascinating notion that almost defies the idea that matter can neither be created nor destroyed. You stick some in a little company, add brains and sweat and before you know it you've got a big company."

"So how do you feel about making money yourself?"

"I've never had enough of it and I can't ever imagine having too much. If I get there I'll let you know."

"What do you know about being an investment banker?"

"From a day-to-day, get-the-job-done standpoint, not much. But on a broader level, I'm more a student of deals than anybody at Michigan, and that's given me a grounding in reality for the concepts I've learned in my finance classes. I don't think my classmates understand the idea of ripping a company apart and putting it back together as more than when you started. I do."

LeClaire looked at his watch. Richard felt his stomach drop, thinking he was going to cut the interview off. Then LeClaire started talking. "I should tell you something about us. Starting with me. I'm a graduate of Ecole Polytechnique in France, was on a fast track at Groupe Credit Generale, then sent by GCG to Harvard Business School, graduating first in my class. I was then seconded by Philippe Delecroix himself to Walker shortly after the amalgamation of Walker, Schoenfeld & Co. and GCG. I am a living example of how a motivated, young banker can excel financially and in creative and career development at Walker. I am on track to be the youngest Managing Director ever elected at Walker, except for Jack Grass himself."

Richard stayed quiet. Interviewers who did a lot of talking always felt the interview went well.

LeClaire continued, "And you know what? If you work hard and focus the intelligence you obviously have, you could be a member of this elite group."

Richard felt a tickle of excitement. *Now he's selling me.*

"Now let us take Walker & Company itself. We are one of the hottest firms on Wall Street today. Four years ago, street-savvy Walker & Company amalgamated with Schoenfeld & Co. and Groupe Credit Generale. The old-school establishment English connections of Schoenfeld & Co., one of the last great English private merchant banks. The powerhouse financial clout of Groupe Credit Generale, my first employer and our French partner, the largest bank in France. The deal that Jack Grass and Mickey Steinberg put together was an amazing coup. They got Walker access to Schoenfeld's and GCG's prestige and capital without giving them control. They got them to put up 51% of the capital for 40% of the vote. In the four years since the amalgamation, Walker has catapulted from a mid-tier firm to a top ten rising star on the Street."

LeClaire paused, as if to say 'What do you think of that?' Richard didn't want to kill his momentum, just nodded.

"Look," LeClaire said, leaning forward like he was letting Richard in on a secret. "Sir Reginald Schoenfeld runs Schoenfeld & Co. like a personal fiefdom, hand-picking his people, preserving the unique culture of the firm. GCG, despite its scale, is carved into individual profit centers run by aggressive entrepreneurs. Philippe Delecroix is on GCG's Board of Directors, and heads two of GCG's most entrepreneurial profit centers: the investment banking business and the merchant banking subsidiary that holds GCG's investment in Walker. Do you know why Sir Reginald and Philippe sought out Walker?"

A question LeClaire would obviously answer himself. Richard didn't dare even nod this time, afraid he might stop.

"Because they wanted Walker's DNA. Because they know it is their unique DNA that drives their own organizations. What we are looking for, Richard Blum, is exceptional people with that same DNA."

"I know what you mean," Richard said, seeing an opening for his final pitch. "I really believe I was born to this. I know I have it in me and I can make a major impact here at Walker. But I won't come in here with the notion I'm entitled to it; I'll work my butt off, learn the business from the bottom up. Give me a shot. I won't let you down."

Now LeClaire smiled again, broadly, his face rounding out.

Richard sensed it was coming to an end and didn't want to screw it up at the last minute. He stayed silent.

"You are sharp," LeClaire said. "You are not full of sheet and you seem to know how to work hard and you definitely have the business under your skin. I like you, Richard."

Richard felt he'd scratched part way through the surface. LeClaire was still smiling. *Close, shut up and leave. The guy just said he liked you.*

"I like you too, François," Richard said. He felt relieved when LeClaire looked at his watch again.

"Well, I need to get ready for my call. I will get back to you. It will be tough, but I will see what I can do."

Richard got another toothy smile in the lobby as LeClaire escorted him to the elevator. Richard left with the feeling he'd passed the initial grilling, then connected. He felt a rush of relief, then a spasm of tension in his guts. It ended well; but well enough to be finally breaking in?

#

Richard got his callback to New York for a day of second-round interviews a week after he first met with LeClaire, and then didn't hear anything until mid-April. When he did, LeClaire's voice sounded ominous on the voicemail message. Richard's heart was thumping as he called him back, sitting on one of the benches outside Sam Wyly Hall.

"Hello, my friend," LeClaire said, "we are hoping you will join us as a member of Walker & Company. Tell me what we need to do to convince you."

Richard felt his body go numb where it touched the bench, the sensation he was floating above it, and then a feeling like laughter rumbling up from his guts. He said, "You don't have to do anything. I accept. I can't tell you how happy I am."

"Excellent. So let me just give you one element of our offer upfront before I lay out all the details."

Richard heard the change in LeClaire's tone and now got a different sensation in his guts, like someone punched them. He was also aware that his butt had landed back on the hard slats of the bench and his legs were rubbery.

LeClaire continued, "I remember telling you in our first interview that it would be tough. I fought hard for you but got significant pushback. So here is what we propose: join us as an Associate in this year's class on a probational basis. That means you have six months to prove yourself. If you accept, we will drive you hard. We will ask you to do things that may make you uncomfortable, even squeamish. We will test you to see if you are Walker material. But the other terms of your employment will be no different from any other Associate's, and none of your classmates will be aware of your probational status."

Richard cleared his throat, thinking on his feet, trying to put his interviewing hat back on. "I have no concerns about my ability to succeed. Of course, I accept."

Richard listened to LeClaire walk him through the other elements of the offer, feeling the strength coming back into his legs. Probation or not, he was going to Wall Street, even if they could throw him out again within six months. But as he told himself there was no way he was gonna let that happen, he couldn't shake the sense of a dull thud in his stomach.

#

Washington, D.C. Roman Croonquist, Director, Division of Enforcement of the Securities and Exchange Commission, sat at his desk, feeling as if things couldn't get any better. Yesterday he'd returned from New York, where he'd acted as government spokesperson at the sentencing hearing in his best insider trading bust since becoming the SEC's top cop six years earlier. In the Ceremonial Courtroom of the U.S. Courthouse on Pearl Street, where Bernie Madoff got 150 years, twenty-eight-year-old investment banker Matthew Kowalski got the maximum: 15 years, plus disgorgement of his share of his 13-member ring's $14 million in illegal gains, plus a $500,000 fine. Croonquist didn't think it was enough for the slimebag, but that's all the sentencing guidelines allowed. Kowalski, the little creep, had also passed inside information to his father, who traded on it through his niece's brokerage account. *Pathetic.* At one point during the hearing Kowalski's mother appealed to him with her eyes to help her son. Like hell. Croonquist had felt nothing but contempt. The kid knew exactly what he was doing. So did his old man. *They're only sorry after they're caught.*

And even better than that, today, the SEC's new $780 million MarketWatch system was officially on-stream, finished with its two-month benchmarking process. He typed a few keys and watched the symbols appear on the LCD screen on top of his desk, new dots in a blizzard of market trading statistics. The screen was one of 250 new MarketWatch terminals. Croonquist had been hand-picked by SEC Chairman Green and Croonquist's old boss, Phil Johnson in Surveillance to get MarketWatch up and running. It monitored trading activity worldwide through electronic surveillance of all major stock exchanges.

Now the bad guys really *don't stand a chance.* He cracked open a pistachio nut and popped the meat into his mouth.

Croonquist looked up and saw Charles Green, the SEC Chairman, walking toward his office. He leaned back and smiled.

"Charlie, what a surprise."

Green sat down facing Croonquist. "Yeah. But it's never a nice surprise when your boss just drops in unannounced, is it?"

"I don't know, you tell me." Croonquist didn't have any reason to feel uncomfortable. He leaned forward and moved the picture of Ellie and the girls to the side so he could see Charlie, then settled back into his chair.

"You keep eating those things, you'll get gout," Green said, pointing to the pile of pistachio shells on Croonquist's desk. "I won't beat around the bush. I just got back from the Hill, and it wasn't lost on those guys that you just pulled off the sexiest insider trading ring bust of the decade."

Croonquist patted himself on the back.

"Time to stop celebrating. Now they're all asking, 'what have you done for me today?' And that fat bastard Carmichael from North Dakota actually referred to the cost of MarketWatch as a 'bad case of gas bloating the SEC budget.'"

"The guy does have a way with words."

"You wouldn't say that if he was sticking them in *your* face." Green leaned forward and put his forearms on Croonquist's desk. Croonquist now started to get a more ominous feeling about this visit. "I need something to take back to them. The Appropriations Committee is squawking about MarketWatch running $280 million over budget—and I know that wasn't your fault, you did a great job—and the fact that the Kowalski ring bust didn't need any fancy technology."

Croonquist nodded, thinking about what he might have.

"So if you don't bring in a big fish with our new pole damn quick, I think we're both gonna land in the drink, my man."

Croonquist let that sink in for a moment. This not only wasn't a social call, but he now saw that Green was breathing heavily, and the big guy was hard to rattle. Croonquist thought for a moment. He saw Green give him a look that said, "Well?"

"I'm thinking," Croonquist said.

"You don't have *anything*?"

"C'mon, Charlie, it's only been two months."

Green sat back in his chair and shook his head.

Croonquist said, "We benchmarked 5,000 deals against 10 known insider trading deals with MarketWatch. It was a lot of numbers crunching, but that's what the big Crays that MarketWatch runs on are for. Some interesting things popped out," and he turned to point at a pile of computer printouts on his credenza, "but we're still analyzing them. It's premature."

"What's all this benchmarking give you?"

"The ability to correlate recent deals with known insider trading patterns. And if anything looks suspicious, then trace it back to the people who did those deals. Then analyze it."

"You've had two months of correlating and analyzing, my man. We need a big bust, and fast. How long?"

"Shit, I don't know. You know as well as I do that catching one of these characters isn't much different than any other form of police work. You have to have a hunch, a great lead, and then trace every piece of information until you find what you're looking for. The only difference between today and two months ago is that we've now got the means of tracing the data trail based on all the trading activity in a stock."

Green pointed to the pile of printouts. "What's the one on top?"

"Walker & Company."

"Why's it on top?"

"Eight suspicious deals in four years. High correlations with previous insider trading deals. I've got a gut feeling about this one."

"Good. Squeeze it until it talks to you." Green stood up. "I'm counting on you, Roman."

Croonquist watched him leave, then picked up his phone to call his computer jocks. He pulled open the bottom desk drawer and fished into the bag for another handful of pistachios.

CHAPTER TWO

New York City. The next time Richard entered the reception lobby of Walker & Company, on June 15th, it was as an employee.

He was one of six new Associates to join that day, two from Harvard, one from Stanford, one from Wharton and one from Kellogg. He entered a series of movable office cubicles; his new world of tan, fabric-covered partitions where his fellow Associates were setting up their desks like rookies at their lockers in spring training. He felt a twinge of nerves as he walked past them. The place smelled like a new car. Nerves or not, his whole body seemed to be smiling. He put his orientation papers down on the desk next to the woman he was told was Kathy Cella, his cubicle-mate, who had started two weeks earlier. Kathy was hunching over her computer screen, typing at the keyboard, squinting, with the light turned off.

"You'll go blind like that," Richard said.

"We all will. You'll figure that out in a week."

"No, your light is off."

"Burned out. And I'm too jammed to go get a new bulb. You'll figure out what that feels like in less than a week." She looked up, extended her hand. "Kathy Cella." She had the thoroughbred looks of the models in the Polo ads.

"Richard Blum. You're from Harvard?"

"Yeah. You the University of Michigan guy?"

"Yeah." Richard felt his face flush. *Yeah, from that 'other' school.*

Kathy turned back to her computer and continued typing numbers into a spreadsheet. "In that case we're cubicle-mates and competitors of sorts," she said without looking up again. "I gather we'll get to know each other pretty well. We're both assigned to George Cole in the Industrial Group."

Richard checked out his other classmates. They all looked human, no different than his Michigan classmates. But he reminded himself their route here was well-worn, with thousands preceding them; his was a grinding, solo trek that was only beginning. *You're the great impostor. They belong here. You don't. You have to work to earn this.*

When Richard was introduced to George Cole, his new boss, a Managing Director in the Industrial Group, Cole grunted a hello without looking up from his desk.

Pretty absorbed bunch, these bankers. "Pleased to meet you. I look forward to working together," Richard said.

When Cole finally made eye contact, it was penetrating. "Strap on your engines, my man. You start right in on a Harold Milner deal. Heard of him?"

"Who hasn't?"

When Cole paused, staring through him for a moment before responding, Richard figured a simple 'yes' would have done. "Good. Because it's the IPO of his Southwest Homes. Not your average deal. And I don't mind saying I'd rather have my only other Associate from this year's class, my rock star—Kathy Cella —on it, but I already put her on two others last week. You screw this up, probational, and you're toast." He looked back down at the papers on his desk.

Dismissed. No matter. He felt like he did after his first beer. His first assignment a Harold Milner deal. *I should savor this. I may never feel this great again.*

#

Kathy and Richard rode down the elevator together that evening. They got separated on the elevator by a crush of bodies. All Richard could see from over someone's shoulder was her hair. It was shoulder-length, brunette. He didn't think it was anything special. They emerged from the elevator and she half turned toward him, waiting. The orange light from the twilight sun reflecting off the former American Express building shone on her hair. He noticed the whiteness of her teeth against the light that glistened on her parted lips. She seemed frozen there as if in an art-directed commercial. Soft-focus. *Wow.*

Richard decided there was something interesting about her after all. He was looking over the curve of her shoulder, his eyes following her bra strap as it ran down toward the whiter flesh at her chest when she said, "You're lucky."

"What?"

"Southwest Homes. I just heard you got assigned to it." She tapped two fingers to her temple as if saluting.

He nodded, then looked beyond her at the light coming off the old Amex building.

She turned to follow his gaze.

He said, "That's the old American Express building. Before they moved to the World Financial Center."

"Uh-huh." She sounded bored.

After an awkward moment, Richard said, "I'm heading up William Street."

"So am I." She gave him a smile.

That's better. Richard guided them through the preliminaries: he was from St. Paul, she a New Yorker. She'd attended some private school, Sacred Heart, in the city, then majored in Econ at Harvard, then Harvard Business School.

Richard noticed small beads of perspiration broke out on her upper lip when she walked in this early evening heat.

"I went to Michigan State," he said. "English major, sociology minor."

"Sociology, the science of common sense." She smirked at him. "Are you a man with common sense?"

Richard noticed her breasts were small and round and that they bounced with her steps. "Depends on the subject."

She went on as if he hadn't answered. "I minored in Italian. I'm Italian. Did a summer of intensive study at Middlebury and then six weeks in Italy. I went to all these little villages, researched my ancestors, visited their graves."

"Ahh. And a historian." He squirmed inside, figuring he'd have to start sounding a lot more clever if he was gonna get anyplace with her. Now he noticed that her nipples jutted through her bra and cream-colored silk dress. At Hanover Square Richard said, "That's where Kidder stood for over 80 years."

"Who?" He couldn't tell if she was putting him on.

"Kidder Peabody. It was an old-line Wall Street firm. They got bought by PaineWebber. PaineWebber got bought by UBS."

"Oh."

"That's Harry's restaurant there on the left, in the basement of the India House. They're both famous old Wall Street institutions, too."

"Sounds like you're the historian," she said. She smiled. Richard now felt thoroughly stupid about the historian comment.

"Not really, I'm just into all this Wall Street lore." They were at the triangular building at the corner of One William Street. "That's where Lehman Brothers was founded and stood until the 1980s." He pointed up ahead to the right. "Up there is Exchange Place, where First Boston was, before they moved midtown and then got bought by Credit Suisse."

"You seem like you're in the right place." She seemed at least a little interested.

They continued on the narrow, curving street between the tall buildings and Richard felt nestled in the history of Wall Street. Marble, sandstone and granite walls cradled him. Gilded ceilings and carved beams showed through the arched windows on either side. *What a feeling.* They made the left onto Wall Street itself.

"This street has quite a history," Richard said, turning to Kathy. She didn't look up, walked in silence. She had a lean body and a firm ass like a competitive swimmer's. It curved tightly from her slim waist, her silk dress clinging to it. "That's Trinity Church framed at that narrow gap at Broadway."

Kathy nodded. She seemed relaxed, enjoying herself, letting it happen.

"The gray sandstone building on the left near it is the old Irving Trust building. And that building on the right with a rectangular patch of bright orange sunlight . . ." Richard paused and turned to look at her again.

"He's a poet, too," she said, nudging him with her elbow.

Encouraging. *The only thing between me and her is about five thousandths of an inch of silk.* "And on the right, at the corner of Wall and Broad, that's Federal Hall, once a U.S. Treasury building. That statue's of George Washington."

"And the New York Stock Exchange is just to the left," she said. He saw her smirk.

"Yeah. I forgot. You've been here before. Born and raised in New York City. So tell me about Italy," he said.

"Beautiful . . ."

Yeah, beautiful. The only thing between me and her is that little tiny dress.

After a few moments, Richard asked, "You free for dinner?"
He sucked in his breath, waiting.

The sun shined off Kathy's hair again like it had in the lobby.
She was about 27, Richard guessed. She smiled. "Sure."

The Polo girl with the swimmer's ass is mine for the evening.

"Where to?" he said to her, holding onto the strap-handle in
the subway car as they headed toward the Spring Street stop.

"I know just the place," she said, smiling.

#

When they walked into Raoul's, Kathy realized Richard was
still checking her out. Even so, she liked how he looked at her: a
fair amount of lust, yes, but also flattering awe, all of it discreet
and not at all disrespectful. It was kind of like he'd never seen a
girl up close before. *Intense, but also earnest.* And not cocky and
pushy like most of the other guys she'd already met at the firm.
She could do a lot worse for a cubicle-mate. At least he hadn't hit
on her in the first five minutes like most guys from New York.
Still, she'd make it clear this wasn't anything more than a dinner
for two new colleagues to start to get to know each other.

Rob, the maitre d' with coke bottle glasses, walked them past
the stainless steel shelving with the restaurant's Provençal china
through the clatter, heat and smoke of the kitchen to a walled
garden in back. It was cool, quiet and intimate. The air smelled
like garlic, French fries and lavender. She was surprised: she
hadn't known the garden dining area existed. She'd wanted them
to eat dinner in the 1950s style booths in front, amid all the bustle.
An unintended miscue.

"You're more serious about Wall Street than most," she said
once they were seated in the courtyard.

"I think I'm flattered. But in what way do you mean?"

"You actually have a respect—almost reverence—for the
history of the business."

Richard sat in silence, as if turning it over in his mind. What
was he thinking? She guessed he had a reflective side to him. He
ordered wine—Riserva Ducali—a decent Chianti. *Does he know
about wine, or is he ordering Italian to cater to me?* He seemed to
have a sensitive side, too.

"And you? How do you feel about the business?" he asked.

"It's not my first job on the Street. I did a three-year stint as
an Analyst at Morgan Stanley before B-school."

He nodded.

"I threw myself into that," she said, "and that's what I'm doing now. Watch out, Wall Street. I've made up my mind I'll be the youngest woman Managing Director ever on the Street."

He was silent again, still holding the menu in his hands, but not looking at it. *Thinking again.* She noticed his hands. They weren't large, but powerful and perfectly shaped. They looked like something a sculptor would use as a model. She remembered feeling his eyes on her as they had walked along Wall Street. If his hands worked the same way his eyes did, that could be magical. *Down girl.*

Richard said, "That's what I'm gonna do, too, throw myself into it." He looked up at her, now speaking directly into her eyes. "I'm gonna really make something of myself here on the Street. And I'm not approaching it from the standpoint of 'don't screw it up', because I'm surer of myself than that." There was that intensity again. But he said it with such clarity that it wasn't corny. He kept his gaze on her. *Still intense.* It made her want to push the conversation on.

She said, "I didn't want to go back to MS after HBS. For me, been there, done that, and I want to do it all. I came to Walker because it offers more opportunity. It's much less structured, more a meritocracy. Particularly for women. And the place is really making a splash. We're hot and getting hotter. You and I are in for quite a ride." He was still looking directly at her. It made her uncomfortable and she averted her eyes. She felt her face start to color and reached for her wine glass, picked it up.

"A toast. To Wall Street to the max."

"To the max," he said and smiled. That was better. He was lighter now.

"I'm from a long line of I-bankers, by the way. My grandfather was a partner at White, Weld before Merrill bought them and my father was Dominick Cella, the international mergers and acquisitions banker." She saw Richard's face show recognition of Daddy's name. He obviously hadn't put it together when they walked up Wall Street, giving her that history lesson. That's okay. He was charming about it and it showed her that he had the business under his skin. "My father was the youngest partner ever at Kuhn, Loeb and then at Lehman Brothers. He died with his boots on, so to speak, at 54, on the Concorde to Italy to pitch a deal to Gianni Angelli." There. She'd gotten it out in the open. She didn't want him to feel stupid later if somebody else told him.

"So, you said you're from St. Paul. Any juicy tidbits in your big town life?"

He shrugged. "Pretty ordinary."

"Scrapes with the law?"

"Studied too much. And sports."

"Family skeletons?"

"Only at Halloween."

"Nicknames?"

"Just Richard." He smiled.

She liked his smile. She'd been right earlier: he wasn't cocky or pushy. But any guy who held eye contact and smiled like that at a girl he didn't know yet must be sure of himself. Maybe it was a Midwestern thing. And she liked his curious mix of sophisticated brains and naiveté. He was like some high school spelling bee whiz, in town for the national championships and walking around Times Square all starry-eyed. But the straight-arrow side of him was appealing.

Kathy tried to talk him out of walking her to her apartment on Sullivan Street, but he wouldn't hear of it. Still, it was quaint in a farm-boy rube sort of way, and she appreciated it. The cobblestones made her footing uncertain. He saw it and offered his arm; she took it and felt her breast press against his side. *Oh my God, I hope he's not going to try to kiss me goodnight.*

"Goodnight, Richard. I look forward to working together. It's been a fun evening." She wasn't going to wait for him to do anything but wish her good night as she spun and slid her key into the latch. She turned her head back, "You know where you're going?"

"Spring and Sixth," he said. "Goodnight." She hurried the door shut behind her and stood in the lobby for a moment. She felt a funny sense in her tummy, like when you swoosh over a rise in the road and drive too fast down the other side. She smiled and punched the elevator button.

#

American Airlines Flight 785 to Houston. From his seat in coach Richard could hear George Cole and Milner's lawyer from Sterling & Dalton, Howard Blaine III, carrying on up in the first class cabin like fraternity brothers. They were laughing and slamming down drinks, overly loud, like, "Notice us. We're a couple of hotshot Wall Street types." They were already shitfaced and the flight was still two hours out from Houston. It was embarrassing.

And distracting. He was trying to re-read the SEC documents —10-Ks and 10-Qs—on the homebuilding company comparables to Southwest Homes, prepping for the visit. The rush of thoughts and the emotions racing his pulse were distracting enough. His first business trip as a banker. *It's really happening.* Who could he tell? Mom and Dad were already proud enough. Joan Godburn —his college girlfriend's mother who'd referred to him as a deadbeat—what do you think now, bitch? He laughed at himself. *What crack in my subconscious did she just crawl out of?*

Richard picked up the 10-K for Pulte Homes, one of the comparable companies he had analyzed as part of their due diligence for the Southwest Homes initial public offering.

A week earlier, Jeannie Peters, the Assistant Vice President who worked for George Cole, had started him through the paces. "You're lucky," she said. "You've only been with the firm for a few weeks and you're already working on your first deal. That might be normal if you were with Morgan Stanley or Goldman Sachs. But at Walker, working on a 1.2 billion dollar IPO is a privilege." She narrowed her eyes. He already noticed she did that a lot, probably thought it was intimidating. "And it's not just any IPO. Milner's selling 100% of the company to the public in the deal."

"What do you want me to do?" he asked.

"Remember we're doing all the real work, first thing. Some senior officers of Southwest Homes will be involved, and everyone will have lawyers. And Southwest's accountants will be around." She said it like Richard was too stupid to understand, but even if he did, it would be too late to save his doomed soul. "But remember, we're doing all the work, which means you're doing all the work." This woman was like an abused puppy that grew up into a nasty bitch. He could see it coming; weeks with her on this deal.

She grabbed a book of financials on her desk, turned them toward Richard. "Run financial comparable on Southwest versus these companies. Have one of the Analysts run the comps model, but I want you checking all the numbers by hand."

Richard was trying hard not to smirk, having a hard time taking her seriously. Not what she was saying, but her attitude and tone: the 'no, asshole' voice. Like 'no, asshole, don't do it like that, do it like this.'

"Are you getting all this?" she asked.

Of course he was, now starting to get pissed. He knew all the numbers and ratios cold from his practice spreadsheets. "You think I'm gonna blow it on my first deal?" he said.

It seemed to surprise her. Then she said through her teeth, "Go tell George I told you to run all the standard stuff, see what else he needs." The 'no, asshole' voice again. Richard realized he should have kept his mouth shut. The word "probational" kept running through his mind. *Dumb.* He reminded himself he was standing with his toes over the edge of a cliff.

Later that day when Richard walked back to Jeannie's cubicle, he heard Cole and her talking. He stood outside to wait for them to finish. When he heard Cole say, "Guess I'll have to start whipping him into shape on the road," he decided to bolt into the Communications Room until Cole left. Managing the Comm Room was Richard's "probational" duty. Something nobody else would want to do, but not something the firm could trust to a clerk; so they gave it to one of the new schmucks who didn't have a choice. The Comm Room was the site of the firm's general faxes and email accounts. With all the crap that came in, overseeing it was like weeding through the daily garbage bin. But once in a while something real found its way: a lead on a deal, a referral or a resume that warranted forwarding to an officer. He listened for Cole; he heard the computer cooling fans whirring, the fax in the corner spewing pages.

He sat down at one of the computer screens in the room and figured he'd check the incoming emails. He could hear Cole's and Jeannie's voices but couldn't make out what they were saying. He hunched over the keyboard and opened the latest email on the screen, still listening. The email message he'd opened was a mundane series of trades being sent overseas with attendant wire transfer instructions. He scrolled down the numbers of shares and prices in the email, still listening.

The computer beeped with an incoming message. Richard turned back and read it.

"walker1@netwiz.net:
Message previously received. Confirmation previously sent. Duplicate, or are we to double positions? Please advise."

It was signed walker2@gcg.com.

Richard didn't know what the message meant, but he checked the computer's outbox and realized he must have inadvertently re-sent the last message. The recipient must have been sitting at his computer at GCG and believed Richard was walker1@netwiz.net, the person he was corresponding with.

He looked again at the message he'd re-sent. It was a series of account numbers with many similar trades, all in common stock and put options in a group of companies. It looked like someone was buying securities in the hundreds of millions of dollars, maybe more. *Oh, man.* Richard didn't want to be any part of anybody taking twice that big a position, so he typed back the answer:

> "walker2@gcg.com
> Message erroneously duplicated.
> Regards,
> walker1@netwiz.net"

He wheeled and left the room fast, feeling his blood pumping in his temples. He'd talk to Jeannie later. But he couldn't help wondering about the emails. Walker had instantaneous electronic trading technology downstairs on that football-field-sized trading floor. Why would somebody from the Comm Room be emailing lists of account numbers and trade instructions to Paris to buy hundreds of millions in stock and put options in some group of companies?

A few days after that Richard plunked himself into his chair next to Kathy's in their cubicle with a sigh.

"Jeannie Peters?" Kathy asked without looking away from her computer screen.

"Yeah. Anywhere else in the world she'd just be another bitchy, wasp-waisted little girl . . . ."

"Bitchy wasp-waisted *woman.*"

". . . but in here she's Queen Elizabeth."

"With attitude. Welcome to the club," Kathy said. "Hates us all. Worked her way up without going to B-school. We're all a bunch of pasty-faced dilettantes from hot-shot schools. Think we're cool but aren't worth a damn."

"Tell me about it. I crank out and hand-check a hundred and forty-four hours of public comparables analysis in forty-eight hours, she takes it without a word, finds a couple of mistakes and looks at me like I should stab myself seven times." Richard paused and glanced over at her. *Always rubbing my nose in it that she was born into the business, but overall she's okay.*

Kathy smirked. "Actually it was about seventy-two hours. I was sitting here crunching my own numbers the whole time. Remember?"

At least she had a sense of humor. And she worked hard, no prissy attitude. They'd gone for beers a few nights at about 1 a.m. on the way home.

Kathy said, "Shouldn't you be getting home?"

"Why?"

"I heard you're flying to Houston tomorrow morning with Cole at the crack of dawn for management interviews on the Southwest IPO."

"Yeah. So?"

"Mind some advice from my grandfather and father that I got around the kitchen table?"

"No. What?"

"A banker misses the plane on his first deal, he doesn't get a chance to miss another."

Richard smiled. Yeah. She was alright.

#

Washington, D.C. Croonquist sat on a stool at the counter facing the windows in Starbucks. Outside, typical no-time-for-anything Washingtonians strode by. Inside, he could barely hear with the noise, but damn, the place smelled great, like some coffee-chocolate-pistachio aphrodisiac. He wanted a coffee, but decided to wait for Mike Dolan to show up before getting on line to order. Dolan arrived about 10 minutes later, totally soaked and looking pissed. Croonquist couldn't help laughing at him.

"The spy who came in from the rain," Croonquist said.

"Kind of a wise-ass for a guy who's asking for a favor, aren't you?" Dolan stuck out his hand. They shook.

"How about that coffee I promised you?"

"I'll take a venti," Dolan said and sat down on the stool next to Croonquist's.

"What?"

"A large, you dinosaur."

"Large what?"

"Something exotic. Gotta prove I'm not a cheap date."

Croonquist had no idea what Dolan was talking about, but got on line, studied the menu. This stuff was expensive. What the hell were they putting in it, cocaine? A few minutes later he brought back Dolan a venti Brazilian Mocha. It's what his young guys in the office drank. Croonquist had one for himself, too. He figured he'd see what the fuss was all about.

"Sorry about the rain," Croonquist started out, "and thanks for coming."

Dolan made a face that said, "Cut to it, I'm busy."

"I need a favor."

"You already told me that on the phone."

Man, Dolan was on edge. He worked for the National Security Agency, the U.S. government's little-known intelligence-gathering arm that monitored all international communications. The agency's budget and manpower exceeded the CIA's. If the SEC had half their financial resources, Charlie Green could have buried MarketWatch as a rounding error. It had been a year since Croonquist had seen Dolan. Then, at Dolan's request, he'd called in a marker for a favor from Stankowitz at the FBI. Stankowitz monitored some guy for Dolan for something that Croonquist couldn't remember and was glad to forget. But Croonquist was happy to set it up, and Dolan was grateful. Anyone who'd been in the federal government for over 26 years had friends in all the various other branches, and those friends did things for their friends that went outside their friends' jurisdictions. Croonquist regularly did favors for CIA, NSA and numerous congressional subcommittees. And they did favors for him, even the Democrats. Croonquist always thought that if the American taxpayers knew about all the black holes in different agency budgets for this stuff, they'd shit their pants, especially the Democrats.

"Why the hell're you so edgy?"

Dolan scrunched up his face. "Sorry. Budget cuts, too much work, too many scumbags trying to kill us all."

"Tell me about it."

"So what can I do for you?" Dolan asked.

"I'm working on a case where I don't have enough to get formal surveillance. It's got international elements to it. If you could monitor this company's international transmissions—phone calls and emails—you could help us break it wide open."

"You say international?"

"I wouldn't be coming to you otherwise."

"Any national security issues?"

"No idea."

Dolan paused for a few moments, looking Croonquist in the eye. "I said any national security issues?"

Croonquist got it. "Absolutely. It's right up your alley. That's why I came to you."

"Okay, what you got?"

Croonquist handed Dolan a piece of paper. He'd written the names Walker & Company, Groupe Credit Generale, and Schoenfeld & Co. on it.

"Who are these guys?"

"Financial institutions. Suspected money laundering, or whatever you need to call it to make it work for you."

"You mean for you," Dolan said, smiling.

Croonquist paused for a moment, sipped his Brazilian Mocha. "Right. I owe you one," he said.

#

Houston, Texas. At 8:15 a.m. the next morning at Southwest Homes' offices in Houston, Richard ate breakfast alone. Except for George Cole and Howard Blaine, who sat at the other end of the table, the team had already finished eating and scattered. Blaine was still making cowboy jokes in his perfect Harvard accent—"Ro-*day*-o, ro-*day*-o." Richard was thinking Cole probably wasn't a bad guy deep down inside; Richard just hadn't seen any evidence of it yet. Like when standing at the curb at the airport with Richard and Howard Blaine, he pointed to Richard and said "get a cab" as if Richard was a bellboy. Like when he'd shown Richard it was he who taught Jeannie Peters the 'no, asshole' voice in reply to Richard asking if he should have the cabbie leave the meter running. This after Cole's admonishment, "Make sure we have a cab to take us to dinner," while they were checking into the Ritz-Carlton and dropping off their bags before heading to the restaurant. Like when he didn't bother introducing Richard to their dinner colleagues—two Associates of Howard Blaine's, Southwest's General Counsel and Southwest's accountant from KPMG. And like when he'd replied, "In the lobby, checked out, ready to get into a cab at 7:00 a.m. sharp," in response to Richard's "goodnight" at the elevator.

Cole said, "We're on in 10 minutes. Two doors down on the right. Ron Peters, the CFO." He and Blaine got up and left.

Richard relished that much peace based on how the last half day had gone. He was beginning to wonder what he'd gotten himself into starting a career in this business. Jeannie Peters and George Cole were a couple of gratuitous ball breakers. They made the Senior Account Execs in advertising seem enlightened. Ten minutes. Then time to get kicked around again. He heard someone come into the room behind him.

"Breakfast for half a brigade, I see."

Richard turned to see Harold Milner walking toward the credenza that held the catered breakfast. Richard stood up. "Hi," he said, not so much tense as caught off guard. "Nobody told me you'd be here. Richard Blum." He extended his hand. "Remember me?"

"The long-suffering Vikings fan." Milner shook Richard's hand with that big paw of his. He walked over to the credenza.

"How was your flight?" Richard asked.

Milner had his back to him, fixing coffee at the credenza. "Long. I hate them." Milner turned and sat down. "But at least I'm not flying commercial. And this little number makes it easier." He held up an iPod Nano.

"We all have one of those. In my generation you're a nerd if you don't. But the sound's disappointing."

"That's because MP3 recording quality cuts out the highs and lows, compromises the sound in order make the data files smaller. Makes it sound tired and sloppy. I record everything in lossless mode. Tons more data, same amount as a CD."

"Yeah, but it takes up a lot of iPod memory."

"Top quality but less songs is a good trade. Listen to this." Milner handed Richard his iPod. Richard plugged in the earbuds and turned it on. The sound was liquid, like he was in the studio, or better, at Lincoln Center. "Amazing." Richard knew the piece. It was one of his father's favorites. Richard said, "Mozart's Clarinet Concerto in A."

"I'm impressed. Go ahead. Keep it."

"You kidding?"

"Nah, it's yours. I've got a dozen or so."

Richard laughed.

"Yeah, not bad for a man who still has to check his emails through his secretary. Richard, you keep that," he said, pointing to the iPod.

"Okay, Harold." Richard still felt odd calling him by his first name. "Thanks."

"You're welcome. Spread the gospel. Music's one of our last uncorrupted refuges. A purity nobody can mess with. In there," he said, pointing to the iPod, "we're all equals."

"Thanks again," Richard said.

"Where's Cole?"

"He just left. We start our management interviews in five minutes." Richard looked at his watch. He'd milk this down to the last second. How many more chances would he get to BS one-on-one with Harold Milner?

"He's a good banker. You'll learn a lot. He giving you a hard time?"

"Is the Pope Catholic? I'm rubbing a lot of tummies."

Milner gave him a questioning look.

"My dad used to say 'sometimes you have to rub people's tummies to get them to accept you.' Part of the game."

"He's right. So keep toughing it out. And if you can manage to get face time with Jack Grass, jump through hoops to impress him and you'll make it. We all pay our dues. Just don't forget where you came from. Rule number one."

"And number two?"

"Never let anybody take it from you once you've made it." The casualness in Milner's manner was gone. He was looking at Richard but his focus seemed elsewhere. Then Milner's gaze went up over Richard's shoulder. "Here's the Pope now." Richard turned to see George Cole in the doorway. Richard's ears burned and he felt his face flush. If Cole heard what he'd said he was cooked.

"Harold," Cole said. "I didn't expect to see you. What a pleasure." Cole's voice went higher than usual, Cole gushing.

"Yeah, well, just slumming." Milner stood up and he and Cole shook hands across the table. Cole had a brightness in his eyes and an eagerness in his face Richard hadn't seen before. *Golly, Mr. Springsteen, I've got all your CDs.* Some hot-shot Wall Street type now.

On the way to the CFO's office, Cole said, "Must be a really important deal to Milner. He wouldn't normally show up in person for something like this." His tone was almost collegial for the first time, Richard wondering if maybe Cole felt like Richard's audience with Milner had rubbed off on him. It wore off when they entered Ron Peter's office. He pointed at Richard's yellow pad and glared at him, "Take notes."

#

New York City. "To the printer's," Cole said as he, Howard Blaine and Richard collapsed into a limo at 9:00 p.m. that night at JFK. Richard had never been in a stretch limo before. The driver took them to Bowne & Co.'s office on Varick Street and they went upstairs to an enormous conference room filled with the rest of the Southwest IPO deal team—attorneys representing Southwest and Walker, Southwest's General Counsel and CFO, and other Walker professionals—to make final the IPO prospectus that was to be filed with the SEC in the morning. Printer's drafts of the prospectus were scattered on the table. Luggage sat against the walls. The place smelled of ink and sweat.

The second hour went like the first one, and the next six after that: Richard observing, following along as everyone read each successive draft of the documents; Richard generally unsure what people were doing or talking about; Richard amazed that Cole kept pushing a button on the wall and some grey-faced schlub in saggy-assed pants showed up to take his and Blaine's drink orders, that Ron Elman, Walker's senior Real Estate MD picked his nose, then tore matches from the CFO's pack and picked his ears, then mocked Richard for loosening his tie; Richard finally making a suggestion in the drafting and everyone acting like he'd never spoken, hell, like he was invisible.

At 5:30 a.m., after rubbing tummies as hard as he could for the last few days, Richard's ego finally surfaced. "Why are you only using me as a gopher? Why won't you let me make a little more of a contribution?" Richard said to Cole as they waited in the limo for Jeannie Peters to come downstairs.

"You're an amoeba," Cole said. "You don't know anything. You're excess baggage at this point."

Richard felt it like a slap from the back of Cole's hand: not meant to hurt him, just insult him. He fumed in silence. Jeannie got in.

"Hey," Cole said to her.

"Hey."

Richard looked up but Jeannie ignored him. She and Cole both extended their legs full-length from the back seat of the stretch limo to the foot rests. Richard sat facing them on the fold-down seat. He had to shift sideways to avoid Cole's loafers. Cole never looked at him.

"Tired," he said to Jeannie.

"Too tired for a nightcap?"

"Maybe one."

She smiled back like it meant more than a nightcap. After that they drove uptown in silence.

"Good night," Richard said when they arrived at his apartment building. They didn't make eye contact. No response, not even a nod, a word or a perceptible movement of their feet. Richard's ears burned red and his jaw set rigid with anger and hurt as he climbed out of the limo.

As he entered his building it was more than his exhaustion that burned moist in his eyes. His pride stung and he felt trapped in Jeannie's sadism, Cole's nastiness, his hatred of Ron Elman and his fifty-five year old adolescent comments, and the collective arrogance of the industry he'd chosen for himself.

In bed he screamed from his guts with his face down in the pillow. It made both his head and his heart feel lighter. He figured investment bankers didn't do things like that, but he did it again anyhow.

#

Washington, D.C. Roman Croonquist finished reviewing the Wells Notice on the Boston Financial Arts case that his new Enforcement Assistants, Starsky and Hutch—it was easier than remembering their real names, and they seemed to enjoy the monikers—had drafted for him.

He liked these kids. They reminded him of his peers and himself when he'd interned under the SEC's legendary Enforcement chief, Stanley Sporkin, back in the 1980s. Croonquist had done two stints under Sporkin: the first when he was an undergraduate Poli Sci major at George Washington University, the second when he was in second year law at Georgetown. The second time around he was proud to be one of the few interns required to wear a beeper under the hard-ass regime of Sporkin.

He remembered the way Sporkin talked about the go-go years of the 1960s when he was coming up, how the SEC brought down a number of the major conglomerate builders of that era with a flurry of litigation. Sporkin would pace back and forth in his office in front of a few young staff members, railing against the abuses of those early takeover artists. Then he would fire them up with challenges about bagging the current-day bad guys.

Croonquist intentionally tried to create a similar esprit for his staff. He wrote "Culture" at the top of his to-do list each day for the six years he'd held the top Enforcement job, a constant reminder to himself that a culture of commitment started at the top. That's why he worked directly with a couple of the younger staff members each year. It was a way of planting seeds, letting the message grow up through the organization. And it also made the more seasoned guys compete for time in front of the boss, which kept them from getting lazy. Now, looking up from the draft across his desk at Starsky and Hutch, he chuckled. Their Starbucks coffees stood on his desk; they couldn't bring themselves to drink the crap that Croonquist did from the kitchenette. Which was why they were always late. In Croonquist's day, the boss wanted you in by 8 a.m., you were there. Not today; the Starbucks generation didn't get into the office until it was done waiting in line at Fourth and F Street NE for its Brazilian Mocha.

"Not a bad first draft." He nodded at Starsky and Hutch. "Okay, I'll send you my comments after the staff meeting." He nodded again and they got up and left.

He looked at his watch. He'd do a quick scan of MarketWatch before the staff meeting. He turned to the monitor and typed in the keys to see if the software flagged anything unusual the previous day.

It showed about a dozen stock ticker symbols, six with big volume and correlation coefficients above 75%, meaning they were suspicious. He double-clicked on the first ticker symbol. The company was Pulte Homes, a homebuilder. After he clicked on the second ticker symbol, he didn't need to go any further, because all six ticker symbols with suspicious volume showed up on the list of homebuilding industry competitors. A half-dozen homebuilders, all the subjects of unusual trading. He loaded all the tickers into another screen and ran the subroutine to access the identities of the firms doing the trading.

Eight firms showed up consistently, including Walker & Company and GCG. A few more minutes research showed the others were a London brokerage firm, two Swiss banks and a few Cayman Islands banks. *Almost all offshore. Interesting.* If they were trading a single stock, the data would be screaming at him that something fishy was going on. He felt his pulse quicken. He slid open his bottom desk drawer and reached in for handful of pistachios, then stopped himself. He looked at his watch: 8:25

a.m. *Time to get out of here.* He typed in all six ticker symbols to initiate ongoing monitoring.

He stood up and started toward the door. He'd check into it more deeply after the meeting. Maybe it was just a big hedge fund playing the sector, but it was worth keeping an eye on. Then he smiled. His gut told him it was more than that: the chase was on.

#

Boston, Massachusetts. Richard learned that Cole and Blaine had played tennis the morning after the printer's. The definition of Wall Street cool: hotshots in tennis whites nonchalantly playing off hangovers and an all-nighter at the printer's. *Hey, look at us, we just filed a 1.2 billion dollar IPO.* Richard hoped he'd never be that big an asshole.

On Monday morning, Richard accompanied Cole on the Southwest Homes road show—five days of presentations by Southwest's senior management to prospective institutional investors in the stock of Southwest when it became publicly traded in the IPO. In the ballroom at the Ritz-Carlton in Boston, the first road show stop, Cole pushed Richard into position where to stand near the door, and had him pass out selling memoranda to everyone. *Here, Spot, go fetch.*

"I said hand them to everyone," Cole said just before the presentation was to begin. Then he saw Cole's eyes brighten as he looked over Richard's shoulder. Richard turned to see Milner walking in with Rusty Munger, Southwest's CEO.

"Harold," Cole said, stepping toward him and extending his hand.

Falling all over himself.

"Hi, Harold," Richard said.

Cole gave Richard his best icy stare square in the eye. "Just do your job," he whispered. "I'll tend to the clients. Do I need to remind you of your status, probational?"

Richard cut him off by turning back toward the door. He promised himself he'd remember this guy. He'd probably always hold Richard's "probational" status over his head. In fact, he'd learned that last year Cole was responsible for washing out all three probational hires. And now he probably had Richard in his cross-hairs. As long as it took, if Richard ever got the chance he'd cut this bastard Cole off at the knees. He thought about what Dad would say to that, then felt bad. A second later decided he'd do it without Dad ever finding out. Then he decided Cole wasn't worth the trouble after all; just walk over to the prick and tell him to take a flying fuck at the moon.

Richard took a deep breath, exhaled and handed a selling memorandum to the next guy who walked in the door.

After Boston came Philadelphia, Chicago, Minneapolis, Denver, Seattle, Los Angeles and then back to New York. Eight cities in five days. Richard didn't think it was possible.

In Philadelphia Richard noticed three guys in the audience wearing investor name tags that showed up asking the same questions in Chicago and Minneapolis, questions that Southwest's CEO just happened to have great answers to. Funny how they asked the same questions at the institutional breakfasts, lunches and meetings in Denver, Seattle and L.A. He wondered if this was how Wall Street really worked.

#

Washington, D.C. Croonquist arrived at his office earlier than usual, 7:15 a.m., because he wanted to do a deep dive on the homebuilding sector trading data. He'd amassed enough information and wanted to decide if it warranted raising to the level of a potential enforcement action. He stood two cups of black coffee from the kitchenette on his desk next to the MarketWatch monitor, settling in. This early and the coffee already smelled like burnt tar.

After about an hour he printed just two summary pages that told him enough. *Yes.* Unmistakable: a group of market players had amassed a huge trading position in six homebuilders, then unwound it over the last few days. He didn't need to see the correlation coefficients versus previous insider trading cases to convince him he was onto something.

He downed the last of his second cup of coffee, then reached into his bottom desk drawer for another handful of pistachios. He dialed Mike Dolan, his friend at NSA.

"I haven't been able to put a lot of resources on this. Favor, you remember," Dolan said. "So I put a new guy on it. He's a sharp young fellow and I trust him."

Croonquist heard it like Dolan was trying to let him down easy, wasn't going to come through. "And?"

"Nothing worthwhile on the phones, but a lot of back-and-forth in emails between Walker, GCG and some other institutions on the Continent. A few other places, too."

"Yes," Croonquist said under his breath. He rolled a few pistachios around in his palm, waiting. *Come on, out with it.*

"A boatload of orders and confirmations for trades." Dolan paused again, like he was reviewing the data. "They used code-names. The pattern is outbound emails from Walker to GCG, then outbound from GCG to the others."

"Any of the others include firms in the Caymans, London, Switzerland, the Netherlands Antilles?"

"Yeah. And a couple in the U.S. Shaw Securities and Beldenfirst."

Croonquist didn't say anything for a moment. He was wondering how far he could push Dolan, see if he could get him to broaden the monitoring.

"You still there?" Dolan said.

"Yeah . . . listen, I was just thinking," Croonquist said, cringing inside, afraid of the answer. "I was wondering if you could maybe keep an eye on GCG's lines inside the States as well. Maybe monitor their New York office."

"Get real. I'd probably be screwed if anybody found out what I'm doing already. Unless you can convince me it's got something to do with national security."

"What would it take to do that?"

"You'd need to convince me." He sounded like he meant it. Croonquist let that idea flutter around in his head for a moment, then let it go. It amounted to domestic wiretapping, and Croonquist knew what it took to get that. "Okay. Thanks, Mike. I'll talk to my techies about getting the data transferred over to our Cray."

The data would give MarketWatch something to work with. He was sure the NSA's data would be a dead match with his own. The code-names would turn out to be the six homebuilders. Once he had the data download from the NSA, it wouldn't take more than a few hours of numbers crunching to confirm that. That meant he'd have trading patterns for Walker, GCG and the other institutions. And specific email addresses for those directing the trading. Probably enough to get authorization for wiretaps.

The next step would be to understand what the hell these guys were doing. They'd purchased various strike prices of put options in the homebuilders as well as bought all the stocks. Croonquist had an idea what that meant, but he knew somebody who could tell him with certainty. He picked up the phone.

#

New York City. Richard tried to keep a low profile sitting in the office of Fred Wall, Walker's Head of Equity Capital Markets. The stock markets had just closed on the last day of Southwest Homes' road show in New York, and he sat among Walker's Pricing Committee members, ready to price the deal in a few minutes. The Pricing Committee members would figure out the price at which Walker & Company would buy 100% of Milner's Southwest Homes shares from him, then re-sell them to the public when the markets opened in the morning. *Man, over a billion dollars*, Richard thought.

The informality in Wall's office impressed him. The Pricing Committee members were scattered around the room in various plush sofas and nineteenth century chairs, a bunch of senior guys lounging, staying loose like boxers before a prizefight. Jack Grass and Mickey Steinberg were there from Corporate Finance as the bankers who originated the client relationship and the deal. Wall, who reported to John Morris, head of Sales and Trading, ran the capital markets trading division that would sell and trade Southwest's stock. Brian Smith was the syndicate manager, who kept the book of institutional client orders for shares of Southwest's stock at various prices. These were the steely-eyed guys who built and ran Walker. Richard told himself it didn't get any better: sitting among the power elite of Wall Street as they plied their craft.

Jeannie Peters posed with her hands in her blue suit pockets and joked with Jack Grass like they'd also attended George Cole's and Howard Blaine's fraternity.

Richard was the only one sitting by himself, not chatting or horsing around, the new kid.

He could distinguish the bankers from the traders by how they dressed, as if they wore the uniforms of different teams. Jack's suit was European cut with pointed lapels; Steinberg's the opposite extreme, classic Brooks Brothers in navy pinstripes. They both wore brightly patterned Hermes ties, Jack's over a bold English striped shirt, Mickey's over starched white. The traders wore traditional solid white, blue or pink button-down oxfords, their ties slid down and their collars open at the neck.

Finally, George Cole arrived, late.

Cole signaled Richard to hand out his brochures of comparable figures and other pricing information. He gave one to each of the officers, avoiding Jeannie's eyes, feeling self-satisfied to be momentarily in the limelight and anticipating the action. Jack and Mickey exchanged a look and Mickey got up and left the room.

Richard reflected on his Capital Markets class at Michigan, eager. He'd learned about the sophisticated alchemy of how an investment banker priced a deal; now he'd see it from the inside. *Well, this is it. Now I'll see what it's really all about.*

Wall asked, "How the hell can you price a deal with such inconsistent EBITDA and net earnings?"

Jeannie opened her mouth to say something and Cole talked over her, said, "It's being priced off growth and potential." Richard felt a swell of victory at seeing Jeannie muzzled.

Jack said, "EBITDA Schmebitda, look at . . ."

Smith, the syndicate head, cut in, "Fuck all the numbers mumbo jumbo, the order book's at $14.50 per share if you wanna sell the deal out. If we price it any higher we don't have enough buyers. We get stuck owning a big chunk of the deal and we take a bath when the stock drops like a stone once it starts trading on the exchanges, 'cause we overpriced it."

Jack said, "$14.50? $14.50, Jeez."

Smith said, "Cut the shit, you know the order book as well as I do. You've been all over my guys checking it all week."

About this time Richard started thinking this wasn't at all how he imagined it would be.

Jack said, "Okay, how's the book at $15.00? Milner's gonna be pissed if we price it too far below $16.00."

Smith said, "If we try $15.00 we'll probably wind up owning five to ten percent of the deal."

Jack said, "That's a chance I'll take."

Morris sat up like he'd been poked in the back and said, "Not on my divisional P&L and balance sheet. You guys in Corporate Finance carry it on yours."

Wall said, "Yeah, in your dreams Jack, that's 50 to 100 million bucks. We aren't taking a potential hit like that."

Jack curled his lip at them both and said, "We're making, say, $75 million in fees, we can't afford to risk a little of it to keep the client happy? Maybe Milner takes his next deal to Morgan Stanley."

Nobody said anything for about 30 seconds, Richard thinking so much for Capital Markets 105.

Smith said, "I think we can get it done at $14.75, but I can't guarantee it'll stick at any higher price than that."

Jack looked at Smith like, 'You and I knew that all along.' Jack looked around the room and each nodded back to Jack in turn and that was it, the deal was priced at $14.75. One hundred percent of Southwest Homes' stock was being bought by Walker & Company for $1,068,840,003, then sold to the public the next morning when the stock markets opened.

Richard looked into his lap at a copy of the pricing books he'd spilled his guts into for weeks, ignored in the brief chaos of the deal pricing. *So much for the elegance of financial theory.*

#

Afterward, Richard walked into the Comm Room to troll through a week of emails and faxes, trying to digest what he'd just witnessed. The Southwest deal got priced in less than two minutes based on some snarling back-and-forth about how many client orders they had for the stock at what prices, rather than any financial concepts. Then Jack, Morris and Wall started fighting over the fee split between Corporate Finance and Sales and Trading like bears over a carcass, the fight over the fee split going on ten times longer than the pricing meeting. Jack finally stared down Morris at the end like a street bully. Not boring, but was that how it always was? *And can these guys stand being in the same room together?*

He turned to the computer he'd inadvertently discovered the trading emails on, figuring he'd check it out again. He sat down and opened Outlook, clicked on an email in the Inbox to walker1@netwiz.net and then sorted by that name. He saw about 10 emails since the one he'd stumbled on a few weeks earlier. Now he was more than just curious. He opened the first five, counting instructions for about 10 million more shares and put options on the group of companies he'd seen before. He also noticed they weren't company names or ticker symbols, but appeared to be code-names. So whoever was doing the trading was trying to hide it. He left, thinking it was all really odd.

Back at the Associate bullpen he stopped at his cubicle to see if Kathy was in. He wanted to celebrate his first deal, and she was the only one he felt like doing it with. She wasn't around so he went straight to Raoul's; it seemed like the most logical place to find her. Rob couldn't get him a table or a booth so he had steak frites at the bar. Ken behind the bar asked where Kathy was. *Rub it in, man.*

After six beers and three cognacs Richard looked at his watch. It was 11:05 p.m. "Leaving," he said and stood up. Kathy or no Kathy, he was going to bed. Southwest Homes would start trading in the morning and he wanted to see his inaugural deal's first trades. He turned toward the door just as Kathy walked in.

"Been looking for you," Kathy said, smiling. She stepped back for a moment, then chuckled. "I was going to buy you a beer, but it looks like you're a dozen ahead of me."

"Looking for you, too. Where were you?"

"Work, dinner, work. C'mon I'll buy you one, Mr. Deal."

Richard nodded, sat back down. Ken set up two bottles of Heineken. "Cheers," Kathy said, clinking Richard's bottle. "Congratulations on your first deal. How's it feel?"

"Exhausted, demoralized, but otherwise great."

"Demoralized?"

"Not quite the glamour I expected. You know, getting kicked around by Jeannie and Cole."

They both paused for a few moments, sipped their beers looking straight ahead. Then Richard could see Kathy observing him, leaning away from him, like she thought Richard might do something irrational. Or fall off his stool.

Richard said, "How about you? How you doing?"

"Good. Fired up. Like my father used to say, 'I'm already on the second rung of the ladder.'" Just like Kathy, that killer ambition. But now that he thought about it, lately he'd sensed her ambition was on autopilot. This drive to be the youngest woman Managing Director ever seemed monomaniacal. And her constant talk about the family heritage in the business; it was almost like she was still building her resume, or maybe using her father as part of hers.

Richard said, "You still sure this is what you want?"

Kathy shot a look at Richard. "Why would you ask me that?"

Richard didn't say anything for a moment. The intensity of her reaction surprised him, and then he realized how drunk he must be to have asked her. But he figured, *what the hell.*

"Sometimes when I hear you talk about your dad it sounds like maybe you feel you have to live up to him, be the son he never had. Or maybe you didn't think you had much choice but to go into the business."

She settled back on her stool. "I've had plenty of choices. This is what I want. And I want to be the best."

Richard nodded.

"But I'm still surprised you asked. Do *you* have doubts?"

"I saw some bizarre stuff at Walker on this deal. This is a tough business." Richard thought about Cole beating up on him, the Southwest pricing meeting, Jack in the turf battle over fees afterward. "Some high financiers. Bunch of guys duking it out over a pot of money."

"Nobody said it's for the fainthearted," Kathy said. He saw her face soften. "But you're a tough guy. And smart. I've seen it firsthand. Getting thrown together into a cubicle with somebody, you see what they're made of."

"Yeah, I think I have what it takes."

"But you still sure you want it?"

"Absolutely. Bad enough to suck in my pride for six months." He realized what he'd said as its came out of his mouth. He might as well have used the word "probational."

Kathy leaned in toward the bar and tilted her head so she could see his face. "Nothing to be ashamed of about that. When I heard, it made me respect you more."

"Does everybody know?"

"Cole talks about it like it's not even supposed to be confidential."

"Maybe he wants everyone to know. I hear he flushed a few probationals last year."

Kathy didn't say anything for a moment. She was looking into Richard's eyes, almost tenderly.

"What?" Richard said.

"Like I said, I respect you, and I hope you make it."

"What do you think of my chances?"

She laughed. "You just did a billion-dollar IPO, the firm's biggest ever, for Harold Milner, no less, arguably the most important financier of his generation. I'd say that's a good running start."

"I'm not kidding myself. I was a low-level grunt on this one. A pencil getting pushed around by Jeannie and Cole." He paused and smiled. "So what do you think of my chances?" Richard teetered sideways on his stool; Kathy put her hand out to prop him up.

She didn't answer.

After a moment Richard said, "Cole's got my number doesn't he?"

She shrugged.

Bastard. What did he have to do to get past this guy? What a downer. Some first deal celebration. He shrugged back at Kathy. No sense feeling sorry for himself. He imagined Dad looking at him with that half-smile, telling him to dig in and show this guy Cole what he was made of. In that moment he made up his mind he was gonna do whatever was necessary, whatever Cole or anybody asked him to do.

#

The morning Southwest Homes went public, Milner had coffee at Cipriani Dolci on the balcony level at Grand Central Terminal, looking out at the Main Concourse. Milner loved Grand Central. Sometimes he came up here to just stand and watch, imagining what Cornelius Vanderbilt would have felt taking in that view of the station his heirs built as a monument to him and his empire. People hurrying across the floor, the brass clock atop the information booth where it had always been. The hum of voices and feet shuffling on marble echoing off the ceiling. The ticket booths still busy, everything much as it must have been in 1913.

He looked up at the three cavernous arched windows sixty feet above the floor on either side. The architect's vision had proposed them as open arches for elevated roadways to connect 43rd Street through the station, instead of stopping it dead at the terminal and continuing it on the other side; a complement to the elevated north-south arteries that encircled the terminal to unite Park Avenue with Park Avenue South. It was intended as a grand-scale tribute to the stature of Vanderbilt's accomplishments: Grand Central as the nexus of all activity in the world's most important metropolis. Milner would like to have seen that, just as he would like to see a similar tangible monument to his own achievements. Now he felt free to get that plan back on track. The hell with "financial engineering on steroids", he was going back to being a builder again.

CHAPTER THREE

New York City. Richard said how much you wanna bet this takes all day? Kathy said not a bet I'd take. Richard said how'd we get ourselves into this anyhow? Kathy said quit complaining, you're the one who was campaigning to be this year's debutante. Richard said I just wanted to be at the top of this year's class and get sent to Europe, not get pins stuck in me all day. Kathy said maybe if you'd spent a few weekends this summer out on Long Island instead of kissing ass in the office you might not be sitting here. Richard said how come you're sitting here, Hamptons girl? Kathy said I'm smarter than you.

They went on like that for a while, like they did next to each other in the bullpen at the office. It helped with the boredom. They were sitting across from each other outside a massive dining room in the rented suite at the Carlyle Hotel where the assembled senior partners of Schoenfeld & Co., GCG and Walker & Company were holding their annual strategy sessions. Richard and Kathy were dwarfed by 15-foot high ceilings, opulent silk wall fabric, the ivory sheen of aged oil paint on chair rails, and two-inch thick polished mahogany doors. They waited for their interviews to be considered for a three-month secundment, as the Brits called it, to the European offices of Schoenfeld and GCG. They bantered to masquerade their tension, tied for top of the Associate class.

Richard was desperate to win the secundment: it was considered a plum and evidence of being on the fast track. That would assure he'd survive his probational period. Besides, he'd heard rumors that if he didn't get sent to Europe he might get assigned to the Mergers and Acquisitions Department. The officers in M&A were even tougher than Cole, who Richard, through diligent focus, thinking two steps ahead and grinding it out, had managed to win over. And while the M&A bankers were considered Wall Street's elite, Richard knew that meant working for LeClaire. He remembered how LeClaire broke his balls when he interviewed him; what would he be like to work for? Richard had a pretty good idea that Jack wanted to see him stick around, what with Jack tapping him for little odd jobs all the time. And he wouldn't put it past Jack to kibosh his candidacy to keep one of his best mules in his own barn. It was a touchy spot.

Jack hitting on him started early on. "Jack's looking for you," Kerry Learned said as Richard walked back into the bullpen with his bag of take-out food one evening. "Said he's heading out to dinner with a client, but he'll be back later." Things like that boosted Richard's status as the alpha male after closing the "Milner deal," as the other Associates referred to Southwest Homes. They actually got quiet when he walked into the bullpen for the first two weeks. It was like his friend's pointer, Rip, when it would walk around the kennel all stiff-legged and cocky after being the only one let out to work the field on a Saturday. The deference of the other dogs was grudging, but unmistakable.

"You busy?" Jack asked Richard after his dinner.

Richard there with his shirt sleeves rolled up, 10 p.m., tie undone, half-eaten boxes of Chinese food on his desk and piles of annual reports all over the place. *The hell you think?*

"Sort of."

"Working for Cole?"

"Who else?"

"Got some time for me?"

"Always, Jack." Richard smiled extra hard to look eager.

"I'm not asking you on a date, bozo." Jack handed Richard a list. "Tomorrow first thing would be great. I'll cover you with Cole. Get whatever help you need. Thanks, tiger."

Richard looked over to say something to Kathy and realized she was gone, having dinner with some guy from Morgan Stanley.

One of those nights Richard stood in a darkened conference room and looked across the river at Brooklyn. He could see the lights of the River Café on the other side, where she'd told him another guy, this one from Goldman, had taken her for dinner, and then walked with her on the promenade at Brooklyn Heights. He turned away, wishing it didn't matter to him.

She'd laughed that off as nothing while Richard and she played squash one evening at the Harvard Club. "It was downright windy and cold out there, even in early September. I couldn't wait to get home." Even hearing her say that, he remembered the ache he'd felt when she first told him about it.

Richard saw her smirking at him, working the ball in her hand, poised for a serve.

"What?" he said.

"You sure you want to keep going?"

"Just serve, smart-ass." He felt as if she'd dragged his lungs around the court for half an hour. His legs were beginning to cramp. She wore a simple t-shirt and gym shorts, but still managed to look killer sexy. Her skin shined with perspiration.

"You're cooked, farm boy," she said.

"Quit calling me that. I'm a Midwesterner, not a farmer."

"Same thing," Kathy said, smiling. "And don't knock it. It's a big part of your appeal." Then she aced him for the fourth time that game. He only learned a few days earlier that she was a tri-state junior squash champ in private school.

Now he looked over at Kathy's profile, the graceful jaw, pert nose and full lips. Whichever of them won the secundment, Richard would miss her for the three months. Aside from the fact that he was trying to figure out a graceful way to put a move on her without killing their friendship, she was the only one in their Associate class that wasn't pretty much an asshole. Not having Kathy to horse around with at midnight or have a few beers with would leave a void. Richard had even brought Kathy into his confidence with the emails he'd discovered between somebody at GCG and "walker1" in the Comm Room. They'd nicknamed "walker1" the mole.

When Richard told her about the first emails he'd seen, Kathy nodded, thinking. "If this is what it looks like, your mole is a crook. The SEC would send him and his friends to jail for what they're doing."

"For a long time. Especially the mole, since he's the one placing the orders."

"And he's here at Walker," Kathy said. "You check out the stocks he's trading?"

"He's code-named them. He's being careful."

Two weeks later Richard sat down in his and Kathy's cubicle in the bullpen and whispered, "Somebody almost walked into the Comm Room while I was checking the mole's emails."

Kathy looked around the bullpen, then whispered back, "I've been thinking about that. I have an idea. Wait till later."

By 1:30 a.m. the Associate bullpen had cleared out. Kathy stood up and started walking out. "Come on, farm boy. I'll show you some stuff they taught us at Harvard."

Richard followed her, feeling a flicker of anticipation.

They could still hear the Analysts' fingers on their keyboards crunching numbers, smell stale take-out cole slaw when they walked past the Analyst bullpen. They entered the Comm Room as quietly as they could and sat down in front of the computer. Richard felt lightheaded. He realized he was clenching his fists. Kathy motioned for Richard to sit next to her. "Write this stuff down."

Richard looked back at her and rolled his eyes. "Since when do I take notes for you?" he whispered.

"What, I can't show you something without you feeling like I'm stomping on your ego? Lighten up."

Kathy turned back to the computer, opened Microsoft Outlook and clicked on the "Tools" menu, then "E-mail Accounts." When the box popped up, Richard saw about 15 email accounts.

"There it is," Richard said, pointing to walker1@netwiz.net. He glanced at the doorway.

Kathy highlighted the account and then clicked on "Change." The new box that popped up showed the email account walker1@netwiz.net, the incoming and outgoing servers, the username "walker1" and nine asterisks for the password. Richard wrote it all down. Kathy clicked on "Advanced" in the "More Settings" menu and pointed to the checked box next to "Leave a copy of messages on the server." Richard wished she'd hurry up.

Kathy closed down the Tools menu, got up and motioned for Richard to follow her. Richard's mouth was dry as they walked out. When they got back to their cubicle, Kathy said, "The netwiz.net server, wherever it is, doesn't care where the mole is or what computer he's using. It'll send his emails to whatever computers have that account set up in them. So all you need to do is set up that account in your own computer and you'll get the mole's emails. That is, after you guess his password." She smirked at him.

Richard geared himself up as if he'd be solving the London Sunday Times crossword puzzle and then was almost disappointed when he got it on his second try: walkerone.

"Look," he said to Kathy, as well over a hundred emails streamed into his computer once he'd entered the account. *This guy's been busy.* He felt a squishy sensation in his stomach, then his legs. What was he getting himself into?

"All those downloaded because that little box was checked saying to leave a copy of all the messages on the server. They've been sitting there, waiting."

Richard clicked on his "Sent Items" folder. "Nothing."

Kathy said, "That's because your Outlook only tracks emails you send from your computer. But if all of the incoming emails are still on the server, I'll bet all of the outbound ones are still on there too."

Richard Googled netwiz.net, found the website and logged in as walker1, password walkerone. It worked and sure enough, Kathy was right. The "Sent Items" folder had all the outbound messages as well. Hundreds, Richard guessed. He printed out hard copies. He felt his pulse quicken. By then Kathy had rolled her chair over next to Richard's to see. Her laugh was one Richard hadn't heard from her before: giggly, like the fastest-promoted woman MD on Wall Street was a 16 year-old girl. Richard felt that squishy sensation again, but more intense because of Kathy's reaction. This mole was into something big, and maybe better left alone.

Amazing old building, the Carlyle. Richard now absently looked up at the ceiling, eyeing 18-inch plaster moldings. He itched to know what was going on at the strategy session in the room next door. He bet Jack was pumped, remembering how Jack had sucked up the tension in the room in the Southwest Homes pricing meeting, like infighting was some drug for him.

#

Jack was so bored he was afraid that if he didn't concentrate on breathing, his autonomic nervous system would shut off and he'd die. These strategy sessions were even worse than year-end bonus discussions. At least in those things you were talking about money. Here it was just Sir Reginald sounding off about "tactics and accomplishing our strategy" and shit like that. *What a horse's ass. Must be a riot getting stuck sitting next to him at a dinner party.*

It was awful, but Jack had to listen. His logic was: even a nincompoop sometimes passed a multiple-choice exam, like when the *Wall Street Journal* had those monkeys pick stocks by throwing darts, and they occasionally outperformed big-time money managers. So Jack felt like he couldn't afford to zone out while Sir Reginald was blathering on, just in case the potato-head, upper-crust Brit moron got lucky and had a brainstorm that could cause mischief.

Sir Reginald was in the middle of one of his monologues right now, acting all dramatic, looking like some stern-faced high school guidance counselor. He droned on about Schoenfeld & Co. and GCG sharing client relationships to springboard the Walker-Schoenfeld-GCG alliance into a global presence. *Global schmobal.*

". . . it may admittedly take some years to do so," and Sir Reginald extended his palms like he was cradling a globe, "but we're building a business and we have plenty of time."

The old guy was talking to everyone like they were little kids. Only the Brits were so arrogant. *Except for the Frogs.* If Jack hadn't sat through a couple of hours of this already it might be comical. He spent half his time looking at Sir Reginald Schoenfeld's belly bulging out of an open button on his shirt. Other than that at least the bald old slug knew how to dress—he wore a Saville Row custom suit, a subtle chalk stripe on a bold blue. But the other half the time Jack spent looking up the old bird's nose, given the way Schoenfeld tilted his head back. Jeez, somebody should buy the guy a nasal hair trimmer. Marvin Garden-Whyte, Sir Reginald's number two man, perched at his side like a lap-dog. Philippe Delecroix, their partner from GCG, was a spindly little wisp who looked like a loud cough would blow him out of his chair on the other side of the 20-foot conference table. How a scrawny stick like that could be such a cagey in-fighter was always a surprise to Jack. Look at him, yawning, talking in French to his guys, waving those pixie arms that looked like you could snap them in half with a good twist. Jack reminded himself the Frog was nobody to mess with even if he did come off as Truman Capote. He glanced over as Mickey jumped up to take another call on his cell phone, heading out for the hall. At least he was getting some work done.

"Would you repeat that part about utilizing our clients? I'm uncertain I correctly heard you," Delecroix said.

Sir Reginald cleared his throat. "Of course, Philippe. Let me clarify." Sir Reginald took a long breath.

And now for a prerecorded message.

Sir Reginald carried on like he was running for President. *Jeez, the way this fool went on.* Jack looked around the room to see if anyone else was as fed up as he was, wishing somebody would fart. He forced himself to stop fidgeting his leg.

Still Sir Reginald went on. After another few minutes Jack couldn't listen to any more. He said, "I don't see where we make a buck on all this. Underwriting profits on Eurobond issues are so tight that you gotta pucker your sphincter to squeeze a nickel out of a deal. Besides, the markets are in a coma right now with this credit meltdown freezing things up. So why go through all the effort if it means there won't be any payoff for any of us?"

Jack searched Sir Reginald's face for a reaction: nothing.

"Well," Sir Reginald said. He leaned forward and set his gaze on the ceiling, the way the Brits did to avoid looking you in the eye when they were about to say something you didn't wanna hear.

Before he could say anything, Delecroix said, "While as Jack says the markets are now frozen, we have made money which is important to us on Eurobond deals. And when you split that into half—or thirds—why, then it should be obvious that hurts us. If we, and Schoenfeld & Co., are to achieve more as partners it must be from an addition from Walker and not merely sliding profits around. Or worse, giving them away." He pushed his chair back from the table. "Our people are not so easily motivated without financial considerations." He poked his index finger on the table for emphasis, "I will not so easily relinquish our lead underwriting position under the GCG name unless we share more disproportionately in the finances."

Jack wondered how anybody could massacre English so badly and still be drop dead clear. Even a stooge like Sir Reginald had to understand it. Sir Reginald turned and met Delecroix's gaze. His face was now stony and his eyes were hard. Jack saw a definite chink in the relationship.

Jack said, "Fellas, regardless of the split, there just isn't a way to make as much money on anything right now as there is on mopping up after this credit mess."

"Go on," Delecroix said.

"You take a step back and look hard at this housing collapse and the worldwide credit freeze and you can see an obvious way to make money out of it. Ask yourself what comes next. My bet is we're headed for a doozy of a recession. And what happens then? Bankruptcies, tons of them."

Jack looked around the room. Delecroix wandered over to the credenza and poured himself a cup of coffee. Jack wasn't sure he had his attention. The little guy was hard to read.

Jack went on. "And our competitors have gotten creamed in this thing. Merrill Lynch: 8, 10, 12 billion dollars of write-offs in mortgage-backeds and more to come. Citigroup: even more losses in mortgage-backeds than Merrill's. Bear Stearns: teetering. Morgan Stanley and Lehman: scrambling not to be the next to get clobbered, with their stock prices off 50 percent."

Now Delecroix was nodding in agreement. *Good.* Jack looked over at Sir Reginald. He was tilting his head back, giving Jack another bird's eye view of his nose bush.

Jack went on. "But us? No losses and it looks we've got almost no exposure."

Delecroix had turned back from the credenza, now scowling at Jack. He said, "Where is this going?"

"We gear up big time to be players in bankruptcy restructurings and refinancings. And not just in the U.S., but Europe, as far as Schoenfeld & Co.'s and GCG's relationships reach. We step into the vacuum and suck out all that business before our competitors can get off their backs."

Sir Reginald said, "That is an unsavory business."

"Since when are we concerned about 'unsavory'?" Jack said.

Sir Reginald looked at Delecroix, then back at Jack. No one said anything for a few awkward moments. Then Sir Reginald said, "But we don't have a restructuring team."

"We've got GCG to provide all the financing, and a crackerjack mergers and acquisitions team in New York. We hire a couple of big shot bankruptcy restructuring guys, then move all the M&A team over into restructuring. We'll all make a fortune on fees."

Jack looked over at Delecroix, who'd sat back down and was looking into his coffee cup, thinking. Sir Reginald shook his head. *But no response.*

"Come on guys whattaya think?" Jack asked. He saw Sir Reginald move in his chair and look over at Garden-Whyte.

"Shall we break, and flesh out the discussions after tea?" Garden-Whyte said.

Sure, why not waste the whole day?

#

Richard watched the senior management team file out of the conference room for a break. He saw Jack pull the door shut, then heard raised voices, then shouting. After a few minutes Jack opened the door.

"I should fire you on the spot," he heard Sir Reginald say.

Jack turned his head and laughed. "Fire me?" he said over his shoulder, "you can't fire me. I'm the firm's biggest producer. You're *my* bitch."

Richard looked over at Kathy. She leaned back in her chair, trying to seem nonchalant, but looked scared stiff. Now she turned to Richard, eyes wide.

"Not like Morgan Stanley, huh?" Richard said.

Kathy didn't respond. Jack strode past, smiling, walking cocky. Richard didn't wait for Sir Reginald to walk by. He went and took a long piss, splashed some water on his face. *This is it.* Europe for three months.

The senior management team was reassembled for about 15 minutes before Jack poked his head through the doorway and motioned for Richard to come in. Richard felt his pulse pound in his temples, a flutter in his stomach. Kathy gave him a thumbs up. Richard thought of her breasts silhouetted in the orange sun in that little tiny dress. As he walked through the door and took his position at Jack's end of the table, he could see Sir Reginald's gigantic nostrils twitching open at him as the old man arched his head backward to observe him. Everything else kind of muddled together after that.

#

Voicemail again. It was the third time Jack called Mickey after they'd scattered following the kids' interviews. Give Mickey an hour before dinner and God only knew how many phone calls he'd jam in. Jack didn't want a drink, but he was headed for Bemelmans Bar anyhow. See if he could jawbone Delecroix a little. He figured Sir Reginald was stewing in his hotel room right now, what with the pistol-whipping Jack had given him earlier. That'd been a long time coming. But even that was too civilized to really satisfy him. Back in Canarsie he'd have called Sir Reginald a soft old fuddy-duddy and popped him in the nose.

The old boob needed it. He had no market instinct, no understanding that these wild-ass markets could make you rich in a heartbeat if you played them right—or kill you just as quick if you didn't. That was a real concern with a moron like Sir Reginald trying to call strategy for the firm with all this volatility and panic out there. Jack knew from watching years of market cycles that you held onto your balls with both hands in times like these, or else. Sir Reginald should've remembered that quote from Socrates: guys who don't read history are doomed to repeat it. *Stupid putz.*

At least spanking Sir Reginald was more fun than sitting through those interviews, the Brits all serious about which of the two kids would get their dumb-ass secundment. Then wanting to talk about it for an hour afterward. The Frogs must've made up their minds the minute they saw Cella walk in. Jeez, Delecroix sitting with his mouth open, looking her up and down. Blum never had a chance. He'd call the kid later.

#

Richard came up behind Kathy at the bar at Raoul's. He'd just gotten the news from Jack on his cellphone.

"Hi. I'm Richard." He smiled, like it was an opening line.

Kathy smiled back, looking confused at first, then her eyes showing a spark of understanding, playing along.

"I'm new in town," Richard continued, "but I'll be here for at least three months."

Kathy's eyes softened, like she fully understood, then coy.

Richard went on. "I don't usually do things like this, but I saw you sitting alone, and I thought, what the hell."

Kathy smiled again, then turned away, sipped her drink.

"How'm I doing so far?" he said.

"Not so great with your spiel, but you're the second best looking guy I've ever seen."

"Who's the first?"

"A girl's gotta keep a guy guessing sometimes." Kathy patted the stool next to her. "Hi, Richard, I'm Kathy." As if she did it all the time. Barfly.

"You drinking alone, or just been stood up?"

Kathy shrugged. "Depends on how you look at it." Still playing along, now looking like she was ready to take the lead. Sucking on the straw of her drink again—looked like a daiquiri—come-on look in her eyes. Maybe she would surprise him tonight. He sat down on the stool next to her and leaned in. Her hair was a little tousled, windblown. She smelled great, that Estée Lauder fragrance she wore. Her eyes were done just so. He could tell she'd reapplied her makeup after the offsite. *All good signs.* He felt warm in his chest.

"So what do you do for fun?" he asked.

"Kick guys asses at squash."

"How's that working for you?"

"I'm drinking alone, aren't I?"

"Not anymore."

#

In the clunky service elevator to her loft, Kathy was still role-playing like the girl taking her pickup home for a drink. She wanted out of it. Not out of bringing Richard home, but out of the game. She didn't need any role-playing to feel the sexual energy between them.

She looked over at him, remembering him as he was that first time in the elevator at work, all business, earnest and serious. She thinking he hadn't noticed her, then all of a sudden him coming alive, attentive. Richard escorting her up Wall Street, his Wall Street. Giving her a history lesson, enjoying himself. He looking sleek in his freshly-pressed charcoal gray suit, foulard tie with the perfect dimple snuggled up against his starched collar. He with his strong hands constantly in motion, and his eyes always on her.

Even now, even knowing him these months, he had that air of confidence with an undercurrent of vulnerability that only she thought she could see. Not cocky, but the undiscovered champion with the gentle look in his eyes.

She had that feeling in her tummy again, that airiness, like driving too fast. Then the same feeling, but lower, as if her legs were disconnected from her brain and were going to wrap themselves around him. She bet he was a great kisser. She was sure he didn't try to force his tongue into your mouth the instant your lips touched, like most guys, trying to act sophisticated. Like they've kissed all kinds of girls, showing you how cool they are. No, she bet Richard kissed you like he meant it. Tonight might be difficult. She didn't want to say yes to him. How silly women could be. Knowing what they wanted, and not wanting it at the same time.

By the time they'd finished a bottle of wine, Conan O'Brien was coming on the television. Kathy was now sitting in an armchair by herself, having gracefully slipped off the sofa when it looked like Richard was moving toward her—twice. If he did it again she was going to get pissed off.

Near the end of Conan's monologue, she bent over in the chair laughing. When she sat back up, Richard had walked over from the sofa and was standing right there. He did it smoothly; leaned over, kissed her. She pulled away.

"Richard, don't."

He didn't move, didn't say anything. He just looked into her eyes and smiled; very confident. He put his hand on her cheek and came toward her again.

"Don't," she said and stood up. She balled her hands into fists, narrowed her eyes and stuck out her jaw. "Stop it!"

"I don't get it." He stood there, eyebrows furrowed.

"What don't you get?"

"Calm down."

"I'll calm down when you back off."

Richard shook his head and put his hands up as if in surrender. He crossed to the sofa and sat down.

"Don't look so shocked. You're acting like you've never had a woman say no to you before. Besides, what were you thinking? God, we're cubicle-mates."

He smiled and chuckled. "It was pretty clear to me we were moving in this direction."

"Maybe clear to *you*. But you're not thinking clearly; you've been pining away over me for a while now. And it's beginning to get in the way."

"I'm not trying to hide that I'm interested, but I'm getting mixed signals here. You were downright coquettish in the bar. And how often do grown women invite male friends over for TV after a few drinks, then a bottle of wine if they aren't at least thinking about something more?"

Kathy let out a long sigh and sat back down. She looked him in the eye and said, "At least once."

He didn't say anything for a few moments, maybe waiting to see if she had anything else to say. All of a sudden she just wanted him to leave. Maybe he was right: she'd probably been putting out what she was thinking as they got to her apartment. But still, after two failed passes he should have backed off.

"I think you should leave. I'll see you at work tomorrow."

"Message received." He stood up. "Thanks for the wine."

She didn't get up to show him to the door.

She felt lousy. But after Morgan Stanley, there's no way she was ever getting involved with anyone from the office again. *My God*, it was downright humiliating with everybody finding out about Frank and her within a few weeks. Separated from his wife or not, a Managing Director and an Analyst was juicy gossip. And it made it worse that she was working for him in the Healthcare Group. *Under him*, some snickered. At the time she tried to tell herself she was above the gossip because she loved him, but it hurt, made her feel cheap.

And she wasn't blind to the fact that it was the only time she let a man get in the way of what she wanted. In prep school, Harvard undergrad, even HBS, her relationships never lasted more than a few years, if that. The shrink she saw for six months after Frank helped her see that a man wasn't important enough to her to let the obligation of a commitment slow her down—at least up until then. When Dr. Oldman started probing her on why it took a man 10 years her senior to open her up for the first time, she stopped going.

Now she wished she could ask Daddy for advice about Richard, but at the same moment she knew what he'd say: that crude aphorism about not shitting where you eat. Thinking of him now made her ache. How could she still miss him so much after all these years? She realized she was just staring at the television. She got up, picked up the wine bottle and glasses and walked into the kitchen.

#

Croonquist got off the elevator on the 47th floor of the GM building. The receptionist at Surrey Capital Management's offices looked like a model on the cover of Vogue. *Only in New York.* She smiled like she was posing, head cocked to the side.

"Mr. Croonquist?" she said.

"I must have that rumpled public servant look about me."

"Not at all, Mr. Croonquist. Jamie said to expect you at noon, and that you were always punctual." She looked over at her computer monitor. "You're two minutes early."

Croonquist smiled and shrugged.

She walked him into the center of the office, which was a single trading floor that took up a full third of the building's footprint. They entered a series of trading stations arranged in concentric circles around a single circular desk raised slightly above them. Croonquist felt cool air from the floor. He knew from prior visits the floor was raised to accommodate the myriad wires and communications cables running underneath the panels, chilled to help dissipate the heat emanating from all of the computer and communications technology in the room.

Croonquist guessed 60 people sat in the trading stations positioned in the circles around the center desk, all in front of multiple LCD screens. Most wore headsets with microphones. Their voices blurred together into a monotone buzz.

Jamie Swift, the founder and manager of Surrey's $15 billion in hedge funds, smiled at Croonquist from the center desk, where he presided over the rocket scientists who worked for him. As he approached Swift, Croonquist felt more cool air cascading down from the ceiling. He smelled nothing. He recalled that one of Swift's rules was no perfumes or colognes: nothing to interfere with the ozone-charged air, designed to enhance creativity and a positive outlook.

"Roman," was all Swift said, standing and shaking hands. He motioned for Croonquist to sit across from him, then sat and said, "Great to see you. Whatcha got?" No extended pleasantries, right to it. Croonquist had known Swift for over 15 years and it was always the same.

"Something, I think. But I hope you can tell me for sure."

"Okay, lemme take a look," Swift said, reaching across for the papers Croonquist pulled out of his briefcase. Swift flipped pages for a few moments. "These must be code-names."

"Of course. But can you figure out what they're doing without knowing the company names?"

"Yup. They put on a colossal bearish macro sector put trade with a long stock hedge. They're real gamblers."

"Care to put that in English?"

Swift laughed. "Somebody made a huge short bet that the stocks in a single industry would all decline."

"Yeah, that really clears it up for me."

"Okay, these guys placed a couple billion dollar wager the stocks in this industry would drop—fast, and made three hundred million or so in profits by the time they unwound the trades."

"How did they do it?"

"They bought puts—options to sell the industry companies' stocks, which increase in value when the stocks drop—and simultaneously bought the stocks, to moderate their loss if they were wrong and the industry's stocks went up. A hedged bet with a major downside bias."

Croonquist slid a piece of paper across the table with the real names of the homebuilding companies on it.

Swift smiled. "Of course, the homebuilders." He flipped back through the first pages Croonquist had given him, then looked back up at Croonquist. "The instant Milner's IPO of Southwest Homes was announced, the rest of the homebuilding sector traded down 10%—because a lotta money managers sold off their homebuilding stock positions in anticipation of buying Southwest's stock once it became publicly-traded."

"What are you saying?"

"Somebody knew in advance about Milner's IPO of Southwest and anticipated the market's reaction. Either that or they're geniuses and guessed that the housing bubble was getting ready to pop, and that the homebuilding stocks would tank."

"What do you think?"

"A short bet this big on an industry sector as hot as the homebuilders were a month ago? Nobody's that smart. I'd say somebody's a crook."

Now Swift was talking a language Croonquist understood.

#

Richard buzzed for entry at the door into the sealed-off Mergers and Acquisitions Department. Cynthia Jackson, the administrative head of the department, waited for him on the other side. She ushered him into the windowless conference room.

"May I see your ID, please?" she said.

"Cynthia, we've ridden the elevator together for four months. You know who I am."

"Do I look like I'm kidding?" She recorded Richard's employee ID number into a loose-leaf notebook, opened it and pushed it in front of him on the conference table. "Okay, Richard this is serious. This is the M&A Department Security Procedures Manual. I need you to read it before you do anything else, even if it takes you all morning. Sign both copies of the form at the front, give one to me and retain the other and the manual for your records. Don't sign the Consent and Waiver of Injunctive Relief unless you fully understand and agree to be bound by the rules of the manual and the applicable Securities and Exchange Commission statutes summarized in it. If you need any clarifications, we'll get you a full text, and we can have the General Counsel of the firm explain them to you in detail. I'll leave you alone now to read."

Remind me to stay the hell outta your *way.* She walked out and closed the door. Richard skimmed through the table of contents. Topics like Confidentiality, Persons with a Need to Know, Document Shredding Procedures, and so on. A section had sample questions and answers regarding preserving confidentiality of inside information on pending merger and acquisition transactions. He signed the forms and called Cynthia.

"I meant it when I said *read* it," she said.

He read through it. He recalled being fingerprinted on his first day of work, like everybody else in the securities business, and felt an ominous rumbling in his stomach when he read the waivers of rights that he would be signing. They meant if he screwed up he was on his own. They included signing away his right to being represented by Walker & Company's legal counsel, and his right to enjoin the firm from testifying against him if he broke the securities laws, particularly for insider trading. He called Cynthia back about 45 minutes later. Cynthia then led him, smiling now for the first time, from door to door of the glass-walled offices of the Managing Directors and Vice Presidents around the periphery of the department, introducing him. Then the rows of movable office partitions that made up the cubicles of the Associates and Analysts. He felt a smile cross his face; hell, he felt it down in his groin and creep upward all the way up to his chest.

She walked him into another windowless conference area. "This is the War Room. The Comm Room in the Corporate Finance Department was the original version of this. As you can see we've got much more high-tech stuff in here now." The War Room was a buzz of activity. The Dow Jones and NASDAQ tickers streamed across the far wall. A row of flat panel plasmas tuned in CNBC, Bloomberg, CNN and a few foreign news channels. Two rows of desks in the center of the room sported flat-panel LCD screens, rows of tickers and trades blinking on them, Associates and Analysts hunched in front of half of them, punching keyboards. A shredder stood in the corner, scraps of paper near it proving it actually got used. A team headed by François LeClaire reacted to some news story impacting their deal.

After Richard was introduced to the rest of the department at the following morning's 8:30 a.m. departmental meeting, he followed François LeClaire to his office for his first deal assignment. Richard had learned a lot about LeClaire since his screening interview back in March. Ecole Polytechnique, where he got his undergraduate engineering degree, was France's equivalent of MIT, Harvard and Stanford combined. It was regarded as the premier engineering school in the world. He'd then immediately gone to work for GCG. GCG soon saw his potential and sent him to Harvard Business School, then injected him into GCG's new investment, Walker & Company. Ron Elman, the firm's resident genius buffoon, said the combination of LeClaire's technical education at quant-jock Polytechnique, overlaid with the all-case-study, touchy-feely teaching method at Harvard, had left LeClaire permanently confused. "So he's syncopated," Elman said, referring to LeClaire's accent. "Puts the em-*pha*-sis on the wrong syl-*la*-ble. Ha-ha-ha-ha." LeClaire was now a respected Senior Vice President. He was feared by the Associates. *White-hot smart.* Richard told himself to be careful, remembering LeClaire grilling him in his interview.

Larry Nivens, a Managing Director in M&A, lounged on the sofa in LeClaire's office when they entered. "How're Elaine and the kids?" Nivens asked.

LeClaire's face softened. He cooed. "Wonderful," he said. His round face beamed the words. His eyes were wide and his mouth open like a child's. "Absolutely wonderful. At least that's how Chloe would say it." His thick accent strained Richard's ears.

"How old now?"

"Nineteen months."

"Well, I can see you're busy," Nivens said, getting up. "Welcome to the department, Richard," he said as he left.

LeClaire sat down behind his desk, motioning for Richard to sit in the chair in front. Richard's stomach tightened, watching as the softness in LeClaire's face disappeared, angular lines showing as he set his jaw. *Here it comes.*

Then LeClaire smiled. "I have good news, young man."

Young man. Funny. He remembered that from their interview. LeClaire couldn't have been more than six or seven years older than Richard.

LeClaire went on, "We are heading uptown to meet with Harold Milner at two o'clock." He looked at a pile of documents lined up perfectly on the left side of his desk, then another on the right. All was exacting order. Richard could see a pad in the uncluttered center of his desk with neatly scrolled words and figures on it, like mathematical equations. And a few structural drawings with arrows and boxes, like physicists' renderings. LeClaire reached to the pile on his right, grabbed a document from about half way down, then lined up the pile again. He handed the document to Richard. "Read the Tentron Corporation Annual Report later. Now swing your chair around here and I will show you what we are up to. This should be a fun day." The corners of LeClaire's eyes turned up as he smiled. His face softened again like it had when he mimicked his daughter. He waved Richard in close to his elbow as he slid the pad to the corner of his desk. He pulled a pencil from the holder containing a bunch of sharpened #2s.

Not a bad start, at the elbow of the firm's rocket scientist. It was a helluva contrast to his first days getting slapped around by Jeannie Peters and George Cole. LeClaire was actually *showing* him something, and enjoying it.

#

Richard and LeClaire got out of a taxi on 45th Street in front of the Helmsley Building. Richard could see the expanse of Park Avenue and the core business district of Manhattan running north through the building's gilded lobby, and through the arches of the eastern and western pedestrian walkways on either side. He looked up above them at the elevated highways that channeled traffic around Grand Central and into and out of the arches through the Helmsley building, then spilled cars out onto Park Avenue. He took in the sound of horns honking, the smell of diesel exhaust, the feeling of the rumble of Grand Central trains beneath the pavement.

Standing between the yin and yang of New York power. Richard looked up at the stone gargoyles surrounding the spire of the Helmsley Building. And Harold Milner up there, on top of them both.

When they arrived at the penthouse floor, Richard saw from the open lobby that the entire floor belonged to Milner. Smoked-glass-walled offices covered three sides. Northern Manhattan up Park Avenue streamed in through clear glass on the northern quadrant. Milner's office and conference room were on a mezzanine level, taking up the whole northern wall of the penthouse. The penthouse had double-floor-height ceilings, like Richard had read the earliest New York skyscrapers featured; this was originally the New York Central building, built by the railroad barons, the Vanderbilts. *For the owner's throne room.*

LeClaire led Richard past Milner's receptionist, who nodded with an air of recognition at LeClaire. Milner and Jack Grass reclined in living room furniture that occupied the initial few thousand square feet of the floor. Steinberg stood to the side, eyes blinking. That ever-present lazy way he had. Milner lounging with his geniuses, and Richard in the midst of them.

"I have to say, Mickey," Milner was saying, "I really admire the Russians' tube technology. I believe it's now the best in the world. Their 6C33 power triode output tube used in the guidance system of the MIG 25 fighter plane is something you just have to hear in a really high-quality stereo amplifier."

"Transistors trump tubes," Steinberg said. "Tubes just don't give you the precise resolution, soundstaging and deep bass of solid-state."

"Maybe if you're into technical perfection. Give me tubes' palpable reality anytime."

"An overly warm and colored reality."

"If you ever heard the 6C33 in my old Macintosh monoblock amps over there, the question would be resolved forever. I have just that much respect for your listening sensitivity." Milner winked at Steinberg. "But the things are just damned hard to come by, and one of my last matched pair just blew out."

"So get yourself a pair of Krell amps and find out what real music sounds like."

LeClaire and Richard waited until Steinberg finished his sentence, then walked up. Butterflies now in Richard's stomach like before a high school track meet. He felt his shoulder tug like the pitch books in his briefcase were an atom bomb.

"Characteristically punctual," Milner said, turning to look at LeClaire.

"I do not wish to keep our most important client waiting," LeClaire said, shaking hands with Milner. That syncopated French accent. "Hello, my friend," LeClaire said warmly.

"Hello, François," Milner said. "Always great to see you. And you, Richard," he said, shaking hands with him, "good to see you again. Still enjoying the music I gave you?" That big, warm paw of Milner's enveloping Richard's hand, now familiar.

"Yes, I'm a convert to lossless encoding."

"Jeez, another one," Jack said under his breath. He stood up. "Let's get to work," he said and motioned toward Milner's mezzanine office.

Milner led them upstairs. Milner had half a dozen well-thumbed manila folders and a few 10-Ks on his conference table. He seemed to have done most of his own research on a hand-written spreadsheet with penciled notations. Richard took a seat at the far end of the table, thinking to keep a low profile, but Milner sat at the end next to him. LeClaire took them all through his pitch book, Richard following along as he went. Richard kept his head down early on, like in class when you didn't want to risk getting called on because you hadn't read the assignment. Most of it was standard stuff he'd seen before: valuation numbers and ratios he'd crunched for Jeannie Peters and George Cole. He figured he could get up to speed quickly. He knew he'd be doing lots of them. The guts of the meeting only took about 20 minutes. Jack threw out some crude concepts after LeClaire finished going through the book, Milner threw them back, and then Steinberg and LeClaire exchanged some stuff that Richard found incomprehensible. Richard did his best to take notes.

At one point Milner saw Richard looking sideways at his one-page spreadsheet. Jack, LeClaire and Steinberg were engrossed in some penned manipulations LeClaire was creating in front of him on his pad.

"This is all I need. My map of reality," Milner said. "If I can't get it on one page, it's not worth doing, because I can't keep it framed in my head."

When it was over, Milner pushed back his chair and said, "So, Richard, what do you think?" He leaned on the table and cupped a hand over his mouth.

Not like he was trying to put Richard on the spot, at least Richard didn't think so. Richard smiled.

"I'm new at this, Harold. It's my first day in the M&A department. I've only read the Tentron annual report, carried the pitch books and sat in here."

"So, you must have some impressions."

Richard was afraid if he looked down the table at the others he might get a twitch of nerves. He didn't want to embarrass himself. But he felt comfortable with Milner, always had since the beginning. He said, "I don't know much about turbine driven generators, but I do think that Nick Williams' CEO letter to shareholders in this year's annual report was a little cocky on their developments in that area this year, especially since they've got a number three market share. I think the guy's got a big ego, and he'll likely put up a fight."

"Not a bad insight," Milner said. "And?" Milner was smiling with his eyes, his hand cupped over his mouth again.

"You could probably take the same approach you did with Berkshire United. Borrow against the hard-asset businesses with asset-backed financing and sell the divisions you don't want. That way maybe you get most of your investment back right away. As I recall on BU, you got more than your investment back after the sale of the unwanted businesses, so the whole deal was playing with other people's money."

Milner smiled, then looked down the table at Jack. Richard hoped Jack wasn't rolling his eyes. "Any other observations?" Milner said to Richard.

Richard still resisted the urge to see what Jack's reaction was, said, "Northern Ash baseball bats in the consumer subsidiary. They're an American icon. Every kid in my, and probably your generation grew up using them. They're the second most popular bats in Major League Baseball. So from a PR standpoint it might be like attacking our national pastime, or worse, mom and apple pie, if you try a hostile takeover."

Richard now glanced to the other end of the table. Jack was looking at him like he was from Mars, it seemed with some admiration. Steinberg was placid. LeClaire, sitting erect, was listening as if Richard was discoursing on a new physical property of argon gas.

"Whattaya suggest?" Milner asked.

"Maybe some colorful metaphors in your press releases and some pithy quotes in the *Wall Street Journal*. I'd avoid words like 'bashing' and 'bludgeon', but maybe use words like 'heartwood' or 'home run'. How about: 'a sufficiently solid company at the heartwood to avoid the decay of mismanagement'."

Milner laughed and slapped Richard's arm. "Not quite there, but a worthy try. Good bullshit, Richard. Glad you're on the team."

Milner was still smiling when he pressed their hands before they left. And nobody looked at Richard like he was an asshole in the elevator on the way downstairs.

Chapter 4

Washington, D.C. Croonquist recognized Charlie Green's cell phone number on his desk phone's caller ID. *Here we go.* He picked up the handset.

"Roman, it's Charlie. You called?" he said, impatient.

"Yeah. I need some air cover."

"I'm up to my eyeballs with these bastards on the Hill again. Can it wait?"

"Not really. I've got something brewing . . . ."

"About time. What you got?" Sounding interested now.

"I've got a potential bust working, and I think it's big. I've got reams of trading statistics in MarketWatch and emails ordering trades from Walker New York, then emails from Groupe Credit Generale to all over Europe."

"Emails? How the hell'd you get them?"

"A friend at NSA."

"You dog, you."

"Yeah, but I'm not sure I can use them all. Stone in Litigation is a real Boy Scout. He might say they're illegal."

"Of course he will. Because they are."

"That's why I need you to talk to him."

"And say what?"

"Tell him NSA uncovered them by mistake in some national security monitoring or something. You'll figure it out. You're the boss, I'm just a humble lawyer."

"Don't be a smart-ass." He paused for a moment. "Shit, Roman, you're stretching it here. Is this worth it?"

"It's had me semi-erect for a month."

"Okay. Anything else?"

"Authority for wiretaps. On phones and emails."

"It'll take probable cause to get it past Judge Weinstein."

"The trading statistics show a clear pattern of insider activity prior to the Southwest Homes IPO. Unrestrained trading. Somebody got a hold of inside information that a filing was coming and front-ran it with a very complex and risky trading strategy. I've had a real pro confirm that nobody's got balls to take a multi-billion dollar position like that without knowing inside information. And our MarketWatch algorithms say an 86% correlation with previous illegal insider trading activity."

"Sounds like you're getting there, but I don't think it's enough to give Weinstein a boner yet. How big is this?"

"Walker & Company, GCG in Paris, some other European institutions and . . ." he paused for effect, "maybe Harold Milner."

Green was silent for a moment, then whispered, "Holy shit."

"I was counting on you to say that."

"Have your guys draft me a brief. I'll get on Weinstein's calendar. You drop everything else and fast-track this thing. And Roman . . ." Green paused.

"Yeah?"

"Don't fuck this up."

#

New York City. Richard and Kathy didn't miss a beat when they saw each other the morning after she'd brushed him off in her apartment. Richard's family called it 'doing the South American,' when you pretended a blowup or embarrassment never happened, going on with things as usual. They bantered, Kathy called him farm boy and Richard wondered why South Americans were so screwed up. Kathy left for Paris a week later.

Kathy phoned two days after she arrived.

"Sa va," she said.

"Up yours, too."

"It means 'how's everything?'"

"Oh, sorry. I'm fine, how's Paris?"

"Gorgeous. I'm trying to drink at all in."

Drink it all in? "How's your French coming?"

"Quite well, quite well. And I picked up a tutor today."

"What?"

"I met a Frenchman at the market this morning. Says he's from the south of France, here for a modeling career. Gorgeous. And he's fluent in French, of course." She laughed.

Richard felt his face starting to color as Kathy said it. Was she breaking his balls, or just reinforcing the message they were only friends?

"Sounds like you're settling in."

"Yes. Hey, our mole has been pretty active, no?"

"Haven't checked up on him lately."

"You should. These guys are trading a lot of options. Representing maybe one to two billion dollars in stock, I can't quite tell. And another thing. I found emails to London as well, signed by walker2@GCG.com over here at GCG."

"Did you crack his password? I'll load that account onto my computer."

"No, couldn't break it." Kathy paused. "What do you think's going on?"

"Looks to me as if it's just plain old-fashioned larceny: insider trading. Somebody knows the takeover targets and he's passing their names along to a couple of others who are trading on it as well."

Kathy didn't respond. Richard could tell she was still connected because he could hear the transatlantic line crackling. Finally, Kathy said, "This is probably just some intercontinental arbitrage strategy the trading guys are doing."

"Sending code-named emails to do trades?"

"I think this is all something you're dreaming up in your head. I mean, stumbling by mistake onto an insider trading ring by just uncovering one suspicious email."

"That's how it happens sometimes. Remember the whole Dennis Levine insider trading scandal in the 1980's? Half the major firms on Wall Street were involved. Guys from Drexel to Kidder to Goldman were indicted. Marty Siegel, an M&A banking star, ex-Kidder then at Drexel, turned out to be dirty. Ivan Boesky, the biggest arbitrageur of his day, paid a hundred million dollar fine and went to jail. Mike Milken, the junk bond kingpin, paid $600 million before they put him away. And it all started with a back office compliance clerk someplace thinking some trades looked fishy, reporting them. And not even Levine's trades. It was some dope who was piggybacking off Levine's trades when he saw how much money Levine was making."

"I think you watch too many movies, farm boy."

"I think you've got your head in the sand."

"Yeah, well." She used the impatient tone she reserved for when she wanted to dismiss a subject.

Richard said, "I'm gonna keep an eye on this and figure out what's going on and who's doing it."

Kathy didn't respond.

#

"What are you doing?" Chuck White, Milner's CFO asked. He'd just knocked on the glass door to Milner's office, Milner motioning him in to sit down. Milner was reviewing the pitch book on Tentron again, for about the fifth time in a week.

"Whattaya mean?" Milner said, playing a little, acting innocent, seeing Chuck look at the pitch book from Walker & Company on his desk.

"You thinking about doing that deal?"

"A pitch. What, I can't get a pitch?" He put his elbow on the table, letting Chuck see him smile.

"Why?"

"It's what these Walker guys do. Never hurts to listen." Still playing dumb.

"Why are you screwing around?" Chuck said. Tilting his head to the side.

"I'm not."

Chuck not saying anything, giving him his 'Oh, come on' look, then saying, "You said you were through with these guys. What happened to pulling yourself out of the sewer they dragged you into? Holding your head high again?"

"Look, all I did was listen to a pitch."

"Sounds like you need another lecture from Sandy. How did he put it? 'The clear bright line between right and wrong'?"

Sanford "Sandy" Sharts, Milner's lawyer, a founding partner of Wilson, Sharts and Devane. The man was tough as a skunk on your side in a fight, but he could be downright pedantic. "Gonna tell on me to Uncle Sandy, old friend." He looked up at Chuck, who was now looking ashamed, like he'd stepped over the line. That made Milner feel ashamed himself. How could Chuck step over the line? He was one of the only guys he confided in. Aside from Sandy, but he was paying Sandy by the hour. He smiled. "It's a really interesting deal." He put his one-page spreadsheet in front of Chuck. "I'd like to get your opinion."

"You're serious, aren't you?"

"How often does something really interesting come along these days? All the hedge funds out there crawling all over every stock. Information available on the internet, CNN, CNBC, MSNBC. Cramer doing his mad money thing. Today somebody farts and you see it on Bloomberg before you smell it. There's no information advantage anymore."

"So?" Chuck said.

"So, every once in a while you stumble on something."

"You really are serious."

"Take a look yourself." He nodded to the spreadsheet he placed in front of Chuck, pushed it toward him further.

Chuck shook his head.

"C'mon, call it a swan song with the Walker guys."

Chuck pulled the spreadsheet toward him.

Milner felt that familiar deal-junkie rush as Chuck picked it up. This Tentron deal had him hooked already.

After a minute Chuck looked up from the spreadsheet. "You're right, it's an interesting deal. But, sorry to be a boor, what happened to breaking away from these Walker guys?"

Milner shrugged.

Chuck kept looking at him.

"I'd use the billion I just took out of Southwest."

Chuck was looking down at Milner's spreadsheet again, studying it harder now. After a moment he scrunched his nose.

"What's wrong?" Milner said.

"Is a billion enough?" Chuck looked back up. "This thing will take close to $6 billion to get done. How you gonna finance all the rest in this environment? Hell, Bear Stearns went bust two days ago."

"And rumors of Lehman not far behind."

"The markets were already bad, now they're totally spooked. Bankers are too scared to lend to their own mothers."

"I don't know where I'll borrow the money. Let's see what Jack and Mickey come up with."

"You better hope they've got dirty pictures of some bank president."

#

LeClaire called Richard into his office. He motioned for Richard to sit at the side of his desk, pulled out a clean yellow legal pad and started drawing little boxes and diagrams with his fountain pen. He wasn't smiling.

"I have just heard from Harold Milner that he would like to see more on Tentron. You will need two Analysts for a week or so," he said, "because this will get complicated." He turned back to his boxes and diagrams. "Now, this is the deal." He drew the name Tentron Corporation in the top box. He wrote 'Project Mary Claire' over it. "Use the code-names at all times, and, of course, the usual Need to Know rules apply. We cannot have any leaks, particularly with one of Milner's deals."

"Uh-huh," Richard said. He was thinking about his first two minutes in the department with Cynthia. *No-nonsense.* Then he thought about LeClaire's reputation. *More than no-nonsense.*

"Now, as you know, Mary Claire has four major divisions." He drew four boxes below the top box. He penned in code names for each—Alpha, Beta, Sigma and Gamma. "'Alpha' is consumer products, including your favorite, Northern Ash Bats. 'Beta' is the heavy industrial equipment, turbine-driven generators. 'Sigma' is specialty carbon and stainless steel. 'Gamma' is mail order." LeClaire paused and looked at Richard to see if he understood, waiting. Richard not moving. LeClaire still waiting. Richard nodded back.

"Now, Milner has done his own division-by-division break-up valuation analysis of the company. Call it a sum-of-the-parts. He thinks the parts are worth about two billion more than the whole company is trading for in the market. We need to tell him if his valuation thinking is correct, figure out who we can sell the divisions to that he does not want—he wants specialty steel and turbines—accumulate a position for him, plan strategy and structure and execute the financing."

Richard was suppressing a smile. He'd see a breakup deal— pulling a company apart and putting it back together, or not—from cradle to grave, if Milner went forward. But he was also seeing his next few weekends evaporating into visions of the M&A conference room strewn with 10-Ks, annual reports, brown lettuce and stale sandwich crusts. And a smell like dirty socks.

"You will do a divisional black book on the company—with a separate section for each division." He looked at Richard to see if he understood.

Richard froze, trying not to betray any emotion. *What the hell is a black book?* He wondered if he was supposed to know what it was.

LeClaire must've seen a glassy look in Richard's eyes. "Relax; we will take this one step at a time. Get your Analysts started and we will revisit this with a first pass at the public comparables in the morning." He smiled. "Okay? Here, take these two black books as guides," he said and handed him two thick, tabbed presentation books from his desk.

Back in his office, Richard thought, *starting over: new desk, new analytics, new boss.* But he felt certain LeClaire wasn't gonna cut him off at the knees. Dissect him with that scalpel-like mind, yes. But slash him, he didn't think so. And yet, he'd need to look sharp.

#

Richard was in the next morning at 8 a.m., earlier than his usual hour. As he unlocked the door to the M&A department he ran into LeClaire coming out of the War Room. It gave him a start, sent a rush of adrenaline through him.

"Shall we get started in about fifteen minutes?" LeClaire said.

"I'll be there in ten." *Shit, not much time for coffee.* Or to review his notes.

Sitting in LeClaire's office, Richard started squirming almost immediately. LeClaire's face assumed those angular lines he'd seen before. "Richard, before we get started I need to make a point." He had his arms on the desk and his hands clasped. He perched forward at the edge of his chair. "Even in proceeding with something that may seem relatively innocuous, such as the selecting of appropriate public comparables for valuation analysis, we must always keep in mind that our clients are relying on us. And they are paying us very, very well to work very hard and to give them our best possible input." He leaned further forward now. That syncopated accent. "As investment bankers, we are supposed to be among the brightest minds, most energetic and most dedicated professionals in the business community. We are to bring both inspiration as well as sheer analytical force to performing for our clients."

Damn. Had he shown he was that much of a novice? Richard had to lick his lips before he spoke, they were so dry. "I understand that, and I do take it seriously."

"Let me continue. Now, specifically, in this case, Harold Milner will be risking hundreds of millions of his money and exposing himself publicly if he decides to pursue this deal. That to a very great extent based upon our advice and analysis." He looked Richard directly in the eyes. "Harold Milner does not like to lose money. Harold Milner does not like to lose."

Richard now felt his ears starting to burn red. He was clenching his fists.

"And so when we advise him, we must evaluate our analysis is if we are risking our own money and not just Harold Milner's. We must evaluate the situation as if we will not earn our fees if we do not perform our job properly, and that therefore we will lose our jobs, and that therefore we will be unable to put bread on the table for our children."

Richard now thought LeClaire was laying it on a little thick, but he still wasn't moving.

"One little number that goes into one piece of analysis that is summarized on one little page which is in turn reflected in other numbers, each into another page, is equally serious and equally important." He glanced at his watch. "And, we must not only be precise, we must be fast. So let's get to it."

Forty-five minutes later, LeClaire said, "Very good outline for your first pass." Richard felt his shoulders relax, realized his biceps were sore from being tensed the whole time. "I must turn to this now," he said, looking at a pile of materials on the corner of his desk. He smiled at Richard. Richard left. *One step at a time.* He had a long way to go. A day and a half to pick some comps and draft an outline. He couldn't become Harold Milner overnight. Back at his desk he thought of Kathy. No Kathy Cella to cut up and laugh with, but a Milner M&A deal, and a big one. Five, maybe six billion. Above the fold in the *Journal*, if it got that far.

#

Eleven p.m. on a Friday night, and everyone in the M&A department had cleared out. Richard had been pretending to be busy for the last hour until Peter Blumenthal finally left. He waited a few more minutes, then went into the War Room. He'd already checked four of the six computers in the center row of desks in the room. He sat down in front of the fifth, starting to wish he'd never gotten into this. He went into Outlook, clicked on Tools and checked E-mail Accounts. No mole.

He moved over in front of the sixth, which always seemed to be turned off. He switched it on and waited while it finished booting up, logged into it using the generic M&A login. He opened Outlook, went to Tools, then E-mail accounts. He sat up straight like someone stabbed him with a fork, felt a rush of adrenaline. There it was: walker1@netwiz.net, one of half a dozen email accounts on the computer. He clicked out of Tools and checked the Inbox for emails, alphabetizing them. He saw that all the mole's activity, as far back as he'd seen it in the Comm Room and downloaded onto his own laptop, was on this computer as well. He glanced over his shoulder, making sure nobody was watching.

He closed Outlook and shut down the computer. He went back to his desk, shut down his laptop and unhooked it from its docking station. He packed it in his briefcase, put on his jacket and headed for the door.

As he turned the corner of his cubicle he heard the M&A Department door open and saw the shadow of someone approaching. He felt a bolt of adrenaline and ducked into the War Room, hid behind the door. When whoever it was walked past, Richard slipped out of the department, not sure if he was seen.

His heart was thumping in his chest as he rode the elevator downstairs. He reviewed in his mind who had access to the locked and sequestered M&A department. Other than M&A department members, it was only the most senior officers of the firm, even though he'd rarely seen one of them in there. That meant the mole was most likely someone in M&A. He hadn't checked the mole's emails since he last spoke to Kathy. Too busy. But now he was itching to turn on his laptop when he got home, see what was going on. He wanted to call Kathy, but it was too early in Paris, particularly on a Saturday morning. But he'd check this out tonight.

#

Washington, D.C. When Croonquist got back to his office from a meeting, the email was waiting for him from Phil Johnson, his old boss in Surveillance. It said he'd put taps in place on 12 phone lines at Walker's, GCG's and Milner's offices. And Johnson had put his best computer hacker onto the Walker/GCG email chain. The hacker had already hacked into the netwiz.net account with the username walker1. From there he'd found the usernames of accounts on three different computers at walker.com that walker1 operated from: commroom@walker.com, warroom@walker.com and richardblum@walker.com. Then he'd hacked into Walker's system, grabbed a mine of useful emails from those accounts, and then set the accounts up for ongoing monitoring. Croonquist smiled and turned on his MarketWatch monitor.

#

New York City. Milner looked out his conference room window, up Park Avenue. Glorious day. If only he could enjoy it. His lawyer, Sandy Sharts, sat with him. Sandy had just called to tell Milner he needed an immediate face-to-face with him about what he'd heard the Feds in Washington were up to. Milner said he wanted Chuck there, too.

Chuck walked in late and said, "Is this bad news?"

Milner shrugged. "Could be. But could also be nothing."

Milner saw Sandy rise up in his chair. He said, "That's not a realistic perspective. In fact, it's a form of denial."

The avuncular Mr. Sanford F. Sharts, Esq. Great guy, careful lawyer, but why always a lecture?

Milner said, "Well, can we review what we know? And what they know?"

Sandy cleared his throat. "I haven't made any of this up." He settled into the chair again like it was for a long talk.

Milner just looked at him.

"Okay, you stubborn old bird." Sandy sounded impatient, rising up again to lean forward with his elbows on the table, looking up at the ceiling, as if reciting, "I got a call from my partner in Washington. Let's leave his name out of it. He has friends inside the enforcement and surveillance divisions of the SEC, reasonably well placed."

Milner was listening out of one ear, seeing Sandy's mouth moving, but now not hearing. He was seeing how things might play out. He sees Mary Claire reading on the sofa in the New York apartment. Sees her look up as he walks in, sits. She reacts to his face: grave. She says what is it? Her look says, Oh my God.

"One of his well-connected friends takes him aside at a cocktail party and informs him he should tell his boy in New York —that would be me—that he's about to become a world champion in billable hours servicing his boy—that would be you, Harold—

because the whole of our government's machinery is about to catch your tits in their ringer, to use his phrase."

Milner tells Mary Claire I screwed up, I'm going to go away for a while. She says what have you done? He says I sometimes do business skating near the edge. I went over it. Her face now shows panic. His guts are twisting.

"My partner has the presence of mind to see to it that his smug friend gets more to drink, and then cajoles a fascinating narrative out of him. Seems they have this new MarketWatch system to track trades, analyze patterns like never before, and his boss in enforcement is using Walker and you as a test case."

Mary Claire is now getting over her anger. No more why? how? what? questions. Now she asks what will happen to you? How long will they put you away? He says a long time. She asks how soon? He thinks for a moment, says weeks, maybe months. He sees her wounded look and feels his throat constrict.

"This enterprising government servant has reverse-engineered the stock and options trading on a bunch of Walker deals, including your last three, and found unusual correlations with documented illegal insider trading cases. He has taken that database plus ongoing surveillance activities to begin to build a case to bring Walker and you down."

Milner now sees Mary Claire some 22 years ago when he'd come home from his office that Friday. She'd been waiting for him. He just felt it. It wasn't that hard to see, Mary Claire sitting on the sofa in the old Fifth Avenue apartment, a martini next to her and the bar open with a bottle of Perrier and a glass ready for him. Not in the kitchen as usual, doing final puttering before dinner. The girls in their bedrooms doing their homework. She had it all set up; crafty.

Milner saw no choice but to seize the initiative. Still, he wasn't sure how she was gonna take this, and his stomach felt a little airy, like before the first round of negotiating a deal. "Can we talk for a few minutes?" he said.

"I was wondering when you were going to get around to it," she said without looking up from her magazine, grabbing her martini and taking a sip. Angry and feeling shut out. Her eye makeup refreshed for the evening, a darker shade of lipstick than usual, and her going-out-for-the-evening Chanel perfume—he couldn't remember which number—heavy in the air. She was trying to make him remember who she was to him, sticking it in his face, in fact.

He walked to the bar and poured himself a Perrier, sat down next to her on the sofa. "Over about the last two weeks—"

"More like six," she said.

"Okay, so over six weeks I've been thinking about our situation. Ticking things off in my mind, seeing how they stack up."

She looked up at him only now. He heard her let out a soft sigh, resolved to listen through it, Milner now suspecting she was fearing the worst. It tugged at his heart. He saw her now as he had across the dance floor 10 years earlier. Not stricken by some thunderbolt, but aware she was a gem, a slim-wasted beauty he wanted to meet. Him having just finished his CPA, six years out of Baruch and on his way as an audit manager at Arthur Young; her out of nursing school, working in the emergency room at NYU Hospital. Then Milner realizing he'd been in neutral until then, waiting, not willing to expend the energy unless the prize was worth it. She made him want to get busy. They'd gotten to know each other over two months, blitzing through it like modern-day speed-dating: I'm from Chelsea; Really? I'm a Brooklyn girl; Then we moved to the Village so we could go to a good public school; Not me. I scraped by at PS 6 on Snyder Avenue, then Edward R. Murrow High School; I went on to Stuyvesant High School; Really? Oh, you were a pointy head, top science program in the city; No. Math, it's what got me the scholarship to Baruch; I love you, you know. They went dancing three or four nights a week because she loved it, and he'd never looked back, or at any other woman. Still hadn't; she was his girl and always would be.

He decided to hurry it up, because whatever she was thinking, it wasn't good, it was hurting her and had been for weeks. He put his hand on her knee. She was rigid, tense.

The room felt uncomfortably warm.

"This isn't about us, hon," he said. "It's about me, my career."

He saw Mary Claire's eyes softening, felt her body relaxing underneath his hand.

"I thought—"

"Don't say it," he said. She leaned back into the sofa and put her drink down. She bent over and wiped her eyes with her fingers. He reached for her and she waved him away.

"You talk," she said.

He remained silent, watching her.

"Talk," she said again.

"I'm 40 years old. I'm told it's normal to be asking myself questions like this at my age. I've been Jimmy Hill's CFO for over six years now. Always at Jimmy's elbow as he built Coastal +Northern. Grinding through the hours. Careful, methodical. While everyone lauds Jimmy as 'corporate America's reigning genius.'"

She looked up at him and he saw her nodding with understanding, attentive, a smile forming on her lips.

"And look at what we have," he said. "Look around, we're comfortable, and I could argue we've slumped into the inertia of a cushy existence. At least I have."

He now saw her eyes take on that steely quality they had when she whittled down the price on new drapes.

"You have to do it," she said.

"What—?"

"You have to do it."

"I haven't said—"

"Go out on your own."

Milner thought, What the hell? How could she—

"You think I haven't seen it?" she said. "You zoning out at the ballet after the lights go off. Curled up in your mind, staring at the television here in the apartment."

Milner felt tension start to ease out of his shoulders.

"It's that obvious?"

"You kidding me? You've been miserable. Bitching about Jimmy for months, even before you started this zombie routine these last weeks."

Milner started to chuckle. *Here she goes. On a roll.*

"And me? You have any idea how sick I've gotten of seeing you standing off to the side at those ridiculous cocktail parties while everyone kisses up to Jimmy like he's the brains around C +N? It's at least as much you as him, maybe more. You have to do it."

Milner saw her smile at him and felt it like she was opening the curtains to let the sun in. He said, "I know. I'm not gonna be Jimmy's number two man anymore."

Mary Claire leaned forward and clasped one of his hands in both of hers, hard, and tears started forming in her eyes. "Damn right."

Milner felt like his whole body was smiling back at her.

Mary Claire sighed and leaned back into the cushions again. "What's the plan?"

"I can take about 1.5 million after-tax out of Coastal+Northern from my stock options. I figure, since I was always taught to save half and spend the other half, I've got about 750 thousand to get started with."

"How much do we need to cut back?"

"We don't. If I keep that cushion, even if I fall on my face it won't dent us a bit. I can always find another job."

She dismissed it with a chuckle and a wave of her hand. "Don't be ridiculous, you aren't going to fall on your face. Keep five hundred and invest a million."

He leaned over and put his arms around her, pulled her close and kissed her. "I love you, you know that?" he said.

Now he couldn't imagine how he would feel at disappointing her, but he was beginning to get a taste and it was awful. He felt the sensation of tiny feet, a thousand midgets stomping on his upper torso, then a thousand more, plodding down inside his chest cavity, then another ten thousand, all of them trudging on his heart.

Now Milner was seeing his picture on the first business page of the *New York Times* and a headline with the word 'Scandal' in it. An article near the top of the first business column in the *Wall Street Journal*. A feature article on the *Journal's* right front-page column, one of their grainy black-and-white drawings of him from a recent photo.

Milner was back with Sandy now. He said, "Doesn't sound to me like reverse-engineered trading data does the trick."

Sandy looked interested, like he had Milner's attention. "Normally they get wiretaps next. On phones and emails."

"Emails? How do they do that?" Milner now intrigued.

"Spook stuff. They hack into the system. Once they're in, they can get any email account from any computer on the system, from any domain, whether it's an in-house system account or not. After that, it's all automated. They track any activity from any email account they want with one of these supercomputers not too different from what the SEC just brought on-stream with its new MarketWatch. Trust me, they can do it."

Milner thought for a moment. Maybe he could use that to his advantage. "How about phones?"

"You kidding? The National Security Agency's got algorithms that can scan all domestic and international phone lines for any hot words it wants. You say 'bomb' or 'terrorist' on the phone today and you're recorded on tape that instant, video camera tomorrow. But if they've ID'd who they want to listen to in advance, that's pre-internet technology. The Mayberry police department can do that. It's as easy as opening your stinking mail."

Milner was now really interested. "How long to get wiretaps?"

"It takes probable cause to get it through a judge. But if my partner's rendition of events is accurate, assume they have them by now." The stern look of Uncle Sanford again.

Milner felt himself smile, tried to suppress it because he knew it would piss off Sandy. "So what happens next?" He wanted to milk this out to the end. He was getting an idea.

"They nail a low level person and get him to give up someone higher up. Work up from there."

Milner shrugged.

"Don't give me that 'Who cares?' shrug. You're the top of the food chain."

Milner thought for a moment, then said, "So how long's it been now, since they've been at this?"

"About two months." Sandy impatient again at this point. Showing he's annoyed with a different stern look reserved for when Milner was intentionally being annoying.

"That's a long time. So maybe they haven't got anything after all. What if there's nothing to get?"

Sandy leaned forward. "Don't bullshit a bullshitter, my friend. If there's nothing to get, how do you explain the couple hundred million Walker sneaked into your bank accounts?" Sandy looked at his watch. "I remind you I'm billing here, and I'll stay as long as you want, but I've got work to do back at the office. You need me anymore today?" He nodded to Chuck, got up and left without waiting for a response.

#

Richard was so busy working on Tentron it was days before he spoke to Kathy again. He still hadn't told her about finding the mole's email account on the War Room computer in M&A.

"Are you still screwing around with that?" Kathy said when he told her.

"Look, all I'm asking you to do is go back to the computer where you found the walker2 email account, see how many emails to and from the mole are on it, print out hard copies and send them to me."

"It's a waste of time . . . ."

"And since you found another person in London that walker2 is sending emails to, print those, too."

"What is it with you and this mole thing?"

"I think something's going on."

"If you think something's going on then tell somebody."

"I'm not going to tell anybody until I'm convinced."

"So you're not going to waste anybody else's time until you're convinced, but you're happy to waste mine?"

"Dammit, all I'm asking you to do is click on an email account in the computer, sort a bunch of emails and print them out. How the hell long can that take?"

Kathy didn't respond for a moment. "Okay, I'll do it. But only if you promise that if there's really any substance to this, you'll tell somebody and put an end to it."

"Done."

#

Jack was sitting in front of Mickey's desk, watching him glance back and forth at his screens. Four flat panels, two at each end of that battleship-sized, glass-topped table he used as a desk. Two more LCD TVs sat on a credenza to his right, piping in CNN and Bloomberg. Wires lashed to the legs of his desk, running up through the floor into the screens made it look like one of those futuristic movies. Jack could imagine Mickey wired to the internet with a big plug in the back of his head, doing deals in cyberspace. This was how he worked, always had been. Sucking in info, thinking, reflecting. Then Mickey and him ham-and-egging it, like they'd done for 20 years.

"I talked to Milner again," Jack said.

Mickey didn't look up from his screen, but nodded.

"He says he'll hear us out on a conference call about next steps on Tentron, but he seems lukewarm all of a sudden."

Mickey shrugged, still looking at another of his screens, then at Jack. "Maybe it's the markets. They're a mess since Bear Stearns blew up. And now Merrill Lynch and Citi look like they're starting to implode."

"That's not it."

"Doesn't like the deal?"

"He loves the deal. But he gave me some bullshit about being a 'builder' again."

"Could be he's spooked by the potential lawsuits over the Southwest Homes IPO. An investor buys the stock at $14.75 and three weeks later it's at $5.25, he's likely to be upset."

"I wish that was it. No, I think he's backing out on us altogether."

Mickey raised his eyebrows like he was asking 'why?'

"He wants a face-to-face with just the two of us after the deal strategy call."

Mickey said, "Maybe he'll need some convincing."

#

"Project Mary Claire," Jack Grass said as he pulled his copy of the black book out of his briefcase and placed it on the desk.

Richard looked around Jack's office. On his credenza behind his desk sat about a hundred lucite blocks containing tombstones, mementos of deals he had done. The entire wall behind his desk was covered with neatly framed, glass-enclosed tombstones as well. Notches in his gunstock. "Ready to get started?" Jack asked into his speakerphone once LeClaire sat down. Steinberg was on the line from Chicago.

"As you can see from the table of contents," LeClaire said, "the first tab of this section summarizes all of our analysis."

"There's a lot of work to do to unbundle the value in this thing," Milner said. "So, François. Let's cut right to it. Your strategy on page 2, the one where I keep the Beta and Sigma divisions."

Richard closed his eyes as LeClaire began outlining the strategy, playing back in his mind his session with LeClaire the day before.

"Come over here," LeClaire had said, pulling a chair beside his desk. Richard smiled and sat. It was becoming familiar territory: learning at the elbow of the young master.

"Now," LeClaire said, pointing to one of his pads with boxes and diagrams penned on it. If Milner bids $45.00 per share it's a total cost of $4.5 billion for all of Tentron. Milner wants to keep two divisions and sell two. That means he sells Alpha—the consumer segment—for $1.5 billion and Gamma—the mail-order segment—for $2.0 billion, leaving him in the deal at a net cost of $1 billion."

Richard came back to the moment as LeClaire finished outlining it for Milner.

Milner said, "I look at it more simplistically. I can probably buy the company for 45 bucks a share. I sell consumer for 15 bucks a share, mail-order for 20 bucks a share, giving me total sale proceeds of 35 bucks a share. That means I'm buying the two businesses I want to keep for 45 bucks less 35 bucks, or a net price of 10 bucks a share."

Milner continued, "I figure I can borrow a total of about 14.50 a share on the assets of the two divisions I want, after I sell the ones I don't want. And because I can borrow 14.50 a share against them, and they only cost me 10.00 a share, I don't have to put up any money at all. Anybody disagree?"

Nobody did. Richard remembered the one-page spreadsheet Milner had shown him in his office, and then LeClaire's lecture about legions of little numbers leading into other little numbers, summing up into one page. As impressed as he was with how his team had summarized their inch-thick book into concise one-page strategies under LeClaire's wizardry of penned boxes and diagrams, somehow Milner's way of saying it had more punch: something for nothing.

"So, guys," Milner said, "I can do the permanent financing once I take control. The real catch is, I need the front money to finance the tender offer to buy the company until I can put my permanent financing in place."

"We figure you'll need about $6 billion, including refinancing their existing debt," Steinberg said.

"Right," Milner said. "So where do I get that kind of money in the middle of the worst credit crunch any of us has ever seen?"

"Our partner GCG has a big balance sheet," Steinberg said.

"I'm all ears," Milner said.

"We have a lot of alternatives," Steinberg said over the speakerphone. "We've outlined two financing scenarios. In the first scenario . . ."

Steinberg went on for ten minutes. Scenario one was easy: Milner borrowed $6.0 billion from GCG, paid $4.5 billion of it in cash to Tentron's shareholders and paid off Tentron's existing debt with the rest. Scenario two wasn't much more complicated. Milner borrowed $5.0 billion, paid $3.5 billion of it to the Tentron shareholders and used the rest to pay off Tentron's debt. Then he paid Tentron's shareholders $1.0 billion in debt of the "new" Tentron as it existed after Milner took control and sold off the divisions he didn't want.

". . . so in summary," Steinberg said, "in scenario two, instead of all cash, you pay the Tentron shareholders $3.5 billion in cash and $1.0 billion in newly issued bonds of New Tentron. What do you think?"

"Clever," Milner said. "Can you guys structure the bonds of New Tentron so they'll trade publicly?"

"I don't see why not," Jack said.

"Very creative," Milner said. "We need to talk about anything else right now?"

"We should discuss Tentron's defensive charter provisions, financial and legal advisers and directors' biographies," LeClaire said.

"I'm not too worried about that stuff," Milner said. He paused for a moment. "I have someone on the inside," he said finally. "And Nick Williams, the CEO, is building a retirement home in Scottsdale. His youngest daughter just got married and he may be ready to pack it in."

Somebody on the inside. Was that how it worked? Richard wondered how you knew who was on whose side.

#

"Eight o'clock." Richard looked back from his watch, sitting in the dim glow of his desk lamp that evening. The Portuguese cleaning ladies were just beginning their routine. He knew it well. He watched them working. One of life's little ironies was that they were so muscular and so overweight at the same time.

His office phone rang.

"Hello," Richard said.

"Sa va," Kathy said.

"Good, and you?"

"Good."

"Really? You sound like shit. The markets got you down?"

"No, I'm okay," Kathy said. She seemed somber, and with an agenda. "Well, you're right about the mole; this is odd. There are hundreds of emails for trades. I printed the whole batch of them out."

"Are they on the way?"

"You should have them by 6:00 tomorrow evening your time."

"Anything unusual?" Richard asked.

"Yes," Kathy said. "Prolific today. Lots of instructions—trading like crazy."

"Are you sure it was all from him?" Richard tried to keep his voice from sounding grave. But for some reason that's the way he felt.

"No, as you know, on any given day he accounts for about 90% of the volume of the trades."

"So if today was a heavy day, chances are he had a heavy day," Richard said.

"Right. I was very tempted tonight to review them all at my end to see what they said."

"Too risky," Richard said.

"Yeah, you're right. No sense in pressing our luck." Richard hung up, put his elbows on the desk and thought about the difference between the last two conversations with Kathy about the mole. *Damn, she sounded downright scared tonight.* He watched the cleaning ladies again. Sometimes when he was in college, then again at business school, he'd wondered what it would be like to be a welder or a cleaning lady, one of those people who just took what came along because they didn't do anything well or didn't have any choice. Nothing much to worry about except going in every day and doing your job. Little ambition, few curiosities, fewer worries. Nothing to twist in your mind, keep you up at night. No reason to feel the nagging sense that you might wake up to something unpleasant.

#

The day the Lehman Brothers bankruptcy was announced, Richard walked into the Analyst bullpen in the M&A Group, looking for Peter and Stella. He could see nobody was getting much done, what with the find-yourself-standing-naked-in-Times-Square-nightmare Wall Street was living out in broad daylight. Half of Richard's friends from business school had called him, worried. Less than two weeks earlier, the feds had pumped billions into Fannie Mae and Freddie Mac. Now Lehman was bust, and rumors about AIG right behind it. So he could understand why the Analysts in the bullpen couldn't take their eyes off CNN, Bloomberg and CNBC. They all had one of them locked onto their computer screens, and Richard could hear their different talking heads speaking in tongues from all directions, like they were prophesying the end of the world. Most of the Associates in M&A huddled in whispering clutches. Some of them talked about friends at other firms on the Street being laid off. Some said, "First it was Bear Stearns, now Lehman," then wondered aloud if Walker was next.

Richard smelled Rick Nunez's sweaty feet, the kid fidgeting and slipping his loafers off and on, like he did when LeClaire hovered over him to check on his acquisition comparables. Richard gave up and walked back to his desk. His phone rang.

"Hi. How you holding up?"

"Okay, Dad. Good to hear from you."

"Your mom and I just wanted to check in on you."

"Thanks. It's been an unusual day."

"I'll say, and on top of an unusual couple of weeks." Dad paused, like he was waiting for Richard to say something that would put his mind at ease. When Richard didn't have any comment, Dad said, "Is it as bad on Wall Street as we're hearing on the news?"

"As far as I can tell."

Dad didn't say anything for a moment. Richard imagined Dad's eyes zeroing in on him.

Richard said, "Schoenfeld & Co. and GCG will stand behind Walker, shore it up if they need to."

Another pause from Dad. He said, "Has Jack taken you aside, told you anything?"

"Yeah, and in fact he asked me to spread the word around that all this will blow over in a week or two." Richard knew that was bullshit and he didn't know why he even repeated it, especially to Dad.

Dad said, "You worried?"

"I'd say rattled to the core. Not just about Walker, but the whole financial sector. This mess looks worse from where I sit than I suspect it does from where you are. They're now calling it The Financial Crisis in the press." Richard thought for a second to make sure what he was going to say didn't come out as too melodramatic. "It makes me realize that life on Wall Street can change overnight. One day you're riding high and the next you could be out on the street."

Richard could hear the air on the line, Dad obviously thinking. Then Dad said, "Your mom will be happy to hear I was so effective in cheering you up."

It stung. Richard wanted to tell him it was okay, but couldn't think of how to say it.

Dad went on. "I'm sure it will work out. I was really just calling to know you're okay with all that's going on." When

Richard didn't answer after a moment Dad said, "Let me know if I can do anything."

Richard remembered saying the same thing earlier in the day to a friend at Lehman Brothers. He realized his throat had thickened, but he managed to say, "Thanks, Dad, I'll be okay."

Richard left the office early and was home by 6 p.m. He thought of calling Kathy, mostly just to hear her voice. It was midnight in Paris; she was probably still up. He imagined her ready for bed, the perfect skin on her face shining after washing up, hair pulled back in a pony tail. The scent of anise-flavored toothpaste on her breath. Sitting on the bed in just a t-shirt, reading an annual report cradled in her lap, her legs crossed at the ankles Indian-style, knees spread apart. Her calves are slim, suntanned, her thighs firm and muscular. His eye moves up her leg to where she isn't tanned, and . . .

Whoa. Richard shook off the image and took out his laptop, then the piles of mole email printouts, the ones he'd printed from the Sent Items folder on the netwiz.net server, and the email printouts from GCG Paris that Kathy had FedExed him. He'd gotten so busy on Project Mary Claire, he hadn't had much time to review them. He figured he'd work for an hour or two.

First he sorted all the mole's emails on his computer in Outlook. That was easy. He sorted by date, sender, and recipient. He offloaded them onto a flash memory stick for safekeeping. The hard copies were more work. He took a half-hour to sort them chronologically. Then he decided to set up an Excel spreadsheet so he could enter and sort them, too. He manually entered them into Excel, organizing them in columns by date, sender, recipient, subject, and summary message. After he got done he went back and added a few new columns: stock, ticker, and volume purchased. When he finished those he decided to add in all the emails he had in Outlook on his computer. That gave him one giant database of all the mole's emails they'd found. *Wow, 752 of them.*

He looked up at the time. It was 2 a.m. "Damn," he said aloud.

He went to bed, too tired to analyze the data. But a number of things had become clear while he was entering it: the emails documented trading back over four years, and started with just Milner's deals in the first two years. And then they got more active, maybe another ten or twelve deals in the last two years. He remembered Dad, with his background writing fidelity bonds to insure banks against employee dishonesty, talking about how embezzlers worked. They started out small, went unnoticed, then got bold. That's when they got caught. Richard figured 752 emails qualified as bold. And he and Kathy had put themselves in the middle of what the mole was up to.

Chapter 5

New York City. Milner decided to meet with Jack and Mickey in his mezzanine office rather than downstairs in the cushy furniture in his reception area. He wanted to make it more of a formal meeting, let them know it was on his territory. He felt giddy and sad at the same time; kind of like breaking up with a girlfriend you had fond memories with but had lost the hots for: itching to move on to someone more exciting.

"Thanks for coming up guys," Milner said when they arrived.

Jack said, "Our most important client calls, we answer."

Mickey said, "Happy to come, Harold."

Jack said, "With bells on our shoes."

Back and forth already. Man, these guys would go on forever like this.

"I'll get right to it," Milner said. "I've been thinking a lot about the Tentron deal, and I've decided not to go ahead."

Jack didn't flinch, just kept on smiling reasonably as if his dry cleaner had just told him his charcoal-gray suit wouldn't be ready until tomorrow. Mickey was blinking and nodding his head. Mickey said, "The financing is structured and we can get it done, if that's what you're worried about."

"I know the markets are dicey, but GCG will still finance all $6 billion of debt," Jack said, flashing Milner a big grin.

"It's not that." Milner looked Jack in the eye. "I just don't want to do it." He saw Jack glance over at Mickey.

Mickey said, "That's not what you led us to believe the other day."

Milner didn't respond.

After a moment, Jack said, "We've already shot a lot of juice into this one. Don't let us down, Harold."

Here we go. He starts with a little guilt, then let's see where they take this. Milner shrugged. "Sometimes the client changes his mind."

Jack glanced over at Mickey again, who sat blinking for a moment. Then Mickey said, "We're counting on you for this one."

Milner shrugged again.

Jack said, "We already got capital in play here."

"I didn't tell you to do that."

Mickey looked over at Jack. Jack said, "C'mon Harold, you know that's how it works."

Milner shook his head. "I'm out. Done."

"It's not that easy," Mickey said.

Jack said, "Yeah, we're stuck with each other."

"No, I'm done. You guys can keep up your little business, trading offshore on your clients' deals, but cut me out."

Jack said, "You back out now we'll take a hit. You trying to screw us?" He was leaning forward in his chair, wearing that tough-guy look Milner had seen him use to bully people.

Milner looked him square in the eye and leaned over his desk. "You guys buy the stock based on a few exploratory meetings, it's not my problem."

Jack said, "It'll be a problem, trust me. We can make it awfully awkward for you if we have to."

Milner sat up straight in his chair and scowled at him, felt a surge of anger tensing the muscles in his arms. "What're you gonna do? Turn me in if I don't do the deal?"

Jack glared back at Milner like he was ready to come across his desk at him.

Mickey talked over both of them. "Okay, okay, let's calm down." Milner didn't say anything, just stared at Jack, who sat back in his chair. Mickey said, "You think about it. We'll think about it." He paused, sitting there blinking, glancing over at Jack, then back to Milner. "I suggest we make Tentron our last deal together, then part as friends." He looked at Jack, who nodded. "Sleep on it. Then we'll talk again."

After they left, Milner paced back and forth behind his desk, then went downstairs and sat in his lower reception area. He felt the post-adrenaline rush sensations of strength surging in his limbs and a flutter of butterflies in his stomach. He couldn't believe how these guys just leaned on him. *Who the hell do they think they are?*

But he remembered who Jack was. When he first started doing business with him he'd put his Devon private investigation guys on it. They'd unearthed a ton of useful information.

The razor-cut hair, manicured fingernails and form-fitting custom suits were a clever way to cover up a street tough from the Canarsie section of Brooklyn. The five public schools young Jack was bounced out of were a mystery until you understood Jack's juvenile police record. Jack ran up a list of misdemeanors: vandalism; underage drinking; and killing a Canada goose in Canarsie Beach Park. He was arrested twice for breaking and entering, but never indicted. Then his background showed a long gap, followed by a B.S. in business from SUNY on Long Island. He never completed night classes for an MBA from Fordham, despite the fact the degree showed up on Jack's bio. After dropping out of a two-year training program at Chemical Bank, he was somehow plucked by Jimmy Walker's grandson as a Vice President for Walker & Company's Corporate Finance Department. He went on the road selling commercial paper programs to major industrials up and down the East Coast. He made Managing Director by 29, and was put in charge of Corporate Finance, based on his uncanny sales skills. Milner didn't quite know how Jack had done it.

But one thing he did know: he was dealing with a thug wrapped in a Saville Row suit. So before he acted, he would think about it. And while he didn't see any reason to take any shit from these guys, sometimes it was better to compromise if it bought you time. He opened a Perrier. By the time he finished it, he made up his mind to take another meeting on Tentron until he could decide what to do about Jack and Mickey.

#

When Chuck White switched off the light at his desk in the northeast corner of Milner's penthouse offices, it was 10:15 p.m. It was Tuesday: Lisa's night out with the girls. By the time he drove to Chappaqua, she'd just be getting back.

With his office now dark, the lights of northern Park Avenue and the East side of Manhattan glittered in through the windows. Halfway to the door, he stopped and looked out. While he was glad he lived up north among grass, trees and winding roads with bluestone rock walls, New York never lost its fascination for him.

As the last to leave the office for the evening, Chuck turned his key in the elevator lock when he got to the basement garage. His Lexus LS460 was the only car remaining—the garage only held 10, the upper basement having been converted to the garage by Milner when he leased the penthouse. As he got ready to start the big Lexus, he saw a man in a dark suit approach. It surprised him, because at this hour he would only have expected to see one of the security guards. He felt a tickle of anxiety. The man motioned for Chuck to roll down the window; Chuck felt better when he saw the man smiling at him. Chuck hit the button and when the window was halfway down, saw the man reach into his suit jacket and emerge with something odd looking. Terror exploded in his brain, then the panicked urge to reach out to start the car as he realized it was a gun with a silencer pointed directly at his head. The word, "No!" formed in his mind and then everything was darkness.

#

Milner sighed and looked out the window of Wilson, Sharts & Devane, his law firm's conference room in the MetLife Building. He looked down at his office in the Helmsley Building across 45th Street. He'd rather be over there. Hell, he'd rather be anyplace than here right now.

"Shot in the temple through the open car window," Sandy Sharts said.

"The police say it was clearly a professional job. Assassination style," Milner said.

Sandy continued, "I have to ask. Do you think this had anything to do with your business?"

Milner didn't want to let his mind go there. But with Jack and Mickey leaning on him about the Tentron deal . . . He hadn't told Sandy about that meeting yet. "It's hard to believe," Milner said.

"Can't be a coincidence. If we found out the Feds are making noises, somebody else may have. And then your CFO, the numbers guy who keeps all your tallies, knows where all the bodies are buried, shows up dead."

The most Milner could do was nod. He couldn't bring himself to acknowledge it aloud. But even nodding caused a stinging spasm of guilt to wrench his chest.

Sandy said, "Or maybe your friends aren't about to let you waltz out of their lives so easily."

How could Sandy piece that together so fast? It forced Milner to think two steps ahead. Or maybe they're worried about taking a fall and they're covering their tracks. *Maybe I'm next.* He couldn't just sit around waiting to find out.

#

Milner bent down to pass underneath the yellow 'crime scene' tape the cops stuck to the front of Chuck's office. He decided he couldn't wait until they were done and out of there completely. The forensic team was basically finished anyhow; after two full days at it since Chuck's murder they'd only been here for about an hour today. Not much chance they'd be back this afternoon. Still, Milner felt his pulse throbbing and an airy sensation in his chest.

He looked around the office. *Man.* It looked like they'd strip-searched the place. They left desk drawers open, showing all the files missing, cables and power cords strewn on the floor, scraps of paper around. Chuck's desktop computer had been removed, showing a dusty rectangle on the glass desktop.

Milner sat in Chuck's chair and spun it around to face the credenza. He pulled out the bottom credenza drawer all the way, lifted it out onto the floor. He got down on his knees, reached in and pressed on the side in the back of the credenza where the drawer had been. The false back opened and Milner pulled out Chuck's hidden files. He poked around with his hand for the laptop computer Chuck always kept in there. It was missing. He got back up, sat at Chuck's desk and put the files down. He thought about it. Chuck's laptop contained all his private spreadsheets and records.

He opened the top file. As Milner expected, it was a raw accounting of all Milner's cut of profits from Walker's trading ring. Chuck always received the data hand-passed from the Walker guys, cryptic stuff buried in deal pitches and memos. Chuck's calculations and confirmations of the accounting were in spreadsheets compiled on Chuck's laptop. Did they take it from his car?

Now he remembered. The day before he was killed, Chuck said he forgot to bring the laptop into the office after the weekend. *So where is it?*

Back in his office, Milner clenched his jaw with resolve, then he realized, anger, has he thought about Chuck and laid out a half dozen of the papers from Chuck's files on his own desk.

He worked into the evening, pulling out his old HP 12c calculator and adding by hand the rows and columns he'd written on a spreadsheet from the raw numbers in Chuck's files. He confirmed they summed to within $15,000 of his cut from Walker's trading ring. Close enough. *So all the records are here.* Could it be that's what the guy who killed Chuck was looking for? He decided he needed to find Chuck's laptop to see if that held any answers. Then he thought of Chuck's wife, Lisa. He hadn't visited her since Chuck's murder, but if his phone call to her was any indication, it wasn't gonna be fun. *Man, I'm not looking forward to this.*

#

Chappaqua, NY. For some reason the GPS system in Milner's Mercedes CL600 didn't pick up all the side streets in the wooded section of Chappaqua off Whippoorwill Road. He turned the high beams on and crept along until he saw a mailbox. *Number 577.* He was close. A minute later he saw the bluestone columns marking the entryway to the White's property, and then the driveway winding up the hill. He drove past the rolling lawn that cascaded down from the house; the lawn Chuck cut himself with his riding lawn mower, not because he had to, but because he enjoyed it.

Three other cars were parked in the gravel circular drive in front of the colonial farmhouse that had been expanded to ramble off in all directions. Renovations he'd heard Chuck talk about over a decade. When Milner got out of the car he felt a cool breeze and a dampness in the air, probably from the stream he could hear on the far side of the house. Milner wanted to turn his suit jacket collar up against the chill, then realized the chill he felt didn't come from the air.

A sharp-featured woman with probing eyes showed Milner into the room off the entry hall. She referred to it as the sitting room; Chuck had called it his den. A minute later the crumpled shell of Lisa White entered and shut the door behind her. "Oh, Harold," she said. Her eyes were reddened puffs of raw meat. Her athletic frame was cowed, like someone had scrunched her down two inches shorter in the last days. She was shockingly diminished from the vibrant woman he'd known for over a dozen years. The sight of her made his stomach feel queasy and his legs weak.

"I'm so sorry, Lisa." Milner crossed the room to her and took both her hands in his, then put an arm around her and showed her to the sofa. He sat down next to her.

"How could this happen?" she said.

"I don't know. I'm trying to figure it out."

"The police have been and gone." She turned away from Milner. He could see she was fighting back tears. She exhaled, turned back to him, said, "Have they told you anything?"

"Nothing. They're asking me for answers, and I can't give them any."

She looked into his eyes, said, "Who would do this?"

Now he started to get angry again. Who *would* do this? Murder his friend and ruin this woman's life? He said again, "I don't know."

She turned away and looked across the room, at nothing.

After a full minute of silence, Milner said, "I can think of one thing that might give me some answers."

She turned her head like a shot, her lips parted and her eyes pleading.

"You know Chuck's laptop?"

She nodded.

"I can't find it, and I don't think the cops have it. Did they mention it to you?"

"No. He had it with him on the boat last weekend."

"Do you think it's still there?"

"I don't know."

"Do you mind if I check?"

"I'll get you the key."

As she walked across the room he wondered if the cops had Chuck's boat staked out. Only one way to find out.

#

New York City. Richard was itching to analyze the spreadsheet he created on all the mole's emails. That night at his apartment he shut off his cell phone, opened his laptop and started sorting. The tally was 17 deals over four years. So the mole started just after the foreign partners invested in Walker. *Interesting.*

He sorted all the deals chronologically, thinking that might make it easier to break the code-names. He was right. LeClaire had told him code-names were assigned using the first letter of the actual company as the first letter of the code-name. Based on that, it wasn't hard to figure out that three of deals the mole and his friends traded on were Milner's—Tungsten Steel Service Centers, Ernest-United and Val-Tech Industries. He surfed the Internet for an hour based on code-names and dates and confirmed his suspicions: all but one of the mole's deals in the first three years were Walker-advised M&A transactions. He couldn't crack the code-names for the last year.

Regardless, it looked like it may not be just a few dirty guys at Walker. Based on this, somebody was trading on almost all Walker-advised billion dollar plus public M&A transactions, where the size of the deals allowed for significant trading volume and meaningful trading profits.

So now he was faced with the reality of blowing the whistle. But what did he really have? And he was still on probation. The last thing he needed was to make a fool of himself if he was wrong, and get fired over it. He decided he wasn't going to say anything to anybody for now. Particularly Kathy, because he knew what her reaction would be.

#

Shelter Island, NY. An hour after Milner left Lisa White, he touched down in a helicopter at East Hampton airport. His car service driver was waiting for him and they made the 9:12 p.m. ferry to Shelter Island with two minutes to spare. They crept down Chequit Avenue into the Shelter Island Yacht Club, where Milner told the driver to turn the lights off but keep the engine running. He walked with his head held erect, trying to look like he knew exactly where he was going. The description his secretary, Stephanie, had given him on the phone from searching the club's layout on its website was all he had to go on. He didn't want to be walking around looking like some guy who didn't belong there; some guy who was looking for some other guy's boat.

He turned left at the first T in the dock and started counting slips. He started wondering about the cops again, if they were staking out Chuck's boat. As he approached what he counted to be slip 13, he recognized Chuck's boat, an Etchells 22, converted from racing to high-performance daysailing.

Okay so far. He still hadn't seen a soul since getting to the Club. He turned down the gangplank, stepped onto the deck the way he thought a sailor might, stuck the key in the lock on top of the cabin and slid the roof open. He slid it shut behind him as he went down the steps. He used his flashlight until he found the switch for the cabin lights. His hands were sweaty when he clicked on the lights.

The laptop was in the second place Lisa suggested he look—on the left forward bunk. He picked it up and turned around. He was back in the car within three minutes from leaving it. He was burning to open the computer on the chopper back to Manhattan, but waited until he sat down at his desk in the office in his apartment.

He plugged into the internet and opened Outlook, then watched the emails download. He saw a series of emails from walker1@netwiz.net on the day Chuck died. His pulse quickened as he opened one, then another. It rammed in his temples as he kept opening emails. They were detailed records of Milner's profits from the Walker ring. That paper trail never existed; somebody created it after the fact for a reason. *A frame.*

His hands were trembling with anger as he searched Chuck's computer to find his spreadsheet files. It took him 15 minutes to find Chuck's master spreadsheet accounting for Milner's profits from Walker's trading ring. He clenched his teeth as he looked back and forth from the spreadsheet to the emails. The new emails from walker1@netwiz.net were an exact match of Chuck's spreadsheet files. *I'm hosed.* If the Feds didn't have him before, they sure as hell would once they saw the emails, and eventually they would. The same emails would be in Chuck's desktop as well, which the cops had.

Who was framing him? Jack and Mickey were still pushing him to do Tentron. Maybe Tentron was a trap. Would their foreign partners be doing it without Jack and Mickey knowing?

One thing seemed certain: whoever killed Chuck was responsible for sending those emails.

#

New York City. Sandy looked across Milner's desk at him. He obviously still thought the phones might be tapped, asking for a face-to-face meeting again. "We need to talk."

Milner said, "That's usually why you come over here and get in my face."

Sandy just looked at him for a moment. Milner looking back at him. Their usual dance. Then Sandy leaned in toward Milner. "I gather you're still moving forward on this Tentron deal. I don't understand. If you're worried about the Walker guys, why still deal with them? And if you really think they killed Chuck, we need to go to the police."

Milner squirmed in his chair, then said, "I think they may be trying to frame me for the trading ring. Maybe even for Chuck's murder. I'm going through the motions on Tentron to buy time, figure out what to do."

Sandy gave Milner one of his sternest looks, one Milner would have thought amusing under other circumstances.

Milner went on, "I didn't tell you, but Jack and Mickey came up here and pressured me to do the Tentron deal."

"When?" Sandy locked his gaze on Milner's eyes. There was no getting away from him on this one.

"Just before Chuck was murdered."

"Jesus, Mary and Joseph."

"And I've done some investigating since then. The cops didn't find Chuck's files on the trading ring; they were still buried in his office. And his laptop was missing, but Lisa helped me find it. Chuck's files match exactly with my totals from the ring as calculated on the spreadsheets in Chuck's computer. Only someone inside the ring could have that information. Except now. I found a bunch of emails to Chuck on the day he died that lay it all out so a second grader could follow it. Only reason for those emails to exist is a frame."

Sandy said, "Sounds like the Walker guys are setting you up for the ring. But why do you say they might be setting you up for Chuck's murder?"

"Just a feeling."

Sandy tilted his head skyward and thought. He looked back down at Milner after a moment and said, "Do you think they murdered Chuck?"

"Who the hell else?"

"To pressure you to keep playing ball with them, or because Chuck knew something?"

"To pressure me. A warning shot."

Sandy shook his head. "Bastards. If I'd never seen anything like this before I wouldn't believe it."

Milner didn't answer.

Sandy said, "You need to go to the police."

"I don't have any proof, just my own speculation. And I'd have to blow the whistle on myself for Walker's ring in order to give my suspicions any credibility."

"If you have material information regarding Chuck's murder, you have to go to the police. If you have to expose yourself, so be it. You're in a helluva pickle anyhow. What's wrong with this: cop a plea and turn everybody else in? Pay a fine and go back to your life when you're out of jail."

"Are you kidding? Jail is what's wrong with it."

"Boesky only went away for a few years. I think Milken served two or three."

"Bernie Madoff got 150 years; maybe they'd only give me 100, but I'll never get out. And I don't have any proof to bring down the top guys in the ring, so I've got no negotiating leverage to cut a deal for myself for reduced time in jail. It'd be my word against theirs, and they'd serve up some poor underling schmucks to the Feds to protect themselves."

"And Chuck's murder? You're going to sit back and let them get away with that?"

"I don't have anything that would help the cops make it stick. I'd be sacrificing myself for nothing."

Sandy shook his head, looking disgusted.

Milner said, "I'd rather run."

"Then you better do it quick. If the Walker guys are framing you, you may not have much time. Remember, the Feds are already onto you. If they come, the Feds and the U.S. Attorney will freeze all your assets. And if the Walker guys have worse in mind than framing you, you might wake up dead one day."

#

After Sandy left, Milner turned and looked through the window up Park Avenue. When Sandy first talked to him about the Feds, Sandy said they would bust a small fry in the trading ring, then squeeze him to give up the higher-ups. *And I'm the top of the food chain.* But there's always a bigger fish.

Milner waited until everybody else in the office went home, then walked downstairs to the wall where the Macintosh amps had been warming up for two hours. He pulled out a good Deutsche Gramophon LP of his favorite symphony, Beethoven's 6th, the

Pastoral, and placed it on his Basis 2800 Signature turntable. By the time he walked back to his chair in the sweet spot, 12.5 feet from the big Wilson Maxx speakers, the opening strains were playing. He sat down, pointed the remote and turned it up. He had some thinking to do, and in about an hour this would clear his head.

#

Milner got to the office at 8:00 a.m., before anyone else would arrive. He turned to one of the foot-high Rolodexes on his desk, cranked it to the card. He checked his watch, dialed the phone.

The secretary put him through.

"I'm surprised to hear from you directly, old boy."

You mean concerned, don't you? Milner didn't respond.

After a moment, old man Schoenfeld said, "Anything wrong?"

"No. I just wanted to speak with you personally to tell you I've decided to do the Tentron deal, and that it's my last with you guys."

"I didn't know it was to be your last, but I knew you've been contemplating it."

"I figured you did."

The line was silent for a few moments, then Schoenfeld said, "Yes, well."

"Are you buying yet?"

"Absolutely."

Milner signed off and hung up. Let's see what the boys listening in do with that.

#

Washington, D.C. It was just after 2 p.m., and Croonquist had his suit jacket on and was already halfway out the door, heading for an already late sandwich, when his phone rang.

"Roman, it's Charlie Holden."

"Charlie. Great to hear from you. How are you?" Charlie Holden, Assistant U.S. Attorney, his partner in prosecuting securities cases when Croonquist was Deputy Director of Enforcement in New York for six years.

"Good. But I'm jammed. Mind if I talk fast?"

"No, I'm on the run myself."

"I just got something interesting from the NYPD on Milner's CFO's murder. It's emails in the CFO's computer showing some kind of accounting that looks like somebody's been keeping tabs between themselves on profits on old deals. I heard you're sniffing at Milner and thought it might mean something to you."

Croonquist started smiling, then walked around behind his desk and sat down.

Holden went on, "I can forward a scanned copy of it to you in an email. You want it?"

"Hell yeah. When can you send it?"

"Right now." Holden paused. "It's on its way."

"Thanks, Charlie."

"Right, gotta go. See ya." He hung up.

Thirty seconds later Croonquist heard the ping in his Outlook inbox. He opened the email. He felt a surge of adrenaline, then a warm feeling in his chest. One look at it told him it was related to his Walker/Milner surveillance. The emails to Milner's CFO were sent from walker1@netwiz.net, the email account at Walker that all the outgoing trades were ordered from. With this on top of his trading data and what he'd gotten from the wiretaps, he had enough. Screw lunch. He'd get Starsky and Hutch to start drafting indictments.

#

New York City. Richard couldn't see any real reason for him to ride uptown with Jack in his Porsche to Milner's office. He figured by that time Jack just liked having him around.

The numbered trading account they'd opened for Milner stood at 4.9% ownership of Tentron's stock, the legal limit without filing his intentions with the SEC. They were heading up to Milner's office for a team meeting on next steps. LeClaire would meet them there. Steinberg was to be patched in by phone.

"It's like skiing," Jack said, tooling the silver Porsche 911 Turbo up the FDR Drive at 60 miles per hour.

"Huh?"

"Skiing."

"You mean this?" Richard asked, thinking Jack was referring to his slalom-like weaving through traffic. He arched his back as Jack raced up to slip-stream a Chevy, tear around it.

"No, the deals, this whole business, the way we live."

"How do you mean?"

"You don't know exactly how you're getting there, no defined route, just the direction you're going in. And fast. Too slow is too late. And who has fun doing anything unless you're scared shitless half the time? Just don't fall down or it's all over. Because even if you get back up, by then the competition's past you."

"What about missing gates?"

Jack didn't say anything. He downshifted the Porsche from 5th into 3rd, slalomed around a truck and a van with the engine screaming, then shot back into the left lane. Richard's stomach felt light from both the acceleration and from hanging on an answer. *Why are you rooting for Jack to fit some mold?* For the first time Richard wasn't sure he wanted to be like Jack.

Finally Jack said, "Depends if anybody sees you."

After another long pause he said, "Relax. Enjoy yourself; this should be a fun meeting. We're getting to the good part." Richard was realizing that Jack's idea of fun was dangerous.

#

Jack and Richard got off the elevator at Milner's penthouse to a blaze of afternoon sun. They walked into a battle command center that Milner's penthouse had been transformed into. Snakes of communications cables were everyplace. A 30-foot conference table was set up in the center of the main floor. Other tables overflowed with catered food. The place throbbed with motion. Stephanie, Milner's secretary, stood at the center of activity, gesturing and pointing, as if directing traffic.

The information agents from Morrow & Company grouped together to the left of the room, clothed in muted grays.

Howard Blaine wisecracked with Shakespearean elocution at Milner. Richard couldn't imagine Milner putting up with it for long. A handful of Blaine's Associates talked on telephones set up in makeshift cubicles lining the east wall. Three guys from Devon & Company, Milner's private investigators, sat in Milner's living room furniture off to the east, looking serious. They wore rumpled gray suits and eyed the table decked out with hot buffet food the caterers were freshening. A cute brunette putting out egg rolls flashed a smile at Richard. She and the heroin-thin tall blonde worked slowly, seeming to enjoy that he was watching them.

The Walker team added the color. Jack was regal in a royal blue suit. LeClaire wore something double-breasted from Zegna, one of those borderline greens that sometimes look blue. Richard wore white collar and cuffs against an English striped shirt and a dark blue Polo suit.

Just before the meeting was to start, Richard stood at the mezzanine rail outside Milner's glass-walled office and conference room. He looked up Park Avenue at all of midtown Manhattan. Cars and people moved noiselessly up and down the streets, Richard wondering how many below even imagined what was going on up here. He turned, leaned on the rail and looked down at the war-room below. One of Blaine's Associates trotted from the phones to a group of professionals clustered at the conference table. Another group watched the plasma screens.

Richard wondered how many of his classmates from Michigan were seeing similar scenes unfold. He was on his way; he'd scrambled from almost not making it to the Street to playing the game on a level he'd never dreamed was possible in that short a time frame. He was on the fast track, ahead of his peers at Walker & Company. The Sterling & Dalton lawyers and all the other professionals on the deal team listened to what he said, because Milner, Blaine, Jack and the others at Walker had accepted him. He was learning directly from masters surrounding him. He was in an industry where knowledge ruled, but where looking and seeming and style were sometimes as important as knowing. He was where he belonged; he'd chosen well.

And he was making more money than he ever imagined. Only a week ago Jack said to him, "Just look at you. Last summer you were a fresh face, but a doe-eyed rube. Young man comes to New York, applies himself, starts to learn the game and gets some strut in his step. You're kicking ass. Keep it up and you'll make a $250,000 bonus this year, be wearing a different suit every day and riding taxis around town with long-legged models."

I'm a success.

Now he thought about Jack's 'skiing' speech on the way uptown. No question, Jack was a master, and maybe that's how they all operated—cutting corners. Richard decided he wasn't doing anything to make waves, screw this up; he'd forget about the mole. Who knew? Maybe Jack was the mole. He remembered LeClaire's words the day he'd offered Richard the 'provisional' job: they'd test him to see if he was Walker material, maybe even ask him to do things that might make him squeamish. And if the mole's operation was really how it worked, maybe soon they'd ask him to send some emails ordering trades. Would he do it?

Milner walked out of his office doorway, leaned on the rail next to Richard. They were both silent, looking at the activity on the floor. "So, whattaya think?" Milner asked.

"You should launch your bid at $45 and get it over with."

"Not advice to give your client lightly. Maybe the guys haven't told you that. But that's not what I was asking about."

"Sorry." Screwed-up. Getting too familiar.

"That's okay, you're among friends. It's just that normally that kind of advice is something reserved for somebody like Jack in a 'dare to be great' speech."

Richard felt himself nod stiffly, tense.

Milner said, "Relax, I said you're among friends."

They leaned on the rail there for another minute or so, watching the activity on the main floor, silent. Finally Milner said, "This was what I was asking you about. It doesn't get any better than this, eh?"

"No."

"This is what life is all about. Not just the deals. What gets me out of bed in the morning is building something that gives guys like these a reason to run around like this."

#

A few minutes later they walked into Milner's mezzanine conference room, Richard watching Jack and Milner. They both seemed different. Milner was subdued, not showing the rapport with Jack he'd seen in the past. Jack seemed sharper, more attuned, if that were possible.

Milner pushed a button someplace on one of the legs of his conference table and said, "Get me Steinberg, please."

After a brief hold, Steinberg was on. Richard was still watching Jack. Jack's gaze was roving around the table, taking in everything. He leaned one elbow on the table, appearing casual, but Richard could see he was poised.

Jack got right to it. "Mickey, Harold's at 4.9% ownership of Tentron. He needs our help to make some decisions."

"Should we begin by reiterating the company's position and details of its situation?" LeClaire asked. Richard saw Jack glance at Milner as if he wanted to push on.

"Go ahead, François," Steinberg said.

LeClaire sat forward in his chair, his hands spread apart on the desk, looking at a notebook with his usual hieroglyphics in it. "All the company's directors are up for re-election this year, so it is vulnerable to a proxy fight to elect our own slate of directors, which would take 90 days or so."

"Or forever," Jack said. He never took his eyes off Milner, even when LeClaire looked up at him, startled.

Then LeClaire's face softened into a smile. "Our CEO is impatient, Mickey," LeClaire said, looking up to where Steinberg's voice appeared to be coming from on Milner's overhead speakers. Milner was waving his hand and shaking his head. "And Harold is already disagreeing with me," LeClaire said. "I am only laying out the situation prior to advising you on your options." Milner shrugged and waved LeClaire on.

Richard was still watching Jack. His gaze was moving around, but always locking back on Milner; oozing purpose, ready to nudge it in the right direction again. He watched Jack watch Milner listen to LeClaire describe Tentron's poison pill defense, then watched Jack watch Milner listen to Howard Blaine describe the applicable Delaware law of Tentron's domicile.

Jack said, "Harold's up to speed on all this. Cut to it."

"I see your options as threefold," Steinberg said. "Number one, make a friendly approach and see if they'll negotiate. Number two, stampede them into negotiating by publicly announcing an offer. Number three, launch an unsolicited offer. Within that last option, I see two possible financing scenarios: first, all cash, and second, a mix of cash and the bonds of New Tentron we discussed early on in our planning."

Richard watched Jack watch Milner listen to himself thinking aloud, mulling the alternatives. Then: "Whattaya guys think?" Milner asked. Richard was now looking over again at Jack and thinking this was Jack skiing like he said in the car. He didn't know his exact route, just the general direction. Then he remembered Jack didn't care so much about how he got there, missing gates, but his eyes were on the last double gate, the finish line. Going for it, getting Milner to do the deal.

"I say launch the tender offer now," Jack said. LeClaire nodded his agreement.

"I agree we should launch, but we should work at the other elements of the offer," Blaine said. Jack showed a twitch of impatience, his jaw clenching.

"Okay, so let's launch," Milner said. Jack was still watching Milner. "So Mickey, what about price?"

Steinberg said, "We recommend as high as possible, say 45 dollars per share, so you can scare off anybody else who wants to make a competing bid."

Jack was still watching Milner. Milner rested his elbow on the table, his hand over his mouth but his eyes not betraying a smile. "I'm thinking 40 bucks to start, give me some room to move up, see what the tone is first."

Richard saw LeClaire look up quickly, Jack's entire body visibly tighten. "Too cute by a half, my man," Jack said.

Milner's eyes were smiling. "Never said I was boring."

Jack smiled back at him. "Or an easy client."

Milner didn't say anything.

Steinberg said, "It's way too low. All you'll do is draw out a competing bid."

"Let's see how it plays out."

Nobody spoke for a moment.

Then Steinberg said, "Because you plan to sell two of the divisions, you'll have to file significant SEC disclosure on your intentions."

"I'm aware of that."

Blaine added, "Including Walker & Company's estimates of value for the divisions you'll be selling, unfortunately."

Richard never took his gaze off Jack, who had his eyes locked on Milner. Jack said, "In other words, you'll be drawing a map for anybody else who wants to outbid you."

"I know," Milner said. "I wanna see what unfolds."

Richard saw Jack's jaw muscles stiffen.

"We'll start at 40 bucks," Milner said. "Howard, get your boys drafting the documents right away."

Jack looked like somebody just made him eat something sour.

#

When he got back to 55 Water Street, Jack headed straight for Mickey's office. Two bankers, Ron Elman and some SVP whose name he couldn't remember were waiting outside, probably for some deal advice. Jack walked past them and closed the door.

"What's Harold up to?"

Mickey looking up, then back at one of the screens. "Not sure." Then looking up at Jack, "Relax, at least he's launching a bid."

"Relaxing is the last thing I'm gonna do. He's not exactly taking the easy way."

"True. Not his usual lights-out approach."

Jack thinking, *No shit.*

Mickey smiled. "Maybe the game's getting to be more important to him than the end result. A test of wits."

"That lowball price. What's with that? Like taking out a full-page ad: 'Here, top me.'"

"He's playing chess, spotting his opponent three moves: 'See if you can beat me.'"

"More like wearing a sign on his butt that says 'Kick me, hard.'"

Mickey shrugged, went back to looking at his screens. Jack tried to think of what Milner could be up to. They already had a shitload of money riding on this one, and he wasn't about to let Milner outmaneuver him.

#

On the way into the office the next morning, Walker's receptionist handed Richard a large manila envelope. "From Mr. Milner," she said.

Richard opened it in his cubicle. He slid out an inch-thick musical score, *Konzert fur Klarinette and Orchester A-dur by Wolfgang Amadeus Mozart,* and a hand-written note:

Richard,

I bought this years ago and thought you might appreciate it more than me. I recall you saying in Houston that this clarinet concerto is one of your father's favorites. The score is old, from the 1820s, and the personal copy of a fairly prominent Viennese conductor of that era, Johann Vermeil. He was an avid interpreter of Mozart's music, and the notes in the margins are his. Enjoy.

Best,
Harold

A takeover maven with soul. Richard eased the score back into the envelope and placed it inside his briefcase. He looked forward to telling Dad.

#

Fire Island, NY. The LeClaires invited Richard to their house on Fire Island for the weekend. When François learned Kathy just returned from Paris, he invited her, too. *Yeah, white-hot smart,* Richard thought. Now to make something of it.

On the ferry, Kathy was the one who suggested Richard and she go out to the railing in the bow as they approached Fire Island. It was Indian summer, but damn, it was freezing out there in the wind. "LeClaire's house is in Point 'O Woods, one of 17 discrete villages on the island," Richard said.

"Uh-huh."

Kathy didn't seem too interested. He watched her hair blowing in the wind, flapping into her face. She squinted against it. A minute earlier Richard had suggested going back inside. She wouldn't hear of it.

"François says that each has its own culture, each its own ambiance. Jewish, jet-set, gay. Point 'O Woods is all WASP."

Kathy turned to face the opposite shore. The wind pressed her windbreaker tight around her breasts. Their firm shape was accentuated, touchable. He could see the outline of her nipples. She said, "Will you look at that sky?" She gazed out on the horizon. Seeing her profile made him ache.

"Beautiful," he said. Watching her. Imagining how she'd feel pressed against him in his arms; she embracing him back. Wanting to tell her how she was affecting him, but the words not coming up. "Point 'O Woods extends from the ocean all the way to the bay side. It has locked gates around it."

Kathy pointed to the clouds. "Are you getting this?"

Why was he stuck in this travelogue? *Shut up, man.* He stood close to her and took in her scent. He stayed silent until the ferry landing was in view.

François, Elaine and children formed an American Gothic picture on the dock as they waited for Kathy and Richard to walk down the gangplank. Elaine held Chloe, the youngest, in arm, and Cynthia by the hand. Renée clutched Elaine's leg.

Richard so wanted Elaine to like Kathy. He'd met Elaine twice before. She was letting Kathy walk Cynthia by the hand. Talking to Kathy with her easy elegance. They walked past wind-battered cottages with railed porches, finally to the LeClaire's, a cedar-sided cottage indistinguishable from the others situated on the beach. The smell of salt air and marshy vegetation rose in Richard's nose.

They prepared a barbecue behind the house that evening. François and Elaine seemed to do everything with Cynthia, Chloe and Renée hanging off them, clutching their legs, sitting in their laps or jumping up and down next to them. Little fingers poked the steaks and the vegetable kabobs awaiting the grill.

"These are times we need to savor, my friend," LeClaire said to Richard, Chloe in his lap squeezing his nose, sticking her fingers into his cheeks. He saw Elaine smiling. LeClaire blew her a kiss. The picture of a happy man. LeClaire motioned to Elaine, handed Chloe to her. "Come on, Richard. Help me with the steaks." Richard and LeClaire walked over to the stone fireplace and LeClaire started putting the meat on the grill. Richard couldn't see anything for him to do. He figured LeClaire just wanted to talk. "She's a great girl," LeClaire said, looking at Kathy, whose nose Chloe was now squeezing.

"Yeah. I'm thinking the same thing, and more."

"We work hard, and we should, but for a purpose."

"I agree," Richard said.

"So get going before somebody else scoops her up."

Sitting in front of the fireplace after dinner, Richard watched Kathy's hair moving in the wind, silhouetted against the flames. He could almost sense how it felt as he imagined running his hands through it, stroking her head. "A walk?" Richard suggested to Kathy. It was already dark.

"Having fun?" Kathy said once they started toward the bay.

"Loving it." Richard thinking Kathy's mind seemed far off.

"Could have fooled me."

"Yeah?"

"Yeah. You were so caught up in your Encyclopedia Britannica routine on the ferry, you didn't seem to notice how beautiful this place is. Or anything else."

"I figured you didn't know Fire Island, what with spending your summers at your dad's ancestral estate in South Hampton."

"Your psyche's still wearing a three-piece suit. Lighten up. Why so tense?"

"Maybe I'm working too hard."

They entered the path to the Beach House and Club, roofed by an arch of bushes and trees, Richard caught up in the ambiance. He wanted to pick up their conversation from earlier, move it toward telling her how he felt about her. They walked slowly, arms brushing, Kathy now seeming approachable. "I guess I am wound a little tight. I'm working on a big Milner M&A deal, and this mole thing is nagging at me."

He saw her tense, then put distance between them and wrap her arms around her as if she were cold. "You had me getting into the mood before you brought up the mole."

"Then forget I said it."

"I can't. I wish you'd never stumbled onto him. But now it looks like something *is* going on."

"There is, and it's worse than you think. Years of trading, tons of deals, mostly Walker's and some of Milner's. And big money, with probably lots of people involved."

Kathy pulled her arms in tighter, focused her gaze downward on the path. "And what are you going to do?"

"Nothing. Forget about it."

Kathy snapped her head to look at him. "What? If you're right you have an obligation to do something."

"Look, maybe this is how it works on Wall Street. You said yourself this is a rough-and-tumble place. The Wild West."

"They're crooks! You have to expose them."

"I blow the whistle without being sure, I could get fired."

"Maybe worse than fired if you don't. Milner's CFO was murdered."

It sent a bolt of shock through him but he went on as if she hadn't said it, "You forget I'm still probational? And now I've got something to lose. I'm doing great, and I'm not doing anything to screw that up."

"I can't believe this. Where's my farm boy now?"

"I'm running with the pack, learning from the top guys in the business."

"Get your head out of your ass, you naive fool. If you don't tell somebody, I will."

Richard just looked at her, surprised. How did stuff just bubble up and erupt out of this woman?

Kathy said, "And don't give me that sad-eyed, lovelorn look."

Uncalled for. He felt a flash of anger. He said, "You're really stuck in your hard-armored shell aren't you? Glib, tough and cool. I try to get close to you and you push me away with talk about fast-tracking your career to be bigger than your dad. It's like your mantra you retreat into . . ."

"Better be careful what you say . . . ."

"Are you doing it for the thrill of the chase, to win, or to be somebody daddy would approve of?"

Kathy stopped and thrust her arms downward, hands balled into fists. She stuck her chin out and said through her teeth, "I don't need to listen to this from some hick who's so crazy to star-fuck with Milner, Jack and Mickey that he's blinded to the fact they're all a bunch of sleazebags! If you'd open your eyes and get your priorities in line with your so-called values, you could use your brains to figure out what you really want. See if Wall Street is anything more to you than some ego trip out of being a dufus all your life!" She spun and walked off in the opposite direction.

When Richard got back to the LeClaire's cottage, Kathy had already gone upstairs to bed. The next morning, she and Richard exchanged awkward formalities over breakfast, then stayed away from each other on the beach all day. They sat in separate sections on the ferry back to Long Island, Richard fuming over her words, regretting his and feeling like his heart was being crushed. When the ferry docked, he decided to catch up with Kathy and talk. His legs felt weak as he trotted down the gangplank. Before he reached the bottom he saw her hop into a cab and pull out. His heart was knocking.

#

Washington, D.C. The next morning, Croonquist spent an hour staring at the MarketWatch monitor on his desk. He ran programs to access the sources and identities of the firms initiating orders on the four stocks he'd come in early yesterday to analyze, and never got to.

At 9:15 he got up, stretched, and sat down to review the sixty pages of output he'd printed. By 9:45 he assessed the situation. SPS Technologies' stock price showed what was probably a normal move based on improving performance. Nothing unusual. His review of Jupiter Fabrics was similar. He decided to drop them both from his watch list. His analysis of Dasher Furniture showed definite signs of unusual buying from the Far East. Not worth bothering with. The Asian governments never cooperated in bringing anything to prosecution.

Tentron was a different story. Walker & Company's steady buying had shown up since a month ago. In the previous weeks, heavy purchasing activity had picked up through two brokerage firms in London and three Swiss, Cayman Islands and Netherland

Antilles banks. The pattern was unmistakable—methodical buying from those firms. Shaw, BeldenFirst, Stuart Halsey and Tucker Securities in the U.S. started the same systematic buying at about the same time. He turned to the keyboard and ran a few more subroutines. He could feel his pulse quicken as the columns appeared on the screen. Prior to a month ago, no buying had been exhibited by any of the European firms, and Walker had shown only modest trading activity indicative of routine customer orders. Yet Walker & Company had purchased for at least one customer over 4.6% of the stock in the last three weeks and the foreign firms had purchased a total of over 13% of the stock during a similar time period. Shaw, BeldenFirst, Stuart Halsey and Tucker Securities customers had accounted for another 7% on just as systematic a basis. If Croonquist was right, that meant that 25% of the stock had been accumulated over the last two months with the stock price moving more than five points, but, incredibly, no one making the mandatory 13D filing disclosing they owned more than 5%.

Croonquist dialed Mike Dolan, his friend at NSA.

"I was wondering when you'd call," Dolan said. Croonquist felt anticipation, reached into the bag in his bottom drawer for some pistachios.

"You have something interesting?" Croonquist asked. So why couldn't Dolan pick up the phone himself if he found something?

"A mountain of trading. Reports back and forth between New York and Paris."

"Which stocks?" Croonquist asked.

"Code-name MCS. It's the same kind of activity we saw in those other half-dozen stocks. Orders going from Walker & Company over to GCG in Paris. Then not much activity and then a whole boatload of confirmations coming back."

"Anything to anyplace else in Europe?" Croonquist asked.

"Nothing I've seen, although who knows where they went once they got to Paris. Some interesting chatter on the phone lines, though. You guys have audio capability in your Cray or you need me to send you some tapes?"

Croonquist sat up straight in his chair. He think they were playing with tinker toys over here? He said, "Yeah, we can download the audio data as well, and we'll play it back over here. I'd like to review everything," Croonquist said, "then I've got a few ideas I want to check out. You in all week?"

"Yup," Dolan said.

Croonquist hung up and dialed his head computer jock to download the NSA's data onto the SEC's Cray. While he waited for the guy to pick up the phone, Croonquist thought about what he had: hard data on order flow on what looked for sure to be a Milner deal, the same pattern as the homebuilding stocks. He was convinced that when he ran the NSA data through MarketWatch it would correlate: MCS would turn out to be Tentron. And he was sure the computer hacker and the phone taps would add input to help it all add up to something. It was coming together. And now Charlie Holden, his old partner, was in the mix. This was looking good.

#

New York City. Richard waited for Kathy at the Teavana across Water Street from the office. He hadn't seen her all Monday and wanted to clear the air. He clenched and released his fists, not just anxious about smoothing over their argument; more at her reaction to the stupid things he'd said about the mole. And if Kathy knew what he'd been thinking that day at Milner's about Jack's skiing speech—that maybe missing gates was okay if nobody saw you, and if that's how it worked he might let himself get talked into sending some emails for the mole—she might never get past it. Like she'd said on Fire Island: Where's my farm boy now? He hoped he hadn't lost her over the crap he'd spouted. He sat on a stool by the counter facing the windows, now sipping his green tea, the only customer. The sharp odor of bleach permeated the place; one of the crew was mopping up. Closing time.

Kathy walked in, looking strained, or impatient, he couldn't tell. Her jaw was taught and her lips were thin lines.

Richard stood up. "Hi," he said, "you want anything?"

"No, I'm good." She motioned with her head toward the door. "Let's just walk a little."

They left, walked side by side. Kathy had her arms wrapped around her. *Closed up.*

Richard said, "I thought maybe we should break the ice. Sunday on the island was awkward." He turned to her and smiled.

She was walking with her head tilted downward, eyes on the sidewalk straight ahead of her. "I . . . regret our argument." She stopped on the sidewalk and looked into his eyes. "I want to know what you're thinking."

Richard decided to just show her. He pulled her to him and kissed her. She didn't resist at first, then pulled her lips from his. She stood encircled in his arms, not moving away, her hands on his chest. She was looking into his eyes.

"No reaction?"

"Okay," she said, "so you're a good kisser." Her eyes showed a hint of a mischievous smile, Richard thinking this was going better than it had at Point 'O Woods.

Then she leaned back and her eyes went distant. She said, "I thought you wanted to talk."

"I do. About us."

She pulled away from him, stepped back. "I need to think more about this."

"Quit thinking. What do you feel?"

She shook her head. "I don't know." Then her eyes narrowed and her jaw clenched. "And I'm still . . . " She paused, then said, "I need to go home." She turned and walked down Water Street without looking back. Richard felt an ache in his chest and started after her, his breathing labored. Then he stopped. *Don't push her now.* He watched her a moment, then started off in the opposite direction. He knew he was getting in deep enough that he needed to resolve this, but this wasn't the moment. *'Getting in.' Who am I kidding?*

Chapter 6

New York City. "Man, oh man," Milner said aloud, sitting alone in his office, looking at his computer screen. All of the press reports—CNBC, Bloomberg, CNNMoney, Fortune, even those yahoos at Yahoo Finance—were universally negative on his Tentron bid. Tentron's stock was trading at $41.50, well above his offer. That spoke volumes more than the press: market expects higher bid.

Sandy called him and said he was coming over. "You seen the press?" Milner said to him when he arrived.

"Like flies on dog shit."

Milner sat back, hooked his hands behind his head. He said, "It's odd, intentionally shooting myself in the foot. Against my instincts."

"I agree. Why don't you just get it over with and take out a full page ad in the *Journal* that offers a $100 million reward to anybody that tops your bid."

"Sanford F. Sharts, I'm surprised at you. Stooping to sarcasm."

"You're bringing out the worst in me, playing around with the public markets, risking both of our hides if the SEC finds out you've made a frivolous offer. That it's to buy you time to figure out what to do about the shit you've stepped in."

"It's no different than bidding for something you don't really want in a charity auction. Coaxing some jerk you can't stand into the bidding, then running the price up on him so your favorite cause gets a higher price."

"Since when is Walker your favorite cause?"

That stopped Milner. "Point taken."

"Sitting around isn't going to solve the core problem. Are you going to cop a plea or run?"

Well, that about summed it up. No hiding from Uncle Sandy. "I don't know yet. I'm still trying to decide."

"Just don't get too cute. Remember you've got a fuse burning, and you don't know how long it is."

About ten minutes after Sandy left, Jack called and asked for a meeting. Milner said sure. It was like *A Christmas Carol*. He wondered when the next ghost would visit.

A half hour later when Jack got there he didn't even waste time grinning and preening himself before saying, "What's going on with this half-assed bid?"

"Not much if you believe the press."

"Quit screwing around. What're you doing?"

"I'm trying to buy a company."

"Doesn't look that way to me."

"No? I've spent a million bucks in fees and committed to six billion in financing. What does that look like to you?"

"At 40 bucks a share? A wet fart. We've got a ton of capital at risk on this one. And not only that, we need the profits to shore up the firm, what with the losses we're taking from this credit market meltdown."

"So now I'm responsible for helping you address macroeconomics?"

"Don't fuck with me. After you called him, Sir Reginald doubled down his position. Jeez, we own over 25% of the stock. If you pull out or blow it the stock will drop like a stone. It could bankrupt Walker. I'm not gonna let that happen."

"You gonna dictate my deal tactics now?"

Jack just stared at him. Milner didn't know if Jack was thinking of what to say next or was just trying to be intimidating.

Milner said, "Maybe you oughtta go back downtown and take care of your business, leave me alone up here to take care of mine." Milner felt like he'd won a round when Jack left. But he hadn't forgotten what Sandy said. And seeing Jack seething like that reminded him of what happened to Chuck.

#

Washington, D.C. Croonquist was tired. Why wouldn't he be? He'd been working his ass off on this presentation to Charlie

Green for two straight weeks. Franklin Stone from Litigation would attend, now an ally whose support he could count on. Phil Johnson in Surveillance, his old boss would also be there, and was on board. Green was still pressing for a big bust, but lately Charlie's mood depended on the direction the political winds were blowing on Capitol Hill that week. So Croonquist wasn't sure how today would go.

At 8:59, Green entered the room, nodded, and took his seat at the end of the table. Croonquist felt a flutter in his chest. He nodded to Starsky to dim the lights, cleared his throat and rose.

He clicked to the first PowerPoint slide. "As you can see here, we're focusing on the stock of just one company, Tentron Corporation, as a potential enforcement action, but there is a pattern that exists from at least one previous transaction we monitored involving Southwest Homes. The similarities in trading provide evidence that the individuals we're targeting are functioning as a group." He clicked to the next slide.

"What you see here are selections from a series of emails over a two month period regarding the common stock and listed stock options of a group of six homebuilders just before the announcement of the Southwest Homes initial public offering. The emails are between Walker & Company's New York office and GCG's Paris office. As you see here, the initial buy orders went out from Walker's New York office and the confirmations started coming in a day or two later." He looked up to see if Green was with him. Green looked bored.

Croonquist clicked successively through four slides, moving it along. "What you can see here is that orders started getting handed out to various Swiss banks as well."

"I never heard of any of these banks," Green said.

"They aren't majors like UBS and Swiss Bank, but they're all substantial in size, none with less than five billion dollars in total assets," Croonquist said. Green nodded.

"The same trading pattern shows up in Tentron's stock." Croonquist clicked through four slides showing the link between Walker & Company's New York office and GCG Paris, then to London, Tokyo, Santiago and Hong Kong. Croonquist was now thinking it was too much information, too many slides.

Green shook his head. "Roman, we talked about these emails a while back. Can we use any of them?"

"Not the homebuilders stuff," Stone said, "but we got wiretaps before we collected most of the Tentron stuff. That's all usable."

Green nodded. "Go on," he said.

"What we have here," Croonquist said, clicking to another slide, "is data produced by our new MarketWatch system and our Cray. It shows documentation of virtually all of the trades in Tentron listed in the preceding emails." He turned back to look at Green, waved his hand in a circle. "Close to twenty-five percent of Tentron's stock has been acquired in activities that appear to be part of a coordinated group."

"Let's cut to the punch line," Green said.

"Okay," Croonquist said, seeing he was getting to the end of Green's attention span, "the Tentron trading appears to be the same group as the homebuilders. Harold Milner launched an unsolicited tender offer for Tentron earlier this week. We think Milner and Walker & Company formed an illegal group operating in concert to acquire Tentron without disclosing their mutual intent and acquired close to twenty-five percent of Tentron's shares without filing a 13D." He paused and waited to see Green's reaction. Green understood.

"What's the relationship to the homebuilders?" Green asked.

Croonquist turned back to look at the screen. "Maybe this will help. The telephone conversations listed here are between the M&A Department in Walker & Company's New York office and GCG Paris. I'm going to play you a tape from one of those conversations," he said and clicked the tape machine on. The sound wasn't great, but he hoped Green could follow.

"Are they on the way?" the first kid's voice said.

"You should have them by 6:00 tomorrow evening your time," the second kid's voice said.

First kid: "Anything unusual?"

Second kid: "Yes. Prolific today. Lots of instructions— trading like crazy."

First kid: "Are you sure it was all from him?"

Second kid: "No, as you know, on any given day he accounts for about ninety percent of the volume of the trades."

First kid: "So if today was a heavy day, chances are he had a heavy day."

Second kid: "Right. I was very tempted tonight to review them all at my end to see what they said."

First kid: "Too risky."

Second kid: "Yeah, you're right. No sense in pressing our luck."

Croonquist turned the tape machine off. He turned back to look at Green. He couldn't read him.

"One of the voices you heard and one of the telephone numbers you see on the screen was Richard Blum, an Associate in the M&A Department at Walker & Company. We think he and one of his colleagues in Paris are part of this group dating back from the Southwest transaction. We have a number of other similar calls between Blum and his colleague, Kathy Cella, who's assigned to GCG in Paris. We don't know if they're couriers or they're privy to the identity of all the other group members."

"So we're recommending we bring in Blum first, sweat him and then see where it leads us," Stone said.

Green said, "You have my blessing. But how do you know that this kid Blum won't tip off the rest of the network?"

"We scare the shit out of him and convince him he can plea bargain for turning everybody else in. That's not a big concern," Stone said.

"Sounds good to me, just keep me posted," Green said. He looked at his watch, nodded at Croonquist, said "good job" and left. Croonquist turned the projector off and felt the rush he always did before a big case. This one was on the way, and it had him tingling all the way down to his toes.

#

New York City. Kathy got out of the taxi at 62nd and Broadway. She knew Richard would be home at his apartment, because she saw him getting into the car service Town Car in front of the office. She heard him decline a drink with Tim Bolton, saying he was heading straight home. She wanted this over with.

Her emotions had been twisting in her stomach for two days, since he kissed her on the sidewalk outside Teavana and asked her what she felt. What was it with this guy? Guys didn't ask her what she felt, they just hit on her. But Richard just kept coming at her. Smiling, gentle, confident, he didn't give up. But he'd said things on Fire Island she had to square with him.

When she got off the elevator, she could see he was waiting for her at the door. His suit jacket was off, tie loosened, hair a little tousled, but still just so. "Hi," he said.

Kathy walked past him without saying anything, got a few steps inside and turned. When he closed the door he said, "Before you say anything I need to talk about the mole. I know what I said on Fire Island was ridiculous."

"That can wait. You hurt me on the island."

"I'm sorry, but you pissed me off."

"What was that crap about my family's South Hampton place?"

"You call me farm boy, razz me for my background all the time. You can't take a poke in the ribs?"

"You call 'stuck in your hard-armored shell' a poke? 'Glib, tough and cool?' And don't ever talk about my father."

"You pissed me off. What did you call me? Lovelorn?"

"Pissed off or not. I think you meant it. Most times, people don't really say what they mean until they're angry."

He moved toward her. For some reason she started to feel like she was going to cry. She clenched her teeth. She'd be damned if she'd let herself.

He said, "I didn't say everything I meant. I love you."

It hit her like a wave of warmth washing over her chest, then down her entire body. She felt like laughing with relief, knowing now it was what she needed to hear, then feeling the tears come. Her eyes were closed when he took her in his arms.

"Oh, God, why are you saying that to me *now?*"

"What do you mean *now?* Why's this any worse or better time than any other?"

He was holding her and she had her hands on his chest, looking up into his face. Why did he have to keep coming at her? "Stop pushing me, please." He kissed her; she didn't respond for a moment, then she let herself kiss him back. She pulled her lips from his and looked into his eyes, smiling. She put her hands in his hair, drew his face to hers and kissed him. She felt him moving her toward the sofa. Now she couldn't wait even that long and pulled him to the floor. "The rug is fine," she whispered, and scrambled to undo the buttons on his shirt.

#

Richard passed 60 Centre Street, the Supreme Court building. He pulled the note from his pocket: Roman Croonquist, c/o Charles Holden, U.S. Attorney's Office, fifth floor 75 Centre Street. At first Richard hadn't believed Croonquist's explanation in his call two days earlier, that Richard could shed some light on a 'problem' the SEC was investigating. But now he didn't care what Croonquist wanted; Richard had his own agenda. After

Kathy stood him on his head on Fire Island one thing led to another. Still ashamed of his reflections about Jack's 'skiing' speech. Then, mortified about telling Kathy he'd just forget about the mole, and worse, realizing what Dad would say about both of those. And finally, deciding to call the SEC himself and get all this mole stuff out in the open. So the call from Croonquist was a perfect coincidence.

He hoped.

As he got off the elevator he felt a rumble in his chest. The place was eerie: everything painted gray and brown, a smell like dust. Not a sound. The receptionist showed him to a conference room, left him standing in the open door.

One of three guys in the room—this one tall and lanky—stood up. He said, "Hi Richard, I'm Roman Croonquist, Director, Division of Enforcement of the SEC." He walked around the table and shook hands, taking in Richard through gray-green eyes like a wild animal's. "Please sit down. This is Charles Holden, Assistant U.S. Attorney, and Charles's assistant, Jeremy Duncan." The two nodded. Neither smiled.

Croonquist said, "Don't be put off by the tape recorder. It's easier for us than taking notes."

"No problem." What is this?

Croonquist said, "As I said on the phone, Richard—can I call you Richard?"

"Sure." Richard started to think Croonquist was overdoing the Mr. Genteel and Polite routine. And he was talking to Richard like he was a teenager.

"The U.S. Attorney's Office is heading an investigation jointly with us at the SEC. Your name came up as someone who might be helpful to us. Thank you for coming." Richard now wished he could get this over with and leave—fast.

Croonquist said, "This summer, in the two weeks prior to the announcement of the IPO of Southwest Homes, our office detected unusual trading activity in six homebuilders' stocks and stock options. We have reason to believe you have knowledge of some of those trading activities. Can you elaborate?"

Richard thought about the mole's emails ordering trades on the code-named companies' stocks and options. They had to be onto the mole. Perfect; he'd tell them all he knew. But now he saw Croonquist staring at him with his wolf eyes, his jaw set like he was cross-examining him. Richard realized he'd been ambushed.

Shit, they must think I'm involved. "I don't understand," Richard said. His stomach gave a nervous flutter.

Croonquist said, "Let me ask the question another way." Holden scowled and made a display of throwing himself back in his chair, muttering something under his breath. Croonquist shook his head at him. He turned back to Richard. "To your knowledge, was Walker & Company involved in any trading strategies in the homebuilders while it had inside knowledge of Southwest's proposed IPO?"

"Not to my knowledge."

Richard saw Holden eyeing him again. His assistant did as well, a faint grin on his face. *Smug little dweeb.* "I don't know anyone who traded in the homebuilders' stocks or options before or after the Southwest IPO. If that's what this is all about, I'm not going to be very helpful to you." Richard tried to smile like that was it, but his nervousness made his face stiff, and he felt his upper lip beginning to perspire. He saw Holden shake his head like he was disgusted.

"Call me Roman," Croonquist said. Now he used that smarmy Mister Nice Guy voice again. "Okay, let's leave that for a minute and move on to Tentron. We detected a similar trading pattern in the stock and options of Tentron Corporation for the eight weeks prior to Harold Milner's tender offer." His gaze was locked on Richard's eyes again. Man, this guy's eyes were creepy. "Are you aware of the identity of anyone who traded in the common stock or options of Tentron prior to the announcement of Mr. Milner's bid?"

Now Richard thought again about the mole's emails, all his trading in code-name MCS. Was MCS Tentron? If they knew about that it might not look good for Richard. Richard said, "Walker & Company is representing Harold Milner on the Tentron transaction. If I knew anything directly about it, I'd be precluded from discussing it with anyone who didn't have a Need to Know. I've signed a confidentiality agreement." Richard looked at Croonquist, who was doing his best to look approachable and sympathetic. Richard was doing his best to look apologetic, probably overdoing it as much as Croonquist.

"This isn't getting us anyplace," Holden said. He pushed his chair back from the table. Croonquist turned and held his hand out as if telling him to calm down. Holden said, "We invited you here today to give you a chance to cooperate. You're in a lot of trouble right now. And if you don't cooperate, you're gonna be in a lot more trouble."

Richard felt his body tense, sensed the urge to rear back in his chair. It pissed him off, this bad cop leaning on him in an obvious good cop/bad cop routine. It helped Richard compose himself. He stared down Holden for what seemed like a minute.

Croonquist said, "Charlie, let's not jump to conclusions and let's not make this into something adversarial."

"We're beyond that," Holden said.

Croonquist looked at Richard, said, "We're still approaching this from the standpoint that you're willing to cooperate. We hear your concern about client confidentiality, that you might need to sort that out. But we're gonna get to the bottom of this one way or another. We also know you haven't been entirely truthful with us."

Richard now resisted the urge to wipe perspiration off his upper lip. So maybe they knew he was aware of the mole's trading. He glanced over to see Holden's assistant openly smirking. *Stick it in your ear, you tool.*

"Let's cut the crap," Holden said. He motioned to his assistant. The kid reached down into his briefcase and came out with two hefty binders of paper, handed them to Holden. Holden slapped the first down on the table in front of Richard. "Ever hear of a Wells Notice?"

"No."

"It's a letter from the SEC outlining the facts supporting an enforcement action against somebody," and he pointed to the name at the top of the letter on the front page, "in this case you. Normally these things are about fifteen pages." He rifled the pile of papers. It was as fat as Richard's thumb. "They came up with a nice chunky one for you."

Richard tried to stay calm. Somewhere in his head he was hearing, *just get up and leave.* He felt his face burn.

Holden slapped the other wad of papers down in front of Richard. "And this is a Complaint. A formal legal action brought by the U.S. Attorney's Office. Misuse of material non-public information, etcetera. We're ready to go. How do you wanna play this?"

Richard didn't know what to say. And he was afraid if he tried to speak no sound would come out.

Croonquist said, trying to make his voice all calm and soothing, "We don't think you've masterminded the scheme here, but if you're someone's pawn, you may be in much further than you think. We can help you."

"Oh for Chrissakes, play one of the tapes," Holden said. Holden's assistant reached into his briefcase again and pulled out a small tape recorder. He switched it on.

As he heard his and Kathy's voices on the tape, Richard was aware his legs were feeling numb, that he couldn't jump up and run out of the room even if he wanted to.

First Kathy's voice talking about finding a bunch of them, then his, then the two of them back and forth, ending with Kathy saying, "Too risky," him saying, "No sense pressing our luck."

Damn, they've been tapping my phone. Panic started to muddle his brain for the first time.

"Do you expect us to believe you're not involved in this?" Holden said. He was staring down Richard.

Richard didn't say anything, but his mind was working again, in slow motion. What was it they thought he had done? They couldn't think he was the mole, because Kathy and he referred to him on the tape. They must just think they were part of the mole's insider trading ring.

"You're in shit up to your eyeballs, kid," Holden said. His assistant started taking notes on a yellow legal pad.

"Charlie, maybe you should excuse us for a minute," Croonquist said. "I'd like some time alone with Richard."

Holden made another display of slamming his chair against the wall as he pushed it back. He left the room shaking his head, sighing. Holden's assistant followed him out the door.

Croonquist turned back to Richard and smiled. He was overdoing his good cop, still standing up. "Please excuse Charlie. He's a very committed and idealistic individual. I won't let him pressure you into doing anything you don't want to." He leaned forward, put his hands on the table. "You heard one of the tapes. We have more of your conversations with your friend, Kathy Cella, about the trading network and your contact you refer to as the mole. Let me tell you what else we have."

Richard was trying hard not to show any reaction, feeling worn-down.

"We have detailed stock and options trading records for a series of institutions in Europe, South America and the Far East, as well as a whole series of U.S. firms. We also have detailed email records between Walker New York and GCG Paris, as well as emails between GCG Paris to and from a number of those institutions ordering and confirming trades. These records exist in detail for Tentron, the homebuilders, and we have somewhat more limited data going back to a number of Milner's previous deals. Ernest-United, Val-Tech Industries, and Tungsten Steel. We've found confirming data on your desktop computer, among others at Walker. Are you following me?"

"Yes." They'd hacked into his computer. They had the mole's emails. *Holy shit. They think I'm him?*

"Since the transactions prior to Southwest predated your employment at Walker, we have no reason to suspect you were involved. But the rest of this is very incriminating. It would be better for you to cooperate. We're going to get your entire network—including Milner—with or without your help. You saw the complaint Charlie has drafted. I can't make you any promises right now, but depending on what you give us, we can offer you a deal."

"But I haven't done anything wrong."

Croonquist gave a long sigh and sank into a chair. Richard wasn't buying it anymore, now feeling better. "Richard, I'm trying to be nice to you. It isn't pleasant for me to contemplate ruining a young man's career, or his entire personal life. What will your mother think when this comes out?"

Bastard. He was trying to push all the buttons. But they didn't have anything on him. A bunch of emails he didn't send, some phone conversations with Kathy taken out of context, nothing. But who wanted to screw around with these guys? They could probably mess up his life even if he didn't do anything. *What can I do?*

Richard lost track of how long he sat there in silence.

"How about I give you some time to think it over?"

"I don't need to think it over."

"That's a big disappointment."

"I haven't done anything. I'm leaving."

"Your choice. You're free to go. I'm here at any time if you change your mind. This is not a formal interrogation and the record will show that you attended voluntarily." He switched the tape recorder off. "But just so you know, if you don't cooperate, I won't be able to intervene on your behalf. I'll have to let Charlie take the lead. Generally what Charlie's boys do is pound on your door at six a.m. and drag you out in your underwear in handcuffs." He got up and left. Richard waited for a minute and then started to leave. As he approached the door, Holden stepped into the doorway in front of him. It jolted him, stopped him short.

"Croonquist just told me you're not gonna help us. Fair warning; you walk outta here and your ass is mine. I won't be coming to you with any deal. Only a warrant and handcuffs."

Richard did his best not to show any emotion, but he was sure the fear was showing in his eyes. He could feel his face wet with sweat. "You're bluffing." He could hear the strain in his voice.

"Yeah? Well here's another thing for you to chew on. In these cases the trading usually becomes a family enterprise. We haul in your father, too, for good measure. Make sure it hits the local papers, and just in case the St. Paul Insurance Company doesn't read the news, we go to your father's boss."

Richard felt it like a punch.

"See how employable a fidelity bond underwriter is after that, whether he's dirty or not. Kind of ironic, don't you think? Dear old dad insures financial institutions against losing money on employee dishonesty like insider trading, and turns out his son's a hotshot Wall Street crook. And maybe even Hank Blum is, too."

Richard felt a visceral urge to call him a son-of-a-bitch and throttle him, but he felt like he had no air in his lungs and no strength in his arms. He stood lead-footed.

"Think about it before you decide to leave," Holden said, then turned and walked down the hall.

Richard left the building looking straight ahead, not making eye contact with anyone. By the time he got to the street he was gulping for air, his stomach heaving. He ran into the alley, bent over and vomited. After a minute he stood up, then doubled over and wretched again. He felt like his guts were spilling out on the concrete. It kept coming up until he was dry heaving. Then he stayed hunched over, hands on his knees, panting, heart pounding. His eyes were teared up. It took him about five more minutes to be able to walk out of the alley and head down Centre Street.

The bastards. So this was how it worked. Use every angle they can conjure up, legitimate or not, and turn the screws. Fire the cruise missile and don't worry about collateral damage—like the kid's father's career, hell, his whole life. Who cares if the guy's worked his way up for 35 years to a Vice President job, making $115 thousand, put four sons through college, and is still paying off the house and the lake house his wife always wanted?

And what about him? Everything he'd worked so hard for, sacrificed for. Whiz kid in advertising but left it and borrowed $50 thousand for business school, finally on his way and still just dreaming of hitting it big, but now tasting enough of it to know he might make it. Screw that. Smash him—and his career—to bits, then see if there's anything incriminating to pick up, anything useful when they rummage through the busted pieces. *This is it. I'm dead.*

He didn't know how long he walked, but his vision started clearing about the same time his mind did. He was aware that all of his senses were at full alert. No doubts, one thing in mind: save his ass, and Kathy's and Dad's, even if he didn't know how to go about it. No panic, no fear. It was awful, exhilarating and fascinating at the same time.

#

Upstairs in 75 Centre, Croonquist said, "That didn't go so well. We gotta work on our routine."

Holden said, "He's a feisty little sucker. Hard to figure how some kid in his twenties could keep his poise like that, pull it off like he was actually innocent."

"Unless he is."

Holden scowled.

"It's happened before. But never mind." Croonquist had seen even tougher guys fake it until the end, then fold.

"Couldn't hurt to haul in his old man."

"That's a lotta paperwork. I say we let him stew about it for a few days before we go through all that. Maybe just worrying about it brings him around. But I say we toss his apartment now. The more pressure the better."

"Way ahead of ya. As of two days ago we didn't have enough to get a search warrant through a judge."

Croonquist raised his eyebrows.

"Not as easy as it used to be."

"Anything come out of today that would change that?"

"Nope."

"Can you have some of your guys at least stake out his apartment?"

"Already done. Anybody on our list shows up, we tail him."

"Him? It's usually the girlfriend."

"Kathy Cella. Even my goons won't miss her. She's a real piece of ass."

Croonquist nodded. They'd have to settle for that, see if it turned up anything. Man, what a setback. He swore the kid would flip and tells them everything he knew. Still, Croonquist knew he was onto something, but now he had no way of knowing how long it would take to unravel it.

He played it right, though. Charlie Holden was the right guy, a natural born SOB. Between the two of them, this kid Blum had no idea what he was up against. He cracked open a pistachio and popped the meat into his mouth.

#

Dad was calm. There were long pauses on the phone, Richard only saying what he had to. Finally, Dad said, "I can't keep this from your mother. But don't worry about me. Holden's probably bluffing, and if he isn't, he's over dramatizing." Then another pause, Dad thinking, undoubtedly wanting to choose his words so he didn't burden Richard with any more concern. Then: "Sounds like you should get a lawyer. I can talk to some of our people in the legal department. That's a start."

"Walker will get me one, I'm sure, but thanks, Dad." He said it right back, without hesitation. Now it was his turn to buck up and sound confident, not let Dad worry. But Richard wasn't so sure, remembering the forms he'd signed in the M&A Department, the rights he'd signed away. His hand felt weak holding the phone. "I love you, Dad. Sorry to get you into this, but it'll be okay. I'll handle it."

"I love you, son. Call me later. Let me know."

Richard hung up wondering what he'd do if Walker didn't get him a lawyer, or worse, turned on him.

Chapter 7

New York City. Richard didn't have a chance to discuss his meeting with Croonquist and Holden with anyone before Jack called him to prepare for a face-to-face negotiation between Milner and Nick Williams, Tentron's CEO. The face-to-face was for CEOs and senior advisers only. Richard rode uptown with Jack and Mickey in Jack's Porsche, got behind the wheel when they got out at Sterling & Dalton's offices, and parked the car at the One Lexington Plaza garage, caddy-corner across 45th Street from the Helmsley building. Jack had a monthly space at One Lex, and always parked there when they went up to see Milner. The garage attendants all knew Richard by now, even gave him the car without a ticket. Richard waited at Milner's office for everyone else to get back from the CEO meeting.

He kept replaying the meeting at 75 Centre Street in his mind on infinite loop. After ten loops he'd figured out what he was gonna do.

#

Milner, Jack, Mickey and Howard Blaine walked the five blocks from Sterling's offices to Milner's after the face-to-face with Nick Williams and his advisors. Milner saw Jack watching him like an assassin, same as throughout the meeting. Jack was obviously trying to figure out what Milner was up to, running it around in his mind. It made Milner feel like fire ants were crawling under his skin.

During the failed negotiation with Nick Williams, his advisors said they'd stay the course with the half-assed recapitalization plan Tentron had proposed to its shareholders as an alternative to Milner's $40 cash offer. Under the recap, Tentron offered its shareholders $45 per share in cash for half their shares, with crappy bonds of Tentron for the remaining shares. A classic last-ditch attempt by management to keep their company out of Milner's clutches to preserve their jobs—in the process loading up Tentron with excessive debt. And it was looking like nobody else was coming off the sidelines to top either his bid or Tentron's recap, so maybe he'd have to decide what to do about Tentron after all.

By Milner's calculations, under the tender offer rules he had four more days to make his next move before Tentron could buy shares under its recap. He wished he could drag it out longer. But with Harrelson of Devon & Company telling Milner that senior SEC enforcement guys had flown to New York, and Jack looking more menacing by the hour, maybe four days was all he had, if that.

Yeah, he had to decide what to do.

#

Jack saw the usual horde of people was at Milner's office when they got there. LeClaire had just arrived from the office. Jack waved for Blum to get his ass downstairs from Milner's glass conference room where he was waiting. Milner insisted on debriefing with everybody on the main floor at that makeshift conference table. Milner sat at the head, Jack watching him. Milner had been almost passive during the Nick Williams meeting. Something was off. This bullshit about doing the deal a nickel at a time wasn't making it happen. What was up with him?

He didn't even wanna think about the consequences on Walker if Milner blew it and Tentron didn't get done at all. With all the capital they had invested in the deal, Walker could go bust if Milner dropped his bid.

"Short meeting," LeClaire said.

"You said it," Blaine said.

"Well, Mickey, whattaya think?" Milner said. He was flat, like going through the motions.

Mickey said, "I think they decided they weren't going to agree to anything yet. Williams is taking it personally, but he'll get over it."

Milner nodded, acting lame, not really into it. Jack thought maybe the competition from Tentron's recap would snap Milner out of his trance, or whatever the hell he was in, but nothing. He might actually have to get somebody to take a shot at Milner, *really* scare him. Milner hadn't made eye contact with Jack since they sat down. Jack kept glaring at him, hoping Milner would look up, see his eyes shooting daggers. "Okay, what next?" Milner said.

Mickey said, "Let's look at your options. If you do nothing, you lose to their recap. Their deal is hard to value because of the bonds they're offering, but we figure it's worth $42 a share." Mickey turned back to look at Milner. "You're still at $40, all cash. So if you don't change something, their $42 beats your $40."

"Game over," Jack said, still watching Milner.

"What can we do to make their deal look even lousier than it is?" Milner said, now starting to look like he had a pulse.

One of the Morrow information agent guys, Walsh, stirred in his chair. "We've been working with your PR people on drafting some press releases and full-page newspaper ads to point out the negatives in their recapitalization plan," Walsh said. "Puts too much debt on the company, no capital for expansion, and so on. All to keep their jobs. You know the story."

"Fine. Circulate drafts to the whole team, get comments," Milner said. Jack exhaled. Was the big guy coming around?

"Be careful, we need to see that material," Blaine said, "you're in the middle of a tender offer. You risk getting fined by the SEC if you say anything in the press that isn't in your 14D-1 filing during the pendency of the tender offer."

Milner made a sour face. "So read the ads and make sure I don't say anything stupid. Just fix them," Milner said, sounding impatient, looking at Blaine like he was a piece of lint to flick off his suit.

Better.

"We also have a lawsuit drafted that attacks their recapitalization," Blaine said.

"Okay, so let's sue them, too, distract the hell out of them. That's good," Milner said. "You were saying, Mickey?"

"Two major options. First, you could increase your cash bid to a price comparable to their blended value—$42. Second, you could make a comparable cash and bonds offer—the second financing scenario we discussed in our initial planning. But whatever you do, you have to make some move or you'll lose."

Milner had his elbows on the table with one hand clasped across his chin. He was looking out the window and up at the sky, a smile showing in his eyes. Jack liked what he saw; the beast *was* coming out of hibernation.

Milner sat for another moment in silence, then started to really act like himself. He said, "Alright, let's keep it simple. We bump the bid to $42 per share, all cash." He looked at Mickey, then Jack. Then to Blaine, "File the lawsuits," then to the Morrow guy, "Run the press releases and the ads. Enjoy yourselves, everyone." And he stood up and walked upstairs to his office, smiling and looking confident for the first time all day. Jack grinned over at Mickey. It was a good day's work. But on second thought, why didn't Milner just pay $43 or $44 per share and get it over with? The difference was a rounding error to him. Maybe like Mickey said a while back, Milner was enjoying the chase more than the catch. But at least he was moving. Jack reminded himself Milner might need a poke now and then to keep some momentum. It was still no time to relax.

Upstairs in his office, Milner looked back down at the main floor. Jack was still grinning as he strutted toward the elevator. Milner smiled, relieved. Hell, he felt like he'd just passed a kidney stone. Why had he held out so long? Why didn't he make it easy on himself earlier, and just exit, stage left. Maybe it took seeing Jack peering down at him from the other end of the conference table like a loaded cannon.

Whatever, it just came to him during the meeting downstairs. He was gonna run. He'd make it look like he was doing the Tentron deal, wire a pot of money offshore, pack up Mary Claire on one of his Gulfstreams and fly away. And by the time Jack figured out what was going on, Mary Claire and he would be sitting in the Hotel du Rhone in Geneva eating fois gras and drinking Chateau d'Yquem. Now he felt giddy.

And yet he couldn't abandon the hope that somehow he'd be able to pull the unlikely rabbit out of his ass: rat out the bigger fish and live happily ever after, sleeping in his own bed on Park Avenue.

#

"You went by yourself? Without a lawyer?"

"Yeah," Richard said. "Like I said, they invited me in to help with an investigation they said they were working on. I had no idea they were gonna lean on me like that." Richard had gone directly to LeClaire's office when he got back from the meeting at Milner's. Now he was seated in his customary spot in front of LeClaire's desk, only this time he wasn't watching LeClaire lay out conceptual structures in his fountain-penned shapes on a notepad. LeClaire was looking at him like he did when Richard did something like forgetting to include deferred taxes in the denominator of a debt-to-total capital ratio.

LeClaire said, "The U.S. Attorney's Office and the enforcement staff of the SEC never invite you in for a chat. If they want to talk to you, they want to talk to *you*. Not about somebody or something else. And you never, ever talk to the SEC or the U.S. Attorney's Office without a lawyer."

Richard nodded. *And how.*

"Did they tape the conversation?"

"Yeah."

"Dumb. The first thing you should have done was get up and leave." He paused. "Besides Southwest Homes and Tentron, did they ask you about any other transactions?"

"Yes, Ernest-United, Tungsten Steel, and there's one other. I forget."

"Burlington Industries? Bethlehem Forge? Val-Tech Industries?"

"Yes—Val-Tech Industries."

LeClaire thought for a moment. "Anything else?"

"They tapped my phone. And hacked into my computer. And I think Kathy Cella's since she got to Paris."

"Go on."

"And Croonquist said they had detailed trading records and emails on those same deals by institutions all over the world."

"Did he mention any U.S. institutions?"

"I don't remember."

"Do you remember anything else?"

"No."

"You say you told him you hadn't done anything wrong?"

"Of course," Richard said. "And I haven't, and neither has Kathy, but Croonquist had taped phone conversations between me and Kathy talking about some guy we refer to as the mole."

LeClaire just looked at him, not moving. Richard had seen that look before, melted under it. Now he wasn't sure what it meant.

"It's a long story," Richard said, "but basically, somebody at Walker in New York sends emails to somebody at GCG in Paris ordering stock trades. We call him the mole. I first discovered it by accident on the Southwest deal and Kathy and I have been observing it as sort of a game. And now it's obvious that the SEC and the U.S. Attorney's Office think Kathy and I are part of some kind of insider trading ring."

"Did Croonquist say the words, 'insider trader ring'?"

"I think he referred to it as a 'network'. But he said he thought they had enough to hold me for insider trading on both Southwest and Tentron. He said if I didn't cooperate, Holden might drag me out in handcuffs at six in the morning. And Holden threatened they might even drag in my dad."

LeClaire let out a long sigh and pushed himself back in his chair. "Well, my friend, we better talk to Jack and Steinberg and get you a lawyer. One more thing . . ."

"What?"

"Who is this mole?" His eyes were probing.

"No idea."

LeClaire nodded. He picked up the phone and punched the keypad.

"Is he there?" he said. Richard could hear Freida, Steinberg's assistant talking to him through the receiver. A moment later he hung up, motioned toward the door.

Richard felt like he always did when he went to LeClaire with an issue: he got clear logic, unsentimental honesty. Same thing with Steinberg. And he'd never seen either of them lose their tempers. But Jack was a different story.

#

Richard heard a knock on Steinberg's door and turned to see Jack walk in. *Uh-oh.* This could get ugly now.

Steinberg said, "Pull up a chair. You won't find this boring."

Jack sat down. Steinberg said, "François and Richard were just briefing me on a visit Richard had with representatives of the SEC and the U.S. Attorney's Office. They tried to sweat him into giving up an insider trading ring they say is centered here at Walker, and linked to Milner's deals."

"Must be a full moon," Jack said.

"And it seems Richard and Kathy Cella stumbled on the same thing the SEC did a few months ago. Nicknamed the guy apparently directing the trades the mole." Steinberg turned back to Richard, asking, "Why didn't you come forward to anybody at the firm about this earlier?"

"I don't know. I've been asking myself that since I walked out of the U.S. Attorney's Office. I guess I just screwed up." Richard could now see Jack observing him, his face blank. *Is he gonna fire me? Serve me back to Holden?*

Jack said, "How's this linked to Milner?"

Richard said, "Trading in a bunch of his deals. Including Tentron." Jack's face was still expressionless.

Steinberg said, "I'm going to call Jim Lawson, the senior partner at Shearson & Stone, our law firm, and set up a meeting with their litigators as soon as possible. Hopefully tomorrow morning." Richard felt his fists unclench. But he was still watching Jack.

LeClaire said, "The guy from the SEC was Roman Croonquist, Director of Enforcement. And he said Charles Holden," looking back and forth between Jack and Steinberg, Jack's eyebrows raising when he heard Holden's name, "at the U.S. Attorney's Office might drag Richard out in handcuffs. We should try and get that meeting with Shearson & Stone soon."

Jack said to Richard, "Better check yourself into a hotel. And get a pair of those Groucho Marx disguise glasses with the moustache and big nose." Jack grinned. Richard felt a whoosh of relief at hearing Jack joke about the situation.

Steinberg said, "Bring all the hard copies of the email messages, your laptop and anything else you've got. I'll call you on your cell when I get the meeting."

LeClaire and Richard got up to leave.

"Close the door behind you," Jack said.

#

After Richard shut the door it took Jack a moment to realize how tense he was, having worked so hard to not show any reaction, and then even joke with the kid.

Flattened by a Mack truck they never saw coming.

His mouth had a funny taste in it. And then for some reason he was thinking of that squishy sound his wet galoshes made on the tiles in the entry hall of the apartment building where he grew up in Canarsie. His galoshes wet from the snow after a street fight. He liked to fight in winter; most of the guys were bigger and stronger, but in the snow they slipped and went down easy. That way he could step onto them and break their spirits while he busted up their faces, blood flying around until they yelled, 'I give.' He realized the taste in his mouth was like after one of those fights; blood mixed with puke. Right now he felt like hitting someone.

"How much you think he knows?" Jack said.

"You heard almost as much as I did. I'd say plenty."

"Enough?"

"Enough. Except maybe who's actually involved. Emails documenting trades going back four years, including emails distributing trades out from Paris to all over Europe, the Far East, firms in the U.S. Including on Milner's deals."

Jeez. Jack had put his blood and guts into Walker, building it up over all these years, now maybe waking up to find it worthless because of these markets. But now he could see it all go down the tubes in an insider trading scandal. And getting his investment in Walker wiped out maybe not the worst of it. He felt itchy, like he needed to get up and walk around.

Jack said, "We gotta get this thing under wraps. If we don't we could lose it all. It was bad enough with this financial mess. Now we're looking at jail on top of going bust."

Mickey was blinking at one of his screens, thinking. After a moment he said, "We'll just have to see how it develops. It sounds like the Feds have a lot of what Richard does."

"After twenty-five years if I get my Walker stake wiped out I'll shoot myself. Anybody tries to stand in my way of protecting against that, I'll shoot *him*."

Mickey just looked at him.

"What?" Jack said.

"If the Feds move on us it'll be soon. I can't see having time to outrun them."

Jack said, "Well, in the absence of any other brilliant ideas, I say we go balls-to-the-wall to bottle this up before it kills us."

Mickey said, "I don't have any other brilliant ideas."

That was a new one: Mickey coming up blank. One of them better think of something quick.

#

Milner sat in the one of the client suites at the UBS private banking office at Park Avenue and 48th Street. He'd finished filling out the paperwork for the wire transfer five minutes earlier, and given it to the assistant to Rolf Kulling, his private banker. Now, staring at polished mahogany walls and smelling oiled leather, he waited for Kulling to get off the phone. A minute later Kulling sidled in with that insinuating manner all private bankers seemed to have.

"Harold, always a pleasure." They shook hands.

"She give you the paperwork?"

"Absolutely."

"Great. You need anything else from me?"

"No, Sir."

"How long you think it will take?"

"One to two weeks. It's hard to say."

Milner felt a burst of surprise. *What?* "One to two weeks? What's the problem?"

"I'm sorry, Harold, but $250 million is an unusually large wire transfer. Ever since September 11th, Homeland Security scrutinizes any wire transfers it deems appropriate, particularly those going offshore. That usually means anything over $10,000."

Milner was nodding he understood, but he still couldn't quite believe it.

Kulling said, "We'll do the best we can."

This sure changed things. Well, he'd have to deal with it. Fake it for a little longer, hang around until he could pack up Mary Claire and get the hell out of here.

#

It was Jack who called Richard about the meeting at Shearson & Stone. Jack told Richard, "Your first lawyer is like your first lover. You never forget. Particularly if you're scared. Wait'll you get a load of Toto."

Karen "Toto" Blanc was Shearson & Stone's head litigator. A rival litigator once yielded to her, saying she was 'too tough.' It stuck. It didn't take long for Jack to abbreviate it to Toto. But even Jack didn't have the nerve to call her that to her face.

Richard had spent the night hiding out at the Carlyle. He arrived at Toto's office on the 7th Floor at 599 Lexington Avenue, across from the Citigroup Building, at 8 a.m. the next morning. *So far, so good.* He wasn't in handcuffs.

About 8:10, a leggy brunette walked out of her office and extended her hand. "Karen Blanc," she said. Richard could see her observing him when they shook hands. She was tall for a woman; he guessed about 5'10". Slim, with prominent features that all seemed too big for her face, but somehow managed to fit together. *Striking.* She wore a stylish wrap dress instead of one of those goofy business suits with the dress shirt and little bow tie that a lot of woman lawyers wore.

"Come in," she said, still observing Richard. She went to her credenza and started fixing a cup of coffee. "Can I get you anything? Coffee, tea, bottled water? . . . OJ?" Asking him, but all business. *Not exactly cordial.*

"Black coffee would be great." She fixed it for him.

"Nervous?" she asked.

"You might say I'm at a high state of attention."

"Doesn't sound all bad." She pointed to a chair next to her coffee table. "Have a seat." She sat down across from him on the sofa. *Blunt.* Guiding him around.

"I hear you had an interesting day yesterday."

"You could say that."

"Well, just in case you have any concerns about it, they can't use anything that you said if they didn't advise you of your rights to have counsel present for an interview."

"They didn't give me any advice. They didn't even tell me what the interview was about. They ambushed me."

"They tried to bluff you, scare you into folding. Mickey briefed me. Sounds like you did fine. I'm going to ask you to tell me the whole story again in a few minutes. Don't worry." Her manner was firm and confident.

"I haven't done anything wrong."

"I believe you," she said. "Sounds like somebody has, though, and we'll need to do what we can to get to the bottom of that. But the most important thing is, if you haven't done anything, you shouldn't have anything to worry about." She smiled for the first time. "Well, young Mr. Blum, now let's get started."

She took the better part of an hour directing Richard through his entire history and understanding of the mole situation, from the initial email he discovered to the meeting with Croonquist and Holden the day before. She interrupted constantly to take him back through various points, getting clarifications, making notes, referring back to them. If this was a friendly attorney-client interview, Richard decided he wouldn't want her cross-examining him. Richard was starting to understand what Jack meant. With Toto he felt like a teenage farm boy learning things from an experienced older woman. She was in command, showing him how it worked.

"Where are your computer and the printouts?"

Richard patted his briefcase.

"Cybil, are you there?" she called through the open doorway. A woman, apparently her assistant, called back, "Yes."

"Get me Martin Springs right away, please." She turned back to Richard. "Are these the only copies?"

"No." He saw her squinting, like sighting him in.

"I don't mean hard copies of the printouts. I mean electronic copies, the files in your computer."

"No. I have one memory stick with the electronic copies of everything with me, another in my apartment."

She nodded, thinking.

Richard thinking, too, trying to stay ahead of her, said, "And, of course the ones on the mole's internet provider's server, and on the computers at Walker."

"At Walker," she repeated. She was looking at Richard but her eyes unfocused, thinking about it. It made him uneasy.

"You represent Walker & Company, don't you?"

"I represent you and Walker & Company, unless you can tell me that there's some reason why your interests should diverge, in which case I could potentially have a conflict." She was eyeing him again now, like maybe she was going to turn on him. Richard felt his pulse quicken. He eased himself back in the chair, trying to calm down.

"I don't know of any reason why our interests would diverge."

"Is there anything you want to tell me about?" She was observing him now like he was a lab specimen. "Is there anything you *suspect* might indicate that your own interests could be divergent from that of the firm's?" Now she was squinting again.

"No. But obviously someone at the firm is the mole. I just don't know what direction this thing will take, and who the mole is."

"Be straight with me. Now, and throughout the rest of this thing." Richard felt like she was looking inside his head.

"I won't lie to you," he said.

"Better not."

A guy, probably the Associate she'd asked for, appeared in the doorway. She looked up. Richard exhaled. He realized he'd been clenching the arms of the chair, relaxed his hands.

"Martin, come in. Martin Springs, this is Richard Blum, our client. He's an investment banker from Walker & Company." Richard stood and shook his hand. Toto pointed to Richard's briefcase, motioned to Richard. He pulled out the memory stick and the hard copy printouts. "Martin, this is critical evidence in this matter. I want chronological transcripts prepared similar to that which we normally do for a deposition, bound in a volume. I need all this by early afternoon. Understand?" Springs grabbed the materials and headed out the door, jumping to it. Richard was certain Springs knew why her nickname fit.

#

"Does this make me a gun moll?" Kathy said. It was good hearing her be a smart-ass, but Richard thought he heard her voice quavering.

"Harvard Business School girls gone wild."

Kathy was silent a moment, then said, "Babe, you alright?"

"Yeah. Yesterday was touch-and-go, today I'm in good hands."

"Where are you?"

"I can't tell you right now. I'm afraid your phone may be tapped."

She paused for a long time before saying, "When can I see you?" her voice airy now.

Richard was seeing her on the bed the other night, smelling her perfume mixed with her scent.

"Soon." He felt better hearing himself say it, but he was uncertain. "Go see Freida. Get the phone number, make sure you aren't being followed and call me."

Ten minutes later she called back. Toto's secretary transferred the call to a conference room across the hall.

"Hi," Richard said, trying to sound normal, but his voice strained.

"I love you, Richard."

"I love you, too, Kath. Everything's fine. I'm up at Shearson & Stone with their head litigation partner. She'll want you here sometime late this afternoon. We have meetings scheduled to go over the whole thing. When we get done I'd like for you and me to get together on this mole thing this evening. I'm staying at the Carlyle under the name Richard Diver. Can you do it?"

"Nah, I've got other plans." Being game, trying to lighten it up, but he could hear the stress in her voice.

"Okay," Richard said. "Here's what I need you to do . . ."

#

Kathy hung up the pay phone from her call with Richard. She crossed Water Street and entered the bank. She cashed a check for $2,000. Then she hailed a cab. As she rode, she was thinking this must be what panic felt like: unable to hold onto a clear thought, buzzing, itchy. She took another cab, got out, then another, all the time checking behind, around her. She got out of her fifth cab at 30 Lincoln Plaza, Richard's apartment building at 62nd & Broadway. She waved to Geraldo, the doorman, acting nonchalant, knowing she wasn't carrying it off, and went upstairs to Richard's apartment.

Upstairs, Kathy stuffed three of Richard's suits and enough shirts, underwear and ties to last him for a week into a garment bag. On his bureau, she found the memory stick with the mole's data, put it into her purse, then ran to the elevator. Downstairs, she hurried out of the building through the service door that exited onto the plaza. She startled a guy sitting smoking a cigarette, saw him jump up when she went past him. As she looked back over her shoulder she saw him motioning to somebody. She had to tell herself this was really happening, felt a wave of shock and ran across the plaza to Broadway, hailed a cab. She saw the same guy from the plaza jump into a car behind her on Broadway just as she drove off in the taxi. "Downtown," she said to the cabbie. "I said downtown! U-turn right here!" she yelled at him as they reached 64th Street.

"Damn, girl, relax," he shouted back as he slammed on the brakes.

"Don't give me any crap, buddy. I'm not in the mood. Drive." The cabbie did a U-turn on Broadway at 64th Street. "Stop here," she said at Columbus Circle and got out of the cab. She ran across the Street lugging the garment bag. She looked back to see the guy get out of the car a block north of her.

She ran down the stairs to the subway at 59th Street, onto a #1 train south that was in the station. Kathy got off at Times Square and walked as fast as she could without breaking into a jog through the transfer tunnels to the Grand Central shuttle platform. She looked around the platform for recognizable faces from the subway car she had just ridden, or the man she'd seen following her. *Nothing.* She then caught the shuttle to Grand Central where she picked up the #4 train south, again checking the faces of the other passengers. After switching subway lines twice more she wound up at Canal Street. In the tunnels there she stopped to buy a copy of *Vogue,* stood thumbing through it to see if anyone else stopped to observe her. She wondered what she'd do if she saw someone.

Then she walked to the #4 train and took it north toward Grand Central again. That was when she spotted the guy. She felt a flash of despair and then anger. *He's still tailing me!* She breathed deeply to try to calm herself. It was no use. When the train stopped at 14th Street she waited in the open doorway until everyone had gotten off; still waited, forcing herself. *Just a little longer.* Then at the last moment she shoved her way out through the entering passengers. She saw the guy jump through the doors at the other end of the car. She turned and leaped back onto the train just as the doors closed. The guy was swearing at himself on the platform as the train pulled away.

She felt a rush of relief. Then told herself not to relax. She got off the subway at 23rd Street and hailed a cab, still checking behind her, and went straight to the Carlyle Hotel at 76th and Madison. She asked for the envelope at the desk in her name, Nicole Diver. On the way to the elevator she pulled two phony driver's licenses and the key to Richard's room out. Upstairs in Richard's room, she hung up Richard's garment bag and sat on the floor next to the bed. Then she buried her face in her hands and sobbed for twenty minutes.

When she finished crying, Kathy let out a long sigh. What a relief, letting go after all that. The things a woman had to do for her man these days. She bet her mother never had to put out like this in her day.

#

Kathy looked like somebody let the air out of her when she walked into the conference room across from Toto's office.

Dazed. Richard felt guilty. If he hadn't starting monkeying around with this mole stuff, he never would have dragged Kathy into it. It sucked, doing that to her, seeing her like this.

Jack and Steinberg showed up half an hour later. They had Ken Stern and Karen Summers, Walker's General Counsel and Assistant General Counsel, in tow. Richard tried to feel out Jack and Steinberg; they seemed okay, the same as yesterday. He'd keep an eye on Jack, nonetheless. The room filled up after that, Toto and team bringing in multiple copies of neatly bound transcripts of all the mole's emails.

"Let me tell you where we are," Toto said. "I've been through the transcripts of all the emails. You each have a copy. It's attorney-client privileged. Essentially, Richard's and Kathy's descriptions seem to be accurate."

Richard sat up straight; he hadn't suspected their account of things was ever in doubt. *Oh, man.*

Toto went on, "Someone is obviously sending trading instructions from Walker in New York to GCG in Paris. The pattern of activities is identical for Southwest and Tentron."

"Any evidence of trades emanating from anywhere else?" Ken Stern asked.

"No," Toto said. "It's all outbound from New York."

"When did the Tentron trading activity start?" Steinberg asked.

Toto flipped open a copy of the transcripts. "Sometime in early September. Here it is, September 2nd," Toto said.

"That's weeks before we opened our numbered trading account on behalf of Milner," Karen Summers said.

"All these emails went from the same email address?" Jack asked.

"Apparently, yes," Toto said. "They could be from anybody at Walker. Richard tells us that the SEC and the U.S. Attorney's Office have traced back similar trading activity to three of

Milner's previous deals—Ernest-United, Tungsten Steel and Val-Tech Industries.

Richard watched Steinberg's gaze move to Jack's like they were communicating in some unspoken way, then back to Toto.

"And evidently someone inside GCG Paris is a critical link as well," Steinberg said. "Okay, what next?"

"My recommendation is that you immediately convene an internal task force to investigate this situation," Toto said. "You can use these transcripts and the tapes of my interviews of Richard and Kathy as a starting point. Next, I should call up Charlie Holden at the U.S. Attorney's Office and tell him that Walker & Company has undertaken an internal investigation of the matter. I can offer copies of these transcripts and anything else we might uncover as assistance to the SEC and the U.S. Attorney's Office in their investigation, in exchange for full immunity for Richard and Kathy and, of course, for Walker & Company itself."

"You're dreaming if you think they'll buy into immunity," Steinberg said.

"Maybe so," Toto said. "But it might get a dialog going. And I'd at least like to get in Holden's face about this scare tactic they pulled on Richard yesterday. That was a cheap trick and I'm going to let them know what I think of it. And I'll tell Holden that if he tries anything like that again, we'll haul him in front of a judge with a motion to suppress and a potential lawsuit for harassment." She spoke matter-of-factly, but her mouth made biting motions at the air. Richard thought of Holden; he'd love to hear Toto laying into him. "I'm also going to see if I can get him off of Richard's back. I'd like his word he won't try any more theatrics. On you, either, Kathy," she said, looking at Kathy. Kathy shifted in her seat and looked at the floor.

Richard looked at Steinberg, then Jack. These guys were like stone; he couldn't read them. He was starting to wonder: *Can I trust them?*

Kathy and Richard took three successive cabs, looking out the back window all the way, before having one drop them at the Carlyle. Richard was beginning to worry about Kathy. She still hadn't gotten the glassy look out of her eyes.

#

In the limo on the way downtown, Jack said to Mickey, "You thinking what I'm thinking?"

"Probably not."

"I'm thinking we might be able to contain this thing if we get immunity for the firm?"

"Dream on. And even if we did, that's not a total shield," Mickey said. "The firm might be okay, but *we'd* get microwaved."

"Yeah, but it's a start. And we're totally fried if we don't get it."

Mickey just looked out the window.

Jack was thinking, *stay inside yourself, hold it together.* He said, "First off, we gotta kibosh this internal task force."

Mickey looked at Jack like he was his dumb little brother. "No. We set it up so it does its job and comes up with nothing."

"Ken Stern is no dummy."

"I know. Dealing with that falls into your department."

Jack thought about it for a moment. He nodded, then said, "If we keep our poise, we just might pull this off."

Mickey said, "Like managing to step on all the stones walking across a stream. Like we always do." Mickey said it looking out the window past Jack, that dreamy look he got in his eyes when he was thinking, eyes blinking.

#

Richard and Kathy ate a room service dinner in Richard's room at the Carlyle Hotel. They didn't talk much. "So who do you think our mole is?" Richard asked afterward.

"Not me," Kathy said.

Richard said, "I guess that eliminates at least two Walker employees." She was sitting cross-legged on the bed, looking sleek and sexy. Richard was looking forward to getting his hands on her later. She must have guessed: she smirked at him. Richard went on, "Should we start eliminating others one by one, or try to guess who he is?"

"Not Mickey or Jack," Kathy said.

"You're hallucinating," Richard said. "I don't see how we can rule out them yet."

"Are you serious?" Kathy asked.

"Jack and Mickey are the firm's biggest management shareholders."

"That's kinda cynical, babe," Kathy said. "As the firm's two most senior guys, they'd be concerned whether or not their pocketbooks were involved."

"Don't be a dope. This is Wall Street. And you already said you think they're sleazebags."

"Yes, but running an insider trading ring when you're worth hundreds of millions?"

"A bunch of back-office clerks didn't set this up."

It stopped her. She thought a moment. "Do Toto's email transcripts tell you anything new?" Kathy asked.

"It's just a bunch of trades. I got more out of the Excel spreadsheet I set up; at least you can sort that multiple ways."

Kathy jumped up, pulled Richard's memory stick with the Excel file on it out of her purse. She went over to the desk, plugged it into her laptop and loaded the Excel file.

"What are you doing?" Richard said.

"Trying to figure out if there's any sequence to the trades. I'm copying the data and breaking the original file into two. I'll sort one by name of the institutions that GCG Paris passed trades out to. The other chronologically, listing side by side all the trades in each of the deals to see if there's any common sequence."

Richard took out his laptop and turned it on.

"Did we have all the confirmations coming back from the other institutions around the world to GCG Paris in the batch you FedExed me from Paris?" he asked. He had an idea.

Kathy said, "I think. But what will they show?"

Richard said, "I'm gonna check to see if we have confirmations coming back from any institutions that we don't have any outbound emails to. That should tell us whether GCG Paris is fanning them all out, or whether there's some other intermediate staging point."

After about an hour they had three completed lists. They kept looking back and forth between them.

Kathy said, "Two of the Swiss banks, Credit Genéve and Stahl Fils & Cie, never showed up in outbound emails from GCG Paris. The same thing's true of Peniche Industrial, a Chilean brokerage firm, and Siu Yan and Sai Ltd., the Hong Kong bank that seems to be executing trades from the Far East."

"So there must be another link someplace," Richard said. "The emails ordering and confirming trades are about a million shares off on each deal."

"It's just noise," Kathy said.

"Each deal? That's significant," Richard said.

Kathy said, "So let's assume your theory is right, that Walker New York is the start of the circle, the origination point and the final confirmation point, with GCG Paris as the primary relay point. So where's the secondary staging point?"

Richard said, "We'll need to juggle the trades again to see if we can find a mismatch on the outbound and inbound to each address. If we have a much higher amount of outbound to some place than inbound, it means it could be the staging point." He sorted the data again. "It's London," Richard said.

Kathy said, "Another thing: these four institutions I mentioned earlier," pointing to the screen, "two in Switzerland, one in Chile and one in Hong Kong sent some of their confirmations of trades directly back to New York."

"So?"

"It has to be London," Kathy said. "The total number of shares confirmed directly to New York from those four sources almost exactly matches the imbalance in confirmations from London itself versus the outbound orders sent to London."

"I knew there was a reason I'm crazy about you."

Kathy said, "So we have New York as the center of the ring, Paris as the main staging point and London as the secondary staging point. And we have banks in Switzerland, Chile and Hong Kong that seem to be getting accessed only through London.

"You think that whoever's staging things out from Paris doesn't know about these four institutions being staged through London?" Richard asked.

"There's so much data it would be almost impossible to keep track of it, unless they sorted it like we've done and figured the totals don't match," Kathy said. "Maybe it's just to conceal the orders better."

"Yeah, maybe, but I still think something's fishy."

Kathy laughed. "The whole thing's fishy. And another thing strikes me. London, Paris, New York. You don't need to be a genius to guess we've got crooks at Schoenfeld, GCG and Walker. A whole kettle of rotten fish."

Richard knew it, too, but hearing it said aloud made it stink even more: no place was safe, everybody suspect.

Kathy stopped laughing. She said, "My God, I can't believe you went to Jack and Mickey with this."

"I went to LeClaire. He brought me to Jack and Mickey."

"So? How can we trust anybody?"

"We're switching hotels," he said. "I don't want anybody to know where we are. Not Jack, not Mickey, not anybody."

Chapter 8

New York City. It was 9:30 p.m. and the guy, Stern, still hadn't come out to the South Street pier parking lot for his car. Preston waited underneath the FDR Drive onramp across South Street, behind the 55 Water Street building where Stern worked. Preston was used to waiting. He had all night. And if tonight wasn't the night—just like the last two nights, when too many people were around—maybe it would be tomorrow night.

There he was. Preston hit his beeper, then watched as Stern crossed South Street. He saw the others get out of the van and follow him. Preston wore a suit and tie, so as not to put the guy off. He picked up his briefcase and walked out of the shadows as Stern approached.

"Hey, buddy, got a light?" Preston said, smiling and holding up a cigarette. Preston stepped into Stern's path.

"No, sorry, I don't smoke."

Preston dropped his briefcase. "Damn," he said and bent over as if to pick it up. When he saw the others were only a few steps behind Stern, Preston jumped up and shoved him in the chest, knocked him over backwards into the others' arms.

"Hey!" was all the guy had time to say before one of the others clamped a hand over his mouth.

Preston hit his beeper again, then heard the truck's engine revving, then coming down South Street, shifting gears, faster. Preston stepped back into the shadows beneath the onramp. He watched as the others dragged Stern to the street and threw him in front of the truck, only doing maybe 50, but fast enough. The other guys scattered and Preston got the hell out of there.

#

Jack sat in front of Mickey's desk, waiting for him to get off the phone. Jack could hardly believe how bad things had gotten, and how fast. "Challenging times," was all Mickey said about it before he took his call.

More like shoveling into a gale force wind. In the last few months, Washington Mutual goes bust and the Fed brokers a sale to J.P. Morgan. Wachovia goes bust and the Fed brokers a sale to Wells Fargo. Bear Stearns goes bust and the Fed brokers a sale to J.P. Morgan. Fannie Mae and Freddie Mac go bust and the Feds take them over. Lehman just goes bust. Next, the Fed sticks over 100 billion into AIG to keep it from going bust. Then, Merrill Lynch, afraid of going bust, sells itself to BofA and the Dow is now 40% off its peak.

The way the last months had gone, Jack wasn't sure he wanted to see how the next few days would go. Then, after all that, Milner finally gets off his ass to get Tentron done, and it looks like that will keep Walker afloat. But now this mole trading thing hits the fan. *Jeez.* Talk about bad timing. Mickey and him would have to do some fancy ham-and-egging to claw their way out of this one. Problem was, you had to have something to start with. Right now, if only they had some ham they could have some ham and eggs if only they had some eggs.

When Mickey got off the phone, Jack said, "The police are calling Ken Stern's death suspicious. They're doing forensics."

Mickey looked at Jack like he was retarded. "Did you expect anything else?"

Jack shifted in his chair, said, "Toto made any progress on immunity?"

Mickey shook his head. "Holden isn't budging. In fact now he's saying he's going to charge Blum—when he finds him."

Jack said, "I've thought about how we firewall this thing."

Mickey looked up. "It's like any deal. We need some negotiating leverage with the Feds. And a sweetener. Then we trade for our immunity."

"Right. What if they had the mole, or thought they did?"

"The only way that works is if we hand them their case in a way that they've got everybody involved, neatly packaged. Or at least looks like it. Enough to get their headlines."

"So we make it look like the mole is the only one at Walker."

"Charlie Holden will never buy that," Mickey said, staring at Jack, eyes blinking.

"All right, so the mole and a few more who helped him out, and it stops there. They think they've got the mole now—Blum."

"You're not serious."

Jack said, "Let's just say they've got so much on Blum he can't talk his way out of it, and so he has to cut a deal, or we make it worth his while to cut one."

Mickey gave Jack one of his impatient looks, glanced over at one of his screens, then back at Jack. "Blum's clean. And he's a straight-arrow. Do you want to be the one to offer him money to pretend he's dirty so he can save all our asses? Even if Blum agreed, he doesn't know enough to make it work. And even if the Feds stretch what they've got on Blum, it won't stick once he's got a good defense lawyer."

"So what're you thinking?"

"That we need to serve up the Feds a little something they wouldn't be able to get any other way."

Jack didn't say anything, just watched Mickey.

"Something that will make it stick," Mickey said.

That Mickey, always figuring things out. Jack sat back while Mickey started explaining.

#

Richard was sitting in their hotel room at the Waldorf Astoria, switching the TV from Bloomberg to CNN to CNBC. Kathy had gone for a newspaper. The Dow was now down 5% for the day, the financial stocks had fallen off a cliff, and the newswires were talking about another federal bailout for Citigroup. The credit markets had ground to a halt and 20% layoffs were happening all over the Street. Two years of B-school, made it to the Street by a hair, work my ass off, finally making it and this happens. *What a mess.* And even worse, this mole thing had him hiding out from the Feds and now even his own firm. His cell phone rang, gave him a start. He looked at the number on the caller ID: Jack. *The mole? Or just Jack.*

"Hi, Jack."

"Hey," Jack said, sounding like nothing had happened. "You okay?"

"Yeah. Bored." Richard now feeling uncomfortable.

"Then I'm about to make your day. Jim Baldwin called Mickey at home last night and asked for a meeting. Sounds like maybe Nick Williams is ready to do a deal with Milner on Tentron. You interested in coming?"

"Of course. You heard anything from Toto?" Richard listening for any inflection in Jack's voice.

"Yeah, but it's not resolved. Holden won't agree to a deal without the SEC being involved. He also says we aren't offering them anything they don't already have. Might take a few days. You may need those Groucho Marx glasses after all."

"I'll figure something out."

"Be at Milner's at noon for a strategy session. Williams and his advisers show up at one. See you there, tiger."

Richard sensed a flutter in his stomach, a tingle in his fingers. He had some things he wanted to discuss with Milner, alone, and this meeting gave him a perfect reason to be there.

But Jack was acting too casual. Walker's General Counsel gets killed by a truck after Toto insists he set up an internal task force to investigate the mole thing. And Jack never mentions it. This was getting scarier by the minute.

"Who was that?" Kathy asked from the doorway.

"Jack."

Kathy clenched her jaw. "Does he know we're here?"

"No. At least I don't see how he could. He called about a meeting at Milner's office on Tentron."

"You're not going are you?"

"Yeah. I think Milner may be a way out of this mess."

Kathy took a few steps toward him, her eyes narrowed, said, "You can't be serious. It could be a trap."

"I can't just sit around. And I need to get to Milner at some point anyhow. What can happen to me with lots of people around for a big meeting?"

#

Milner sat in his office, looking up Park Avenue. He checked his LCD screen. Tentron was trading at $41.50. He glanced down at his watch: 11:15 a.m. Sandy had asked for a meeting. Stephanie buzzed the intercom. "Mr. Sharts is on the way up."

"I take it you heard about Ken Stern?" Milner asked before Sandy even sat down.

Sandy didn't answer, just gave him a grave look and a nod.

"That's part of what I wanted to talk to you about. This is out of control. You should go to the police, and the Feds."

"And that's the good news, I assume."

"You decide. The other reason I came over is that my partner in Washington got wind that Charlie Green, the SEC Chairman, was briefed on a major pending insider trading case."

Milner nodded, then sat very still.

Sandy went on, "Once the Chairman gets briefed it's hard to keep a lid on it. They usually make a move shortly after that."

"Shortly could mean weeks, couldn't it?"

Sandy just stared back at him.

"And so you think they're ready to . . ." Milner's voice trailed off. He couldn't think of the right word. Pounce? Spring? They sounded so dramatic.

"I don't know for sure," Sandy said. "But I can't understand why you're still screwing around with some deal. Start talking or start running."

Milner leaned back in his chair. "Anything else?"

Sandy shook his head.

"Okay, message received. Thanks. I have a meeting coming up. I'll call you later." He watched Sandy turn and leave. Sandy had a point: why *was* he still screwing around with this deal? Then he felt his throat constrict. He had some uncomfortable, if not inevitable decisions to make.

#

At Gale's Uniforms on 86th and Lex, Richard bought a dark gray pair of coveralls big enough to fit over his suit. He also bought a gray baseball cap with "Otis" in big letters on the front, and a soft duffel bag large enough to hold his briefcase. He stood in uniform outside Grand Central where he could see the lobby of the Helmsley Building across 45th Street. At 11:55 Richard saw Jack, Steinberg and LeClaire walk into the lobby. At 12:45 he saw Nick Williams and his advisors arrive for the 1 p.m. meeting. He walked into the building at 1:45.

By the time he changed out of the coveralls in Milner's men's room, the meeting was already breaking up in Milner's mezzanine floor conference room. Everyone was shaking hands, smiling, slapping backs. They obviously had a deal.

Now Richard's heart was pounding, not from nervousness. This was gonna be it: the hell with a $6 billion deal, one he helped hatch and was a player in. He was here to save his ass.

After everyone came downstairs to the main floor and most of them left, LeClaire, Jack and Mickey stood around near the elevators, chatting. Then LeClaire waved goodbye to Richard and got into the elevator. Jack walked over to Richard. Jack was wearing a we-just-did-a-deal smirk. Richard's guard was up.

Jack said, "Where were you before the meeting? We stopped at the Carlyle to pick you up, but you weren't there."

"I must have already been on the way." Kathy and he kept their rooms at the Carlyle in the event they got phone calls from anyone at the firm, so no one would know they moved. Just in case. Now he was glad they did.

Jack nodded. He paused, seemed to be thinking. He must have known it was bull. "Why don't you come back downtown with me and Mickey?"

Did Jack think he was stupid? Richard wasn't about to get shot, or hit by a car, or whatever.

"No thanks," Richard said. "I'm gonna head back to the hotel once everybody leaves."

Jack shrugged, nodded and walked back over to Mickey.

As Jack and Mickey got into the elevator, Richard's heart started pumping hard again. The most important part of his day, maybe his life would come in the next few minutes.

#

Richard crossed the room to Milner and waited until he finished chatting with Harrelson, one of the Devon guys.

"Harold, there's something I need to talk to you about," Richard said.

"Sure." He motioned toward the living room furniture in the center of the penthouse. "You wanna listen to some music? The amps are warmed up and everyone's leaving."

Richard shook his head. His mouth felt sticky, dry. He realized how tense he was, and must have looked it, because he saw Milner's face change, go blank. What if this turned into a negotiation? *With Milner. Damn.*

"No?" He pointed up to his office. "Let's go upstairs."

Richard followed Milner to the mezzanine, now thinking this might not have been a great idea. How well did he really know

Milner? Sure, Milner thought he was a nice kid, maybe even considered himself an older mentor to Richard. But in the dark of night, what was he really capable of? He certainly wasn't the mole, but even worse, could be the center of the mole's group. Well, if that was so, Richard would be talking directly to the source. That's what he decided last night. And he wasn't about to change his mind now, nervous shits or not.

"What's on your mind?" Milner asked as he sat down behind his desk.

"I've had an unusual few days. I'm not sure where to start."

"Go on," Milner said. He wasn't moving, looking directly at Richard. Richard with a hunch that Milner had an idea what this was all about. He couldn't turn back now.

"The SEC and the U.S. Attorney's Office hauled me in a few days ago, believing I was part of an insider trading ring at Walker. They'd uncovered emails from Walker New York to GCG Paris and then to all over the world. The emails involve trades on homebuilders around the time of the Southwest deal, Tentron and a lot of other deals. They include at least three more of your older deals. They also have tapes of telephone conversations between a friend of mine and me. We stumbled on some of these email messages and were following the situation. In fact, we've got a whole computer file of them showing trades on 17 deals going back four years. We might even have more than the SEC does. They think my friend and I are involved. We aren't."

Milner was now nodding, still making eye contact.

"They tried to pressure me into turning in others in exchange for a deal. I have a lot of respect for you, and so this is an awkward conversation for me, to say the least."

"Go on," Milner said. Milner leaned forward, put an elbow on the table and clasped one of his big hands over his mouth, his eyes smiling. Richard realized Milner was too experienced a deals guy not to know it showed. In this case, hopefully the smile was genuine. But how many guys negotiating with him saw it as an unintentional slip, took the head fake?

"I don't know if you're involved in this, and whether or not we have anything to discuss. But I think we can be helpful to each other. One of the last things the senior enforcement guy from the SEC said to me was that they'll get the entire network—including you—with or without my help. I'm potentially in a lot of trouble even though I haven't done anything. In fact, I'm hiding out at a hotel to keep the U.S. Attorney's Office from hauling me away in handcuffs."

Milner didn't respond for a moment. Then: "That's it?"

"That's not enough?"

"You're learning, but you're not there yet." He was now leaning forward with both elbows on the desk, smiling. "You're supposed to ask for something. You never wanna give something up in a negotiation without asking for something back. And the information you just gave me is worth a lot."

"In the past you said I was among friends."

"Times like this you can't assume that, even though you are."

"You negotiate with friends?"

"Sometimes. Maybe you're not supposed to, but in this business it becomes intuitive. I know some guys who don't even know when they're doing it."

Richard thought of Jack for a moment. *Intuitive.* But maybe the word was compulsive. Richard said, "I'm not sure what to ask for, other than your help if you can give it."

Milner said, "Okay, I'll think about it. Thank you. I'll try to think of some way I can reciprocate."

Richard nodded.

Milner smiled again. "Pretty hairy. But you look like you're doing okay. You are, aren't you?"

"Yeah."

"You got balls, kid."

#

Milner rode the elevator up to his apartment. The thing seemed so slow and wobbly tonight. In a high-end apartment building like this it should be smooth as silk. The smell of oil on some mechanism—they must have just serviced it—made his stomach queasy. That made him think about dinner, the last thing he felt like doing. He and Mary Claire with Mindy, Mary Claire's sister, and her coat-hanger-smile husband, Eddie Resnick, senior partner at Moron, Knucklehead and Resnick, who never met a waitress he didn't wanna grope.

He realized the elevator had nothing to do with anything. He was haunted by the conversation, no, tip-off, from the kid, Richard. *Man, they're all over Tentron and at least three more of my old deals.* And the senior enforcement guy said he'd get me. That, and the kid saying he was hiding out to keep from being hauled in by the U.S. Attorney's Office. And all on top of Sandy telling him the SEC Chairman had been briefed on a major insider trading case.

It could be any day now they'd come for him, maybe even any moment. The hell with waiting for his 250 million to get wired out. He could walk in, tell Mary Claire, fire up one of the Gulfstreams and they'd be in Europe within eight hours. The elevator doors opened at their penthouse. He turned the key and stepped into the entry hall. Now his stomach felt light and his legs heavy, the scent of the lilies in the vase on the breakfront sickeningly sweet. His mouth felt dry. It was time. He didn't see how he could put off talking to Mary Claire about it any longer.

When he crossed the foyer he could see something was wrong. Mary Claire sat shrouded in semi-darkness on one of the living room sofas. She wasn't dressed for dinner, or even hard at it in the bedroom as usual, contemplating her choice of dresses sprawled over chairs and the bed. Her face was in shadow.

"What's wrong?" he said, switching on a lamp.

She looked up, and in the light he saw her lips were taught and her eyes were hard with anger. He felt a flash of alarm, tension in his chest. Then he saw her face relax. She smiled.

"Less, now." She patted the sofa next to her.

He walked over and sat down.

"Talk to me, hon," he said. He kissed her, then pulled back to observe her. No makeup on, but she could still pass for her late 40s. Not so slim-waisted anymore, but still a beauty.

"Dinner's canceled. I know you won't mind that." She rolled her eyes, as if to say she couldn't stand Eddie either. "It seems Eddie's rubbing a showgirl in Mindy's face."

"Kind of a cliché, isn't it?"

"She's not really a showgirl, but you know what I mean."

Milner nodded.

"She always said he could do what he wanted as long as he didn't go around publicly embarrassing her."

Milner shrugged.

"Now she can't ignore it, and for some odd reason it's actually broken her heart."

"I can't see how he wouldn't have done that ages ago."

"Nor I, but we girls are funny creatures sometimes." She clasped one of his hands in both of hers. "Like me. I'm just a simple girl. All I really need is you to believe in." She smiled at him and clutched his hand harder, then said, "Don't get me wrong,

I'm used to all this," and she waved a hand around the apartment, "and I'd never go back to living without it, but I haven't lost sight of what's really important to me."

Milner was becoming aware of the sensation that his legs weren't there and that some pressure on his chest was pushing him downward through the sofa to the floor, it seemed.

Mary Claire continued, "Something like this, well, even though it may not seem major to you, really strikes home for me." She moved closer, put her face up to his, looked straight into his eyes. "I've never had any reason to lose faith in you, and I know I never will. That's something I could never say to my sister right now, because I know it would kill her. But it doesn't keep me from feeling how lucky I am, and from saying it to you." She kissed him.

Milner couldn't speak. He felt his heart pounding and his breathing labored, wondering if she noticed it.

Mary Claire stood up. "Well, let me go see what I can whip us up for dinner." She headed toward the kitchen.

Milner sat back into the sofa and felt his pulse ramming, his chest heaving. How could he tell her after that? He'd rather step in front of a bus than endure seeing her face as he destroyed her belief in him. Eddie a common cheat. Milner a crook and a fraud. The difference in scale was hard to fathom.

Milner got up, walked into the powder room off the foyer. He opened the tap and felt his hands shaking as he splashed water onto his face, then again, and again and again. When he finished he avoided looking at himself in the mirror, then sat on top of the toilet as he dried his face. He'd have to go for broke. He couldn't hurt Mary Claire, wouldn't risk betraying her trust if he had a way to avoid it. This kid, Richard, might be the answer. If he could get a hold of the information the kid had, he might be able to crawl his way out of this with his reputation at least partway intact. And more important, face Mary Claire with the truth. He got up and walked out to the phone to call Harrelson from Devon & Company.

#

"You know what?" Kathy said as she entered their room at the Waldorf, "I think you *are* the best looking guy I ever saw." She crossed the room to him, hooked her arms under his and kissed him. She leaned back, "Let me get a better look at you." Richard started laughing; the warmth in his chest was magic to him. "Yup." She pulled away from him, giving him a coy look. "And I've got a present for you."

"I was hoping you did." Richard was smirking at her now.

"Not that. Later." She turned and retrieved her briefcase from where she'd dropped it next to the door, pulled out some papers. "This. You remember the list of foreign institutions we developed last night?"

"Yeah." What did she have?

"The names stuck with me, so I checked the spreadsheet files on my laptop. I also checked the dates on Milner's previous deals that you told me Croonquist mentioned to you versus the capital accounts of Walker & Company."

Richard was flipping through the pages. The bottom page was a spreadsheet showing dates, names of the four institutions they had identified last night as linked only to the London staging point, and dollar amounts. *Where is she going?*

Kathy went on, "The two Swiss banks and the Chilean and Hong Kong institutions are majority-owned by Schoenfeld & Co."

Richard said, "But the London staging point we identified last night is called Golding & Co."

"Yes, and if I'm right, it's also owned by Schoenfeld & Co. But the other interesting fact I uncovered relates to the dates of Milner's deals the SEC says are involved. Shortly after each of those three deals—Tungsten Steel Service Centers, Ernest-United and Val-Tech Industries—GCG and Schoenfeld & Co. put more money into Walker."

Richard said, "So there's something more fishy going on than we suspected last night."

"Right. Every time Milner did a deal, not only did Walker make money, but Schoenfeld and GCG made money, and they reinvested the profits into Walker & Company shortly afterward.

Richard was trying to put it together.

Kathy went on, "I had Walker's capital accounts and financial statements because I worked on a potential IPO of Walker for Jack last summer." Kathy was standing with her hand on her hip, probably not trying to look sexy, but Richard wanted to kiss her again. She raised her hand as if to stop him. Did she know what he was thinking all the time? "There's more. Each of those times they reinvested, their ownership came out the same. Parity at 51% for Schoenfeld and GCG combined."

"This is fishier than I thought. That means our mole is passing information to our foreign partners, who are using it to create illegal trading profits to finance their worldwide expansion via Walker & Company."

Kathy laughed. "It just sounds so laughable that anybody would be using an insider trading ring to finance the development of a global investment bank."

Richard said, "GCG is an entrepreneurial place. Lots of little profit centers, and very decentralized. The Walker stock is held in the merchant banking subsidiary, which reports directly to Delecroix. And Schoenfeld is the quintessential, old school private English merchant bank."

Kathy just looked at Richard.

"Global schmobal," Richard said.

"What?" Kathy asked.

"Global schmobal. That's the term Jack used to describe Sir Reginald's worldwide plan."

"The mole can't be Sir Reginald."

"No, but the foreign partners may be at the top of this whole network. I wonder if Milner knows this."

"Milner? Why would you ask that?"

"I told him about getting dragged in by the SEC and Holden. Told him about them targeting him, too. And about the data we have. I said if any of this was helpful to him, I hoped he'd help us out." Kathy was scowling like hearing this was hurting her. "He said he'd get back to me. He played his cards close to the vest, but I think he knows more than he's saying."

"That was a lousy idea. Does he know where we're staying?"

"No." The thought that Milner might feel threatened hadn't crossed Richard's mind. He felt a whoosh of realization wash over him. *Stupid.* What if Milner had him tailed? Came after him? He knew how the Devon guys worked. And Kathy here, too. He shook his head at Kathy as he said, "No, he doesn't know where we're staying." At least he didn't think so.

\#

Richard got out of bed and crossed the hotel room to retrieve his laptop from the desk. After five minutes of sorting he said, "Holy shit," aloud.

"You are so damn compulsive," Kathy said.

"Sorry, I didn't mean to wake you."

"What is it?"

"The mole. See these code-names?" He turned the screen toward her.

"Chloe, Renée, Elaine and Cynthia. LeClaire's wife and kids."

"The mole's LeClaire."

"How do you know?"

"The code-names. LeClaire told me that for the last year or so the new convention at Walker was to give code-names based on family members of the client. The mole code-named those four deals for his wife and kids. And MCS is Mary Claire Stepshus, Milner's wife's maiden name. Project Mary Claire is Tentron. All the mole's trading in MCS is Tentron. The mole is LeClaire."

Richard was thinking of work, the late nights; LeClaire obviously sneaking off to send his mole emails. Richard's mind had gotten around it, but he was still stunned, trying to absorb it.

#

Richard watched the financial news channels at the Waldorf, unable to take his eyes off the unfolding train wreck in the markets, when the story that crossed shortly before noon about stood him on his head. *Oh, no.* The Enforcement Division of the SEC and the U.S. Attorney's Office announced they were pursuing a major insider trading case with the cooperation of a central member of an insider trading ring they were calling 'Source X'. Source X was cooperating as a result of a plea bargain and limited immunity agreement with the SEC and the U.S. Attorney's Office. At least one prominent U.S. corporate business figure was implicated and perhaps others were involved. Further announcements would come soon. He saw himself back at 75 Centre Street, then with cuffs on.

"I've been looking for you at the Carlyle," Toto said when Richard called her after seeing the announcement. "Get your butt over here. Bring Kathy. Jack and Mickey are on the way."

"Right away," Richard said, not liking the sound of any of this. This had to be the mole. And Milner.

Richard hung up the phone and turned to Kathy. "That was Toto. She wants us at her office."

"I love you," she said and kissed him.

No spunky remark. She was worried. Richard was trying to get his mind out of slow-motion. He grabbed his Otis baseball cap, seeing himself do it and asking himself why at the same time, then his briefcase. A glance over his shoulder at Kathy's face told him how he must have looked: tears were welled in her eyes. He walked to her and hugged her. "Let's go," he said.

When they entered Toto's office she motioned for them to close the door, and put her phone call on the speakerphone.

"Source X is an employee of Walker & Company. We've granted him limited immunity in exchange for a plea bargain in which we've made very few commitments to him . . . ."

Toto was scrawling names on a piece of paper. Franklin Stone, Head of SEC Litigation, Roman Croonquist, Head of SEC Enforcement, Charles Holden, Assistant U.S. Attorney. Richard's muscles twitched at seeing Croonquist's and Holden's names. He kept shooting glances from Jack to Steinberg to Toto, not seeing much reaction from any of them.

"Gentlemen, let me interrupt you for a moment. I have put you on the speakerphone with Messrs. Jack Grass and Mickey Steinberg, my clients at Walker & Company. I'm prepared to continue this conversation with them on the line."

"Up to you," Croonquist said. "Our limited immunity for Source X doesn't extend to other individuals at Walker & Company. To be perfectly clear, any other members of this ring are subject to prosecution independent of whatever arrangements we have made with Source X. Understand?"

"Understood, but not agreed to," Toto said.

"We aren't asking for your agreement."

That got Richard's attention. He glanced at Jack and Steinberg again. *Still calm.* Richard wasn't.

"What about Walker & Company itself? You were starting to say something as my clients entered."

"Well," Croonquist said. "In our agreement with Source X we have come to some unusual arrangements for Walker & Company."

"Go on," Toto said.

"One of the stipulations Source X required in order to cooperate was immunity from prosecution for Walker & Company itself." Toto looked at Jack and Steinberg, who both smiled and shrugged. She pushed the mute button on the speakerphone. Jack and Steinberg looked at each other.

"We have no idea what's going on," Jack said.

Toto didn't look convinced. Richard wasn't. He continued to look back and forth between Jack and Steinberg. Nothing. He might as well have been looking at concrete. Toto released the mute button. "Go on," she said.

"Harold Milner is at the center of this investigation and has been implicated by Source X for violations of the securities laws, including conspiracy to engage in unauthorized trading on material non-public information. Any other Walker employees, including Messrs. Grass and Steinberg, will be treated on a case-by-case basis based upon their involvement and on their cooperation. Any information which corroborates Source X's information and which supports our case—which is already strong—against Mr. Milner will be treated as helpful to the government and likely to lead to favorable treatment."

Toto said, "In short, you don't think your case is airtight, so you're offering anybody at Walker a deal if they'll help bring down Milner."

"Interpret it any way you want. We're here to discuss the possible interest of any of your clients in cooperating. I don't think we have anything more to offer in this conversation at this point. Charlie Holden at the U.S. Attorney's Office is on board with this approach. You can contact either one of us."

"Thank you gentlemen. We have no more questions for the moment," Toto said, looking up at Jack and Steinberg, who nodded, "we'll be back in touch if we have anything for you."

"If that's your response, we think it's only fair to tell you that we're currently processing warrants for the arrest of certain individuals in this case." Richard recognized the voice as Charles Holden's. It made him twitch. "You may not wanna wait too long to make up your minds about your course of action." Why did these guys talk like that? 'Certain individuals.' 'Course of action.' No wonder the papers Holden slapped in front of him at Centre Street were so thick.

"Thank you, we'll be in touch," Toto said, and hung up.

"Will someone please tell me what on earth is going on?" she said, looking back and forth at Jack and Steinberg.

Steinberg said nothing, but looked at her, blinking slowly. Richard exhaled, now feeling more grounded. This wasn't the kind of thing he wanted to get used to, but he sensed he was adjusting. He looked over at Kathy, who seemed paralyzed.

"We're telling you everything we know as soon as we learn it," Jack said, "And we—at least I—can't figure it out. Why would their Source X insist on full immunity for the firm? Not that I'm complaining or anything."

"Unless he's someone who has an interest in the firm being unencumbered by any liability as a result of this scandal," Steinberg said.

No one spoke for a few moments. Richard wondered if Jack and Steinberg were playing dumb about Source X.

"Richard, Kathy, does any of this make sense to either of you?" Toto asked.

Richard was juggling pieces in his mind, trying to line them up. The mole had to be LeClaire, so wasn't the mole Source X? Or could Source X be somebody else involved who got caught or turned himself in? Was it possible Jack and Steinberg weren't involved after all? The scheme started when the foreign partners invested in Walker four years ago; maybe LeClaire was their boy on the inside and Jack and Steinberg were clean.

"Richard?" Jack said.

Richard decided he'd get at least part of it out in the open and see how Jack and Steinberg reacted. He'd taken a calculated gamble with Milner the other day. This would be another one. Richard said, "We did some analysis of the trades you all have copies of. Four of the institutions doing trading are each owned in part by Schoenfeld & Co. And those four institutions had their trades funneled to them from a staging point in London called Golding & Co., rather than from GCG Paris. We also believe that GCG Paris' messenger in the network doesn't know the other Schoenfeld-owned banks exist."

"What are you getting at?" Toto said.

"I don't know what we're getting at; these are just the facts for now." Kathy was looking at Richard like he was nuts.

"Go on," Toto said.

"We were able to figure out that the foreign partners—Schoenfeld and GCG—made additional investments in Walker stock shortly after completion of three of Milner's deals that the SEC says were part of this investigation. Tungsten Steel Service Centers, Ernest-United and Val-Tech Industries. And the amounts they invested correspond with the amount of profit we estimated on the network's insider trading."

"When were you thinking about telling us this?" Toto said. Her nostrils were actually flaring. She was looking at Richard now like she might smack him. Jack's and Steinberg's faces didn't show any emotion.

"We couldn't quite believe it ourselves," Kathy said.

"They were just keeping their equity percentage at the same level after management took bonuses in shares instead of cash," Steinberg said. "We were allowed to do that under the agreements with Schoenfeld and GCG when we put the amalgamation together." Richard looked at Kathy, who rolled her eyes. She wasn't buying it. Toto looked Steinberg in the eye for a moment, and then sat down in her chair behind her desk.

"Have a seat everyone, please," she said. She leaned forward, put her forearms on her desk while they all sat down, looking like she was ready to leap across at one of them. Richard wasn't sure she trusted any of them at that moment. He didn't blame her. Then Toto sat back in her chair, sighed.

"Is there any reason to believe any of you is likely to get hauled away in handcuffs by the U.S. Attorney's Office in the next twelve hours? I'd like to know so I can plan my evening," Toto said. Richard saw Kathy wince and arch her back. He wanted to go over to calm her down, then realized he wasn't exactly cool himself.

Jack muttered, "The perfect ending to a perfect day."

"All right, let's regroup," Toto said. "We should try to stay one step ahead of this thing. There's no sense in seeing it unfold before us in the newspapers."

"No shit," Jack said.

"You all better get out of here," Toto said. "Charlie Holden is likely to shoot first and ask questions later. I'm nervous that he's processing warrants. I'll call him."

"What are you up to?" Steinberg said.

"In the first place, I'd like to see what else I can get out of him. In the second place, if somebody's going to give Walker & Company immunity, I'd like to know what he has in mind, and negotiate the whole thing out. I am, after all, Walker's attorney, aren't I?"

"Absolutely," Jack said.

Richard thought about the forms he'd signed at Walker upon entering M&A, and his initial conversation with Toto. She was still Walker's attorney, still Richard's attorney, as long as no conflict existed.

#

After leaving Toto's office, in the limo back downtown, Jack decided. These kids could screw up the whole deal. They were supposed to be given up to the Feds with the Source X deal. LeClaire, a bunch of junior stooges, and, of course, Milner, neatly packaged. So the whole thing would be firewalled; it would hurt, but wouldn't kill Walker. But now these kids: they knew more than the Feds. And once the Feds squeezed them, they'd tell everything they'd figured out. They'd unravel the whole Source X deal and bring it all down around them.

"These kids know too much," he said to Mickey.

Mickey nodded. "More than the Feds," he said.

"At this point they're our only loose end."

"Milner's still out there someplace, as far as we know."

"Yeah, but I don't care if Milner gets caught or gets out. He can't prove anything past what the Feds already have. But the kids can. They have to go."

Mickey just looked out the window, nodding, blinking.

Jack would drive to Canarsie this evening, talk to Preston. Jack hated this shit; he liked Blum, but sometimes you had to do lousy stuff to cover your ass. It wasn't any different than back in Canarsie when they set up Splits Duncan for the fire Jack and Bucky Pierson set in the Timex warehouse on Avenue L.

#

Richard and Kathy sat in the corner of the Bull and Bear bar at the Waldorf, Richard looking over Kathy's shoulder at a guy who glanced over at him before sitting down. *Anything?* He didn't think so. Richard had seen the corner booth and walked straight for it. He slid into the high-backed seat and crawled in all the way to the wall. He wasn't taking any chances. Well, they were; Kathy and he could just as easily be having a drink from the minibar in the room, but when Richard said he felt like getting away for a half hour, Kathy agreed. They hunched together over the table, sheltered in the corner among dark mahogany paneling in dim lighting. He smelled beer nuts, spilled wine and the sweaty tourists who kept comparing New York to St. Louis at the booth next to them.

Kathy said, "I never imagined things could get turned so crosswise."

"This is pretty high on the weird scale." He checked out the guy again who'd glanced at him.

"I guess the good news is that the mole turned himself in and we're eventually going to get off the hook." Richard didn't respond. He was turning the last few days over in his mind. Kathy went on, "Whoever's at the top of this thing, it looks like they've packaged it for the Feds in such a way that it's going to get resolved without us getting screwed. Once Toto gets the immunity negotiated and all the arrests get announced, we can go back to—whatever."

Richard looked over at Kathy, couldn't believe what he just heard. "You're dreaming," Richard said.

"What do you mean?"

"This isn't over yet. I feel like we're in a labyrinth. Stuck wandering around. And when we get to the exit, somebody's gonna be standing there with a baseball bat."

"You mean other than the Feds?"

"Think about it. Ever consider they might not want us to get out?"

"Who? Jack and Mickey? You said yourself you think it's possible they're clean."

"I was kidding myself. Think about it. We said it before: it looks like it goes all the way up to the foreign partners. You said yourself, crooks at Walker, GCG, Schoenfeld. What if they're all in on it—Sir Reginald, Delecroix, Jack, Steinberg? And we already know LeClaire's the mole."

"What good does it do them to screw us?"

"Negotiating chips. We're expendable anyhow. You know how Wall Street works better than I do."

"But the Feds already have the mole—LeClaire."

"And he's protecting the firm. Why?"

Kathy thought for a moment. "Walker's paying him off."

It was exactly where Richard came out. It fit with Source X holding out for immunity for Walker. "Yeah. He cops a plea, goes to jail, and he collects his $200 when he gets out."

"It's too farfetched. God, he's got Elaine and the kids to think about. Way too extreme medicine for LeClaire just for some money."

"Probably a lot of money. And if he's guilty then he's hosed already anyhow. Might as well get something out of it."

"And we're an extra bone to throw the Feds." Kathy was finally getting it.

"Yeah. His word against ours. Plus the wiretaps, plus the emails. Add my desktop computer with all the mole's emails on it. And if they could get a hold of it, my laptop."

"A couple of bodies."

"A few in New York added to those in Paris and London they'll throw in. Makes a nice neat package."

Kathy thought for a moment. "But in these things you always follow the money. They can trace the money to all of those institutions, the trading accounts."

"How much you wanna bet they'll never find it? It's buried in numbered accounts in Switzerland, the Caymans. They'll never find out who owns them. Or if they could, it would take years. So the Feds get some quick convictions, look like heroes and everybody else goes back to business as usual." Kathy's eyes were unfocused, glazing over. Richard went on, "Or worse, they could see us as a threat and try to get rid of us completely."

"How?"

"Permanently. Kill us. Look what happened to Milner's CFO and Walker's General Counsel."

Kathy's face went blank. She stared at the wall above Richard's head for a few moments. When she finally spoke her voice was jagged. "You're just speculating."

Richard nodded. "Speculating, yeah. The situation is highly ambiguous, I agree, but we need to act or we're gonna get swept away." Richard saw Kathy smirk. Then it grew into a smile. What had she figured out? "What?" Richard said.

"I'm just remembering what Jack said in the *Fortune* article on Milner."

It dawned on Richard, too. He smiled. "Something like: 'This business takes a high tolerance for ambiguity. Markets are uncertain. People are untrustworthy. Your ally today could be your adversary tomorrow. You need to make judgments based on imperfect information, and act.'"

"So we can't go to the Feds. And if you're right, not Jack or Mickey," Kathy said.

"That leaves Milner. He's the only angle I see."

"That's nuts if he's really at the center of this thing."

"Even better. Go directly to the source. And he's the one who stands to lose the most. I say we go to him." Richard was speaking, but no longer to Kathy. He was thinking aloud, then to himself, deciding how to go about it.

#

While Kathy took a shower, Richard walked up Park Avenue to 55th Street, then crossed to the West Side, still thinking about the profits he'd just calculated for the mole's ring. He'd never totaled it before, but all it took was a minute to add the formula to his Excel spreadsheet. He only now understood the scale of this thing. He got a creepy feeling in his guts just thinking about it again. The body count was two so far. He didn't want it going higher.

He had to walk all the way over to 9th Avenue before he found a pay phone that worked. He pulled out Roman Croonquist's business card, put his watch on the platform of the phone and dialed Croonquist's 24-hour emergency number at the SEC. He kept his eye on the second hand of the watch.

"Been doing some thinking, I gather," Croonquist said.

"How could I not."

"You've come to the right conclusion. I'll arrange for someone from the U.S. Attorney's Office to bring you in and we can talk everything through. Where are you?"

One minute, 30 seconds. He wished Croonquist had picked right up, that Richard didn't have to go back and forth with the woman at the SEC switchboard on the reason for the call; she'd said she'd see if he was available, Richard finally having to insist, "Just give him my damn name, he'll know who I am." And Croonquist was wasting time now, too.

Richard said, "Let's cut to it—what if I can deliver the heads of Walker's trading ring?"

"We have them," Croonquist said, sounding confident.

"Bullshit. You've only scratched the surface. Will you deal?"

Croonquist didn't respond right away, sounding maybe confused, then saying, "Maybe. What've you got?"

"I can prove it's a $2.0 billion scheme with links all over the world. And I've got more data on more deals going back more years than you do." Two minutes, five seconds.

"We'll need proof. Come in and we'll talk. If it makes sense, we can go easy on you if you cooperate. If you help us bring in Milner we can make it very, very painless for you." He was back to his smarmy mister nice guy routine again.

"So you still don't have him?" Richard laughed.

Croonquist didn't say anything.

Richard waited a moment, said, "Can we cut the bullshit? I haven't done anything, whatever line of crap LeClaire is feeding you, and I've got enough to bring down the *real* guys who put this thing together. So will you deal?"

Croonquist didn't respond right away again, apparently thinking about it, then, "We'll need proof. Bring everything in and we'll give you a wire to wear."

"You're not getting it. When I call you next about a deal, I'll have reams of data you don't have, full proof, and I'm not listening to any crap about you going easy on me because of my cooperation. I'm not cooperating. I'm the friggin' Texas Rangers solving your stinking case." And he hung up. Two minutes, 47 seconds. Probably not enough time for a trace. Richard headed back to the Waldorf, feeling every part of his body as he walked. He felt the muscles in his legs contracting and releasing as he trudged, heard his breath flowing in and out like he was in the last mile of a marathon. He needed to deliver. He hoped like hell he could find Milner.

#

Richard had left Kathy a note saying he stepped out to use a pay phone while she showered. He wanted to get back as soon as possible. He was troubled about her. Kathy had swung from complacent to twitchy with worry during their conversation at the Bull and Bear. It didn't show much on the outside, but Richard knew her well enough to see it: it was twisting her up inside. The silence, distraction and fixed gaze weren't Kathy. Richard knew now he'd need to get to Milner alone. Besides, he was the one who knew Milner, and the only one Milner would talk to. And this whole mess was on his head. He'd gotten Kathy and Dad into this by nosing around. His job to get them out.

He walked into their room at the Waldorf to see Kathy with her brow furrowed. *Damn.* He wasn't gone that long.

"Everything okay?" he said.

"I'm not sure. Here's a little salt to the mix. The front desk just called. There's a package for you downstairs."

He got the chills. Who found out they were here? "That's odd," Richard said.

"That's not odd, babe, that's scary as hell."

Richard walked over to the phone, picked it up. He said, "I might as well have them send it up. Whoever dropped it off already knows where we are."

The bellboy delivered a large manila envelope with something rattling around inside. Richard felt his pulse quicken as he tore at the paper. Out of the corner of his eye he saw Kathy lean forward to see as he pulled out a cell phone and a note. He read the note aloud. "'Richard. I thought about it. Let's talk. 646-263-2764. Harold.'"

Kathy crossed the room to a chair and sat down, exhaling. Richard could see the tension in her movements. "What do you think it means?" she said.

"Only one way to find out." He turned on the cell phone and dialed it, wondering who else might know they were here if Milner had figured it out, where they might go next.

Kathy said, "Are you sure . . . ?"

Then the phone connected. "Hello, Richard," Milner said.

"How'd you know where I was?"

"I have guys whose business it is to find out things."

Devon & Co. He thought about the Bull and Bear downstairs with Kathy, how exposed they'd been.

"You still there?" Milner said.

"Yeah."

"Don't worry. You're still among friends, although . . ."

"Although what?"

"You should be careful. Not everything's what it seems."

No shit. "Or everyone."

"Yeah. I assume you're current with the news? Walker and Source X? A prominent figure in U.S. business implicated?"

Richard hesitated for a long moment. He wanted to see if Milner had anything else to add. "Yeah," he finally said. He started to think about how to steer the conversation.

"I sense you're tentative. I understand your hesitation. So let me get to the point. I thought about our conversation and I believe we can help each other. We should team up."

Milner was heading straight where Richard wanted to go, saving him the effort. And Milner had an agenda. So he had to know more than Richard did. *Play it out, learn something.* He didn't respond. See what else Milner had.

Milner continued, "We have common interests. The information you said you had, copies of emails, computer files, all that is critical to getting us both cleared with the Feds. I have crucial information, too."

"I figured out LeClaire's Source X."

"Yeah, he's your mole, reporting directly to Schoenfeld and Delecroix. Jack and Mickey are in this with both feet, too." He paused, then sighed into the phone. Richard was clasping his own phone so tightly his hand hurt; he switched hands and ears, then wiped the sweat from the hand he'd just freed. "The stakes are high. I'm sure they killed my CFO and Walker's General Counsel. Now that LeClaire's talking to the Feds, who knows what he'll say to cover it up."

"He's probably getting paid off to protect everyone else." Angry at LeClaire and torn up about it at the same time.

"At least to protect Schoenfeld, Delecroix, Jack and Mickey, but he'll most likely fry anyone else, including you."

That hit Richard like a thud in the gut. He'd told himself that LeClaire could turn on him, but now hearing Milner verbalize it felt like a body blow.

Milner said, "I've got some ideas. I'm sure you do, too."

"I talked to Croonquist fifteen minutes ago. I told him I calculated that the ring's made two billion in profits over four years, that LeClaire's only giving him a fraction of the story. I might've overreached, but I said I can deliver the top guys."

"What'd he say?"

"I think I stood him on his head. It sounds like he'll deal, but we'll need to get indisputable proof. He's an intimidating guy. A real crusader."

"I can get a meeting with Schoenfeld and Delecroix. Let's meet and plan strategy. Someplace safe."

"Okay. Where and when?"

"Tomorrow. 7:30 a.m. at my office."

Is he crazy? "You call that safe? They have to be watching it." Now he was getting a bad feeling about all this.

"Where is the last place you'd look for me if you wanted to find me now? The Feds probably think I've already left the country. I've got a private elevator in my building; it's got a secret stop in the sub-basement the Vanderbilts built to access the tunnels to Grand Central. If you can get in, we can get out. If my building's staked out, the Devon guys will steer you off and take you to me. Hang onto that cell phone."

Richard was working it in his mind. Was Milner setting a trap? Why bother? He knew where Richard was now; he could sick the Feds on him if he wanted to. And it sounded like Milner needed the data. Getting Richard hauled in wouldn't do Milner any good. "Okay," Richard said.

"Bring the data. See you." They hung up.

Afterward when he explained it to Kathy, he was laying out his logic as much to assure himself as her. When he finished telling her, he turned on his laptop and logged onto the internet.

He wanted to check the mole's emails on the netwiz.net server one last time, see if there were any more to add to his files before getting ready to meet with Milner. When he got onto the mole's walker1@netwiz.net account, what he saw made him suck in his breath and arch his back in the chair. *What the . . . ?* All the emails were deleted from the account. That certainly ratcheted up the heat, and maybe explained why the data was so critical to Milner. All he could do was meet with Milner, see where it led. It took a high tolerance for ambiguity, he reminded himself. *And like Milner said, balls.*

Chapter 9

London, England. Jack bumped his head on the doorway of the Lear 60^{XR} as he climbed down the stairway out of the business jet, still the top of Learjet's line.

"Watch your head, sir," the attendant said.

"Thanks for the warning," Jack said.

When the limo picked him up at 8:00 a.m. London time to deposit him at the Bristol, his mind started chewing on the day's events, kept grinding for an hour after he went to bed. *Jeez.* He's in the knife fight of his life to keep them all from going down the tubes with this mole thing. And the markets maybe running the firm into a brick wall anyhow, his entire career building up Walker maybe for nothing. Back and forth with Mickey about ten times on how to keep the mole thing packaged just right for the Feds, fine-tuning it. Then seeing this shit with Source X splayed all over the newswires before they were ready. Obviously old fart Sir Reginald and his toxic little gnome sidekick front-ran Mickey and him.

Unbelievable. Now he wondered if maybe they were setting Mickey and him up. He couldn't wait to figure out a way to get rid of these douchebags. When he got to Schoenfeld & Co.'s offices at St. James' Square at 12:30 p.m., he stopped in front of Elvira's desk outside Sir Reginald's corner office.

"Good morning, my love," Jack said, trying to play it cool.

"Jack, lovely to see you," Elvira cooed back. "He'll see you right away." She lowered her voice, "Delecroix and my knight. It looks like an ambush."

Jack was at full alert as he entered the room. He focused on body language and the room's lighting. The blinds were drawn. Sir Reginald sat erect behind his desk. *All formally British and shit.* Delecroix puffed on a big Havana in the sofa beside Sir Reginald's desk. *Looking edgy.*

"Jack, old boy," Sir Reginald said. Delecroix offered a flat, "Hello."

"Have a seat, old boy, pull up a chair in front here."

Jack didn't like it. He didn't want to be positioned between them. He sat down next to Delecroix on the sofa.

"Little early for that Churchill, isn't it Philippe?" he said, seeing if he could take his temperature.

"I have to be twice as bad when I'm not in Paris to make up for being so good when I'm home. My wife," he explained, "she smells them on me. It isn't worth listening to the lectures." Jack chuckled and slapped Delecroix on the leg.

"We should get right down to it," Jack said. *Assholes.* "So do you guys have a lid on this? Since Mickey and me gave you our plan on how to handle the deal with the Feds, I've heard more on the news about it than from you guys."

Delecroix said, "The situation, it is at a delicate stage."

"You couldn't have kept Mickey and me in the loop?"

"Absolutely not," Delecroix said. "At times like this we need to restrict knowledge to the innermost circle."

"You think I'm your water-boy?" *See if the Frog knew what that meant.*

Delecroix settled down into the sofa, sighed like it was the tenth time he was repeating a lecture to a kid, like Jack was some twerp he could talk down to. Jack was tired, in no mood for this. He watched Delecroix blow out a big puff of smoke from his Churchill, curl his bony little fingers around the cigar. From where he sat, Jack could just reach out and break one of his skinny fingers right off if he wanted to.

Delecroix said, "LeClaire is taken care of adequately. He has agreed with your officials to cooperate under terms that require immunity for Walker & Company. And of course François will keep the involvement of any senior officials from GCG, Schoenfeld and Walker secret. Certain clerical individuals must unfortunately be exposed as part of his arrangements."

"You sure you took care of LeClaire?" Jack said, looking back and forth from Delecroix to Sir Reginald.

Delecroix puffed up his cheeks with air, blew it out. He scowled at Jack and said, "We have compensated François appropriately. He is a French citizen. When he is released from jail in two to three years based on his cooperation, his money will be waiting for him in France where he can live in high style. Very few people care about scandals in France. In fact, such things often lend an aura of prestige and mystery to an individual. Something you Americans do not appreciate."

Talking down to Jack again. Maybe Jack would snap off two fingers; see if the Frog could appreciate that.

"And it is an inconvenient accident about your two young people learning as much as they did," Sir Reginald said.

"I'm on that," Jack said.

Sir Reginald said, "They could present a problem for—"

"I said I'm taking care of it," Jack said.

"Who do you think you're talking to?" Delecroix said.

"A couple a crooks. Who're you guys to act so high and mighty?"

Delecroix pulled his cigar out of his mouth, gave Jack a look like he expected Jack to wither and back down. *Arrogant little runt.* Why had he danced around this guy so long?

Delecroix squinted at Jack and said, "What are you doing about it? We need this fixed, not made worse. We cannot afford another incident like Milner's CFO or your General Counsel."

Jack leaned in closer to Delecroix, saw Delecroix arch his head back. "I said I'm taking care of it."

Delecroix just stared at Jack.

Jack grinned.

"What's wrong? You don't like one of your employees talking back to you?"

Sir Reginald said, "Oh come now, let's not deteriorate into unpleasantness."

Nobody said anything for a few moments.

Sir Reginald shifted his weight in his chair behind his desk. He said, "Well, then, we'll let you get back to it, old boy," looking away from Jack like he was dismissed.

Jack stood up, headed toward the door. "I don't need you to tell me my business," he said.

Delecroix said, "I remind you, I expect this handled discreetly and properly or I will take actions."

Jack stopped and turned back to look Delecroix in the eye. "Don't even think about trying to fuck with me. You stab me in the back, I got nothing to lose. If I'm dying already, what do I care if I gotta blow my brains out for the bullet to nail you in the heart? I'll hand you to the Feds in a New York minute."

Delecroix smiled and blew another big puff of cigar smoke.

Jack said, "Don't look so smug. Even in France they don't let you smoke those things in jail."

#

New York City. Richard walked out of the Waldorf, down Park Avenue and crossed 46th Street toward the Helmsley Building. He carried his laptop in a Redweld folder under his arm, his gaze shooting back and forth from beneath his sunglasses, looking for anyone standing around. He wore street clothes and a baseball cap, hoping to look like a messenger, even though Milner said it was safe.

Then as he passed the East Helmsley Walk on 46th Street, he saw a guy about fifteen feet away wearing an earpiece with a wire running down into his shirt. He turned fast and faced Richard. *Shit!* The guy looked startled for a second, then angry as he broke into a run straight at Richard, his arms spread like he was gonna tackle him. It must have been muscle memory from high school football that told Richard to cross his package from under his left arm into his right and run straight at the guy. Just before they collided, Richard jammed his left arm up, stiff-armed him hard in the face and then executed a perfect spin move, doing a complete circle as he bounced off him and headed across 46th Street. Then another would-be tackler appeared straight ahead about five yards away. He had time to wonder if this was a trap all along. Richard threw him a head fake north up Park Avenue, which the guy bought, and then faked a cut left until the guy leaned back that way, then broke right past him. Richard heard the loud *snap!* of a tendon in the guy's leg. *He won't be chasing me but the first guy will.* Then another came running full tilt out of the West Helmsley Walk. Richard stopped short and reversed his field. His first pursuer hurtled past him as Richard hunched underneath him.

Richard ran back east across 46th Street. *Get out of here now. Now, now, now!* Richard cut right up the ramp toward the east encircling roadway around Grand Central Terminal. He darted across the roadway, barely being missed by a taxi speeding down on its way to Park Avenue northbound.

Richard got halfway up the ramp toward the ninety degree turn to the right that started the roadway around Grand Central. He heard screeching tires and blaring horns. From the corner of his eye he could see his pursuer was only seven or eight yards behind him. He guessed the guy would overtake him on the long straightaway down the east side of Grand Central. He felt a moment of hopelessness, then pushed it back. *Run!* He dashed straight across in front of another taxi, slowing down to force the cab to swerve hard at his pursuer. He heard the *crunch*! of the cab's fender on the concrete wall and the sound of the guy's body slamming on the steel of the cab. Richard looked over his shoulder to see the guy sprawled on the hood.

Go, go, go! He ran as fast as he could along the straightaway down the east side of Grand Central Terminal. More horns, more screeches of tires and then the race of an engine filled his ears. He looked back over his shoulder and saw a car coming after him the wrong way on the roadway, and cars and taxis spewing in either direction to make way for it, crashing into each other and the side railing. Richard kept running.

The car pulled alongside him and now a guy was waving his hands and his head out the passenger window shouting something. Richard heard him call his name but the rest was just noise. He waved a gun in his right hand. *They're gonna kill me!*

He looked up and saw a taxi speeding forward with its tires smoking, trying to stop. He lurched toward the car and at the guy waving the gun, causing the driver of the car to swerve left away from him. The taxi crashed head-on into the car and Richard kept running without looking back. He reached the south turn, followed the roadway's ninety-degree right and then left and ran down the descending ramp toward Park Avenue South.

He gasped for breath as he ran and now felt perspiration soaking his shirt, still pushing himself not to slow down. When he was thirty feet from the bottom of the ramp a man in a grey suit jumped out into the roadway and held his arms out wide. Richard felt desperation flood through him and then immediately called up some reserve. He gritted his teeth, ran straight at the man. He was big, maybe 250, so he'd have to hit him hard.

"Mr. Blum, I'm a friend," he called as Richard got near him, still at a full run. "Mr. Milner sent us. We're with Devon & Company." He raised his hands above his head as if in surrender. "We can get you out of here."

About ten feet from him Richard cut hard right and crossed to the other side of the ramp. The guy didn't make a move to try to stop him. Richard ran to the bottom of the ramp where it deposited traffic onto Park Avenue South and crossed to the west side of the street. He stopped on the corner with his chest heaving, dropped to his knees. The taste of stomach acid filled his mouth. His lungs burned. He kept looking at the guy standing there motionless on the ramp.

"Let us help you," he called. Richard didn't respond, still panting. He looked around, got to his feet. The man walked to the side of the ramp and looked over the railing.

"There's not much time," he said.

"I don't recognize you from the Tentron team," Richard shouted between gasps. His panic had subsided. He started thinking what to do next, where to go. He looked from side to side, picking his route, ready to bolt if the guy came any closer. His legs were trembling, the left starting to cramp.

"I wasn't on the team, but you'll recognize Mr. Harrelson there," he said, pointing to the corner of 42nd Street and Park Avenue South. Richard recognized the man in the grey suit he pointed to. It was Harrelson, now jogging up from the corner. He waved at Richard. Richard was ready to run again.

"There's not much time, Richard. Either come with us now or get out of here fast," Harrelson said. People were now looking at them from all directions, some pointing. Richard decided; he jogged toward Harrelson.

"All right, let's go," Richard said to Harrelson.

"The van is up the street on Vanderbilt Avenue," the other guy said. He trotted up.

They ran across 42nd Street and now saw a beat up, grey van on Vanderbilt Avenue near 43rd Street surrounded by cops, two police cruisers near it with lights flashing.

"We got a problem," Harrelson said.

Richard felt a blast of adrenaline, then remembered Jack's Porsche. It was worth a shot. "I think I can get us a car," Richard said. "Follow me." He jogged through Grand Central out to 45th Street and toward the One Lexington Plaza garage, Harrelson and the other man following.

Richard felt a wave of relief as he approached the garage. The silver 911 was there in its usual spot near the manager's office, heading out, ready for 'Mr. Jack's' call. He slowed to a walk, trying to look casual, realizing he was sweating, panting. "Angel," he said as he approached the attendant. He pointed to the Porsche. Angel look confused at first, then recognized Richard. He waved and ducked into the office, a moment later coming back with the key. Richard tried not to squeal the tires pulling out.

"Sorry, we wanted to try and intercept you long before you ever got to 46th Street. We saw you too late," Harrelson said.

"Who were they?" Richard asked.

"We don't know. Maybe somebody Walker set loose on you. But by now I think we've also got half the NYPD after us." He looked out the back window as Richard drove west across 45th. Richard checked the rear view mirror again, ready to gun the engine if he saw any police. He thought they'd get away with it, though. Nobody would be looking for a silver Porsche 911.

"Thanks," Richard said.

"Head downtown," Harrelson said.

"I need to know where we're going."

"Downtown. Location One." He smiled. "I assume that's the package," Harrelson said. Richard had the Redweld folder wedged between his left leg and the door.

"Yeah," he said, looking in the mirror again. He heard sirens in the distance behind them. Harrelson looked back through the rear window.

"Don't worry, Richard," Harrelson said, "we aren't up to anything. We've just been asked to take you to Mr. Milner."

They were approaching 45th and Vanderbilt, two blocks from the van. It still sat in the middle of the street, surrounded by police, the two police cruisers still there. A cop directed traffic at 45th and Vanderbilt. Richard felt his stomach muscles tighten as he entered the intersection, then a bolt of panic as the cop looked directly at him, did a double-take and started toward the car, reaching for his radio.

"Now would be a good time to tell me where Location One is," Richard said. He gunned the engine and turned south on Vanderbilt, winding the Porsche out to 6,000 rpm before shifting into second gear. They shot past the van with the engine screaming near the top of second gear and in an instant they were to 42nd Street. The light was orange, cars jamming up in the southbound lane, so he swerved into the uptown lane and shifted into third as he crossed 42nd Street, laying on the horn. Pedestrians crossing Park Avenue South at 42nd scattered as he shot through the intersection. Richard was amazed at what the car could do, realized it was him, then wondered if he could keep it up. He swerved around cars, then a truck as he continued down Park, the car leaving the ground for a moment, then bottoming hard as they passed 41st Street. He slammed on the brakes to avoid a taxi, swerved left then cringed as he squeezed between two cars, unable to stop. He heard the crunch of metal and horns as he raked both sides of the Porsche on the two cars, tearing off both mirrors. He hit the gas and was past them, Park Avenue clear for a few blocks.

"Where the hell are we going?" Richard yelled.

"Wall Street heliport!" Harrelson shouted, "take the FDR if you can get to it!" Richard stomped the accelerator to the floor, heard the engine screaming again. He checked the rear view mirror and saw a police car behind them. He shifted into 3rd, ran the light at 35th Street and slowed down to turn onto 34th Street. "Too much traffic," Harrelson said, "take 30th."

Richard revved the engine again and they were at 30th in seconds. As he turned left onto 30th he saw another police car in the rear view mirror, lights flashing. He felt a burst of despair. Thirtieth was blocked with traffic. "Hang on," Richard said. He backed up, stomped on the gas and shot down the uptown lane of Park Avenue South, cars swerving out of their way, horns blaring. He turned onto 28th, tucked into traffic crossing east, seeing the police car make the left onto 28th just as he got to Lexington. *No time.*

He turned left the wrong way up Lexington just as the light changed, laying on his horn, swerving around traffic, then right onto 30th Street, then straight across Third Avenue with the light. They bogged down in traffic again between Third and Second. "Clear behind us," Harrelson said. Richard felt his heart pounding, his pulse thumping in his temples.

"C'mon," he said aloud, waiting for the light to change, palms sticky with perspiration as he squeezed the steering wheel. He felt another surge of adrenaline crossing Second, seeing flashing lights and hearing sirens up the avenue. He gunned the engine and in a moment was on the FDR Drive.

Harrelson said, "Better get off at Houston Street."

"If we get that far." Richard was doing eighty miles per hour on the FDR, the car responding to every twitch of the wheel. At Houston he slowed down to the speed of traffic, cutting across all the way to West Street. No sirens, no flashing lights. His mind was still racing, looking at each side street, ready to stomp on the accelerator again. He kept to the speed limit down West Street, finally starting to relax when he entered the underpass to the East

Side at the bottom tip of Manhattan. He looked over at Harrelson. Harrelson nodded and smiled. What a weird business these guys were in. Even more weird than investment banking.

#

Richard eased the Porsche into the Wall Street heliport. They all got out. A gloss-black Sikorsky twin prop helicopter was warming up. Richard squinted against the rotor airwash. The air was thick with the smell of jet fuel and heat from the chopper's engines. Harrelson guided Richard up to the Sikorsky, Richard not sure about this now. But when he got there Milner was seated inside. He extended his hand as Richard entered.

"Richard, good to see you," he said. They shook, that massive hand of his enveloping Richard's. He'd forgotten how big a guy Milner was, now seeing him outside his larger-than-life office. "I was beginning to think I'd have to leave before we found you. I hear you had a scare up there."

"Yeah." That *was* a scare uptown. What the fuck, man, that guy in the car was waving a gun. Richard glanced sideways at Harrelson. Was he gonna chaperone them? He wanted to get right to it.

"Let's talk in the chopper on the ride over to Teterboro."

Richard nodded, feeling uneasy, but not seeing any alternative. Harrelson got out, closed the chopper door. The chopper headed out across the Hudson River toward New Jersey.

"That the package?" Milner said.

"Yeah."

He nodded.

Richard gripped the Redweld folder in his lap with both hands, then said, "You said you had crucial information."

Richard was anxious for him to respond. He wasn't sure where this was going.

"As far as I've pieced it together, Schoenfeld and Delecroix were startled by how much money Walker was making on my deals. LeClaire was Delecroix's boy, and he was always on my deal teams. Delecroix convinced him to be the conduit to feed information about my deals. They started front-running me— buying up stock in my acquisition targets before I made my move. It was beginning to piss me off that I always had leaks running up the stock prices on my deals, making me pay more, so I put the Devon guys on it. They traced it back to LeClaire. When I confronted him he told me the drill. I can remember I was really pissed about them sucking LeClaire into this thing. I liked him. Still do. You remind me a lot of what he was like early in his career."

"Thanks," Richard said. His voice broke as he said it. "Why didn't you go to the Feds?"

Milner didn't answer right away. He tilted his head forward. He didn't appear to be feeling sorry for himself, just feeling stupid about it.

Milner said, "I was gonna. I had a little 'interview' with Schoenfeld and Delecroix. I was gonna tell them I'd turn them in if they didn't knock it off. I felt so ripped off that instead I demanded payback. Stupidest thing I ever did. They paid me off over time with their trading profits. Two hundred million. I *should've* turned them all in. Now I'm dirty, too. Once they paid me off I tried to get out; they wouldn't let me."

"When was that?"

"Two years ago," he said, "and they finished paying me back just before the Southwest deal. That was when I tried to cut and run from them."

Just before Tentron. They rode in silence for a few moments. The chopper had crossed the Hudson and was heading north on the Jersey side.

"Whether you know it or not, you may have saved my ass— our asses." He pointed to the folder in Richard's lap. "That's our leverage. Schoenfeld and Delecroix obviously wanna keep themselves out of this whole thing, and out of jail. Jack and Mickey, too. I'm sure they bought off LeClaire with enough money that he'll be able to live like a French prince when he gets out, in exchange for keeping his mouth shut about them. He also bargained for immunity for the firm; that'll assure the trail never gets traced back to any of them. And LeClaire bought off the Feds. I already know he turned in some low level guys at GCG and Schoenfeld. They probably got paid off, too. But I'm the big prize, and he's turned me in. That's where the Feds will get their headlines."

"How does my stuff link it to Sir Reginald and Delecroix?"

Milner smiled. "That's where we need to be clever."

Richard was getting a feeling in his gut, a tickle of anticipation, like Milner and he were gonna work a con.

"They've agreed to see us. Come with me to London now."

"To negotiate a deal with Sir Reginald and Delecroix?"

"Yeah. I said we had information to trade with them. Your data, much more than what the Feds have—and an accounting of the profits of the ring going back four years. I told them you hid copies, so if anything happens to either of us the data finds its way to the Feds the next day. Told them I'm gonna live out my days in Switzerland, but I wanna cut a deal to keep quiet. And you want them to lay off you—for good."

Richard tried to digest it. "I can see how the data helps, but where do I come in?"

"Just like any deal. You've got command of the information. I can talk broadly about it, but you've run your fingers around in it. Be my second in the negotiations. Cut a deal for yourself."

"It's not these guys I need to cut a deal with. We get the goods on them and do a deal with the Feds." Richard pulled out his pocket Dictaphone. "We'll get them to talk."

Milner pulled out a tiny recorder and a wire. "My PIs have better technology; it's digital—but wake up, kid. You don't cut a deal with these guys you'll never be sure you're off the hook. If it turns out we can't do a deal with the Feds, we still need to use our leverage with these bastards, or we'll be looking over our shoulders the rest of our lives."

That hit Richard hard. But Milner had a point. Richard's fingerprints were all over this: the mole's email account in his computer at work, the Feds' wiretaps. They weren't conclusive by themselves, but tough to explain away if LeClaire still maintained Richard was involved. Kathy, too and maybe if the Feds really stretched it, somehow Dad. It made him want to throttle somebody.

"Got it. I do know this stuff cold. I can talk much more convincingly about it than you could on your own. And I can trace trades to Schoenfeld-owned entities, too. Ones even Delecroix may not know about. Maybe give them something to fight about between themselves."

Richard saw Milner smiling at him with his eyes, hand cupped over his mouth. He said, "We'll work out our strategy on the way to London. I already put you on the flight manifest. I got you a passport, too. I'm not traveling on my own, either."

Richard saw out the window the chopper was landing at Teterboro Airport next to a big Gulfstream G550. Richard looked back over at Milner. *This is gonna be some show.*

#

On a G550 over the Atlantic. Richard had called Dad before he left for Milner's office; he was a rock. But Richard was worried about Kathy, what she must be thinking. Probably sweating it out. The Feds still breathing down their necks and him off to see Milner, then disappears, out of touch. He couldn't risk contacting her at this point, but hoped the Devon guys got her a message. Milner said they'd think of some way.

Might as well get ready. He watched himself in the mirror of the guest bathroom as if seeing a movie, putting on the suit Milner's guys brought for him. Feeling numb inside, but calm.

This was it. If Milner and he pulled this off, they were safe. Otherwise, he wasn't sure what would happen.

What kept preying on him was LeClaire. He still couldn't get past the idea his friend would turn on him. He wondered if that might cloud his thinking at a critical moment, cause him to screw up. He tried to put it out of his mind. *Get over it.*

#

The kid was still in the other bathroom when Milner finished dressing and went out to his seat. He felt an anxious sensation of lightness in his legs. Richard had shown moxie up until now, but Milner wondered if he'd ever been in the kind of hand-to-hand combat he was about to walk into. Milner had a lot riding on this meeting, and an inexperienced slip-up by the kid could cost him big time. Still, no sense second-guessing his decision to bring him. And in a few hours it would be all over one way or the other. He stood up; he'd see if he could walk it off before Richard got out of the bathroom.

#

London, England. Milner thought it was kind of funny, the private dining room at Schoenfeld & Co. set up for them as if for a client dinner. Mahogany walls, polished inlaid table, crystal and bone china. A choice between white or red wine. The waitress was laying out their appetizers, celery root remoulade. He could see Richard sitting next to him, looking down at his plate like he was wondering what it was. Now he glanced across the table at old man Schoenfeld. Big bags under his eyes, shoulders hunched over. *Worn down.* Then he took in Delecroix, who seemed tense.

He was glad to be on his side of the table. Richard looked pumped up, ready. The spreadsheets he'd prepared on the plane sat in stapled piles in front of him.

The waitress left. *Here goes.* He shot a glance at Richard.

"Well, then," Schoenfeld said, "you called this meeting, old boy. We understand you want to undertake some form of exchange. Suppose you tell us what you have in mind."

Milner said, "As I told you, I'm planning to retire to Switzerland. Not my first choice, but it's a circumstance my business with you has put me in."

Delecroix said, "We are not responsible for your business decisions." He didn't look up from his appetizer.

"I'm not responsible for your systematic front-running of my deals costing me hundreds of millions over the years." Delecroix now looked up, locked his gaze on Milner's eyes. *Guy thinks he's got a cold stare.* Milner said, "Do we need to cover that territory again? We worked that out, what, two years ago?" Milner saw Schoenfeld nod. Both he and Delecroix were being cautious. Milner said, "Let's get to the point. I have reams of data, some of which our SEC probably has, some not." He looked at Richard, pointed to the papers in front of him. Richard handed copies across the table. Schoenfeld picked his up, looked at the top page. Delecroix didn't move, looking at it with his lip curled, like it was cancerous.

Delecroix said, "It is of no consequence."

"Let me spell out the consequences. I also know things that would totally screw you guys if I disclosed them, and put you in a position similar to the one I'm in myself."

Delecroix said, "Your position is one you put yourself in."

"A position you and your trading network put me in."

"You accepted your position as compensation for services."

"Services my ass. I was going on about my business doing deals and you and your stooge, LeClaire, picked me off. I only got payback from you guys for what your scam cost me."

"Describe it any way you wish," Delecroix said.

"I just described it dead-on."

He got the icy stare from Delecroix again, like Milner was supposed to quake in his boots. *This guy overestimates himself.*

Schoenfeld said, "Come now, we don't need to dispute the facts. We are where we are. What are you proposing?"

"Yes, what do you want?" Delecroix said, looking irritated.

Good. He was getting someplace now.

Milner said, "A deal. But not the same deal as before, because I'm out of the business." He paused for a moment to see if they reacted. "What I have to offer is my silence, and keeping these records locked away."

Delecroix said, "What are these records you refer to?"

"Pages of them, right in front of you. You don't want us to take this data to the SEC and the U.S. Attorney's Office and tell them it was you guys who dreamed up the whole scheme, got LeClaire to be your flunkie to set up the trading network. That you guys directed everything and made the bulk of the money."

"We already heard you. We don't need you to draw us a map, as you Americans say it," Delecroix said.

"Okay. Just making sure, what with the language differences between English and French, and our crude American English and the refined Queen's English. I don't want there to be any misunderstandings."

Now even the old man was looking fed up.

Milner turned to Richard. Richard said, "We have copies of all the trades of your network going back four years." Richard flipped open the pages all the way to the end, 22 pages in total. He turned back to the first page. "All LeClaire's emails to order trades distributed out through GCG, and from which he kept records of the profits of your network. I've re-created it all here, including the separate network of Schoenfeld-owned entities operating through Golding & Company."

Delecroix looked startled, scowled and picked up the papers for the first time. Milner suppressed a smile, and leaned his elbow on the table, put his hand over his mouth and grinned as broadly as he could. He wanted to let them see his eyes twinkling. *Chew on that, Philippe.* He saw Schoenfeld and Delecroix shoot sideways glances at each other.

Richard went on, "You'll see on page one I've summed the profits of the network by deal—17 in total—and then totaled it for the overall network, with separate subtotals for the trades fanned out through GCG and Golding. The totals are $2 billion; $1.5 billion of it through GCG, $500 million through Golding."

Delecroix was staring at the first page. After a long hesitation he said, "Enterprising, Reginald."

Schoenfeld didn't say anything.

Richard was glancing between Schoenfeld and Delecroix.

Milner was enjoying himself. The kid was doing great, like taking a client through a deal analysis. He came across crisp and confident, without betraying any of the nervousness or anger he must be feeling. Milner said, "Any questions on the data?"

Schoenfeld said, "No, it seems quite clear. I'm not certain if these figures agree precisely with ours—"

Delecroix cut in, "I am certain not with ours. They are off by 500 million or so." He narrowed his eyes at Schoenfeld.

Schoenfeld said, "As I was saying, the figures are close enough so as not to dispute them. So what are you proposing?"

Milner said, "I'm proposing I keep quiet. As I understand it, you're both in the clear. LeClaire is the Feds' Source X. I gather you've made it to his advantage to keep you out of this, that he'll offer enough of your network to get a splashy bust, including me, and headlines. So what're you offering me?"

Milner saw Schoenfeld turn slightly to look at Delecroix. He could sense the tension between them, see the anger in Delecroix's taut lips. *Good.* Richard had worked the power of information brilliantly. Now they'd see if the feisty Frenchman would act impetuously.

Delecroix said in a low voice, "For the fourth time, what do you propose?"

"That I keep quiet. What are you offering?"

Delecroix stared at him.

Milner stared back.

Richard was loving it, Milner and Delecroix each waiting for the other to blink. Richard felt juiced. The fatigue he'd felt at the beginning of the dinner was gone. It didn't get much better than this. Milner—he and Milner—had these guys cold. Then he remembered what Milner said on the plane: stay alert. Don't get cocky if it starts going well.

Sir Reginald cleared his throat, said, "I rather think we can make it worth your while." He turned to Delecroix and said to him, "I suggest we make the proposal we discussed."

Delecroix nodded. "But not with the split we discussed." He waved Richard's spreadsheet at Sir Reginald. "Let us say two thirds, one third, to account for your side profits?"

Sir Reginald gave a sheepish smile.

Milner said, "You want us to step out for a minute so you guys can work this out?" The waitress came back in. She cleared the appetizers, put down their entrées, medallions of beef. No one spoke while she was in the room. She hurried out.

Sir Reginald said, "No, that won't be necessary. We're in agreement between ourselves." He nodded to Delecroix.

Delecroix said, "We're prepared to offer a full 10% of our enterprise."

"Based on this information, that's an additional $200 million," Milner said.

Sir Reginald nodded. "An acceptable figure," he said.

"I don't think you're hearing me. I'm leaving everything behind, worth an estimated $5 to $7 billion. And $1 billion of it in cash I can't get out. That would be a nice round figure."

Sir Reginald and Delecroix looked back and forth at each other. Sir Reginald's eyes were wide. "One billion? You can't be serious, old boy."

"That's less than 20% of my assets. And I've got a lot of good years left. What's the present value of what else I could make if I didn't have to pack it in?"

Delecroix said, "We don't keep that kind of cash lying around. It's absurd."

"You're a big bank, with lots of pockets. I'm sure you can figure it out." He turned to Sir Reginald, "And you're a privately owned company. You can do whatever you want."

Sir Reginald said, "It's too much." He looked at Delecroix again, who raised his eyebrows, pursed his lips. "We will offer you $300 million."

"No way," Milner said. He started cutting his beef, chewing quickly as he ate it, Richard wondering how much Milner wanted, how much longer he'd play this out. He wanted to get to his own deal. But they agreed to let it wait until the end.

Delecroix said, "I encourage you to look realistically on what is feasible for us."

"A billion is feasible."

Richard was watching Delecroix and Sir Reginald, seeing no more glances back and forth between them. Sir Reginald slumped over in his chair, looking at his plate. Richard figured they were at their limit.

"I'll tell you what," Milner said. "Five hundred now, plus 10% of your business going forward."

Sir Reginald looked at Milner. "What business?" he said.

"Your investment in Walker. And your overall profits in Schoenfeld & Co.," and, turning to Delecroix, "and yours in your merchant banking subsidiary."

"Outrageous," Delecroix said. Sir Reginald didn't say anything. He was looking at his plate again, his jaw slack.

Dead meat. Nobody said anything for a moment.

Then Delecroix smiled, took a swig of his wine. "Three hundred million plus a 10% interest going forward is workable."

Milner nodded.

Sir Reginald lifted his head and looked straight ahead. The color was gone from his face. "Done," he said.

Milner smiled. "I'm glad you're both seeing reason. I'll have my banker get in touch about wire transfer arrangements. And a couple more things. Richard and his people—his family and his girlfriend—are kept out of this. They haven't been involved and you know it. Tell LeClaire to keep them clean or there's no deal." Milner looked over at Richard. "And Richard's got a longer memory than mine." Milner reached into his pocket and then handed a piece of paper across the table to Delecroix. "And finally, this is a bank account number and the phone number for a Swiss banker, Mr. Schott. To show your good faith I'll need each of you to send an initial $5 million deposit to this account by tomorrow at noon. I'll be checking. If it's not there, no deal and we blow you guys sky high."

Richard saw Delecroix puff his cheeks out, then blow out air through his lips. Sir Reginald waved his finger.

Done deal. At least as long as Richard held onto the data.

#

The limo came to a stop between two Gulfstreams on the tarmac at Heathrow. "This is where we say goodbye for now," Milner said. "You sure you don't wanna come to Switzerland with me until we do a deal with Croonquist? I'm gonna have Sandy call him first thing in the morning to set it up."

"No. I'll go back to New York, keep up the front with Jack and Mickey." Richard figured he'd take his chances Croonquist didn't haul him in until Sir Reginald and Delecroix got to LeClaire to call the Feds off his back. And Jack to call off whoever had chased Richard in New York.

"Okay. We'll see how things turn out. Whatever happens, it's been a pleasure knowing you, kid. You'll go far."

Richard felt his throat go lumpy. He extended his hand. Milner took it in that great palm of his. "Thanks," Richard said. "I've learned a lot from you."

"I'm glad. And if this was my last deal, not a bad way to go out. We did a pretty good ham-and-egg." He pointed to the G550 on Richard's side of the limo. "That's yours," then pointed out his window, "this one's mine." He opened the door, turned to go. "Oh, I almost forgot." He turned back. "I have a gift for you." He pulled a bag out of his raincoat pocket and handed it to Richard. "I hope someday you get to buy a world-class stereo system." He turned again, opened the door and left. Richard saw him hurry up the steps of a G450. The stairs were pulled up and the door closed within seconds of Milner getting inside. When would he see Milner again?

Richard opened the bag Milner gave him. It contained two boxes with Russian letters on them. He opened one. A 6C33 audio tube was in it. He laughed, then realized tears were falling onto his hands as he put it back in the box.

#

Milner collapsed into a seat on the G450, feeling drained, his lower back stiff. He sighed, loosened his tie, then reached into his breast pocket to feel the digital recorder. He reached with his other hand to hit the intercom button.

"Let's get outta here," he said to the captain.

"Right," he heard back, and the engines started warming up.

He thought of calling Sandy, then realized at this hour he'd still be asleep in New York. Besides, he'd rather call him from a landline from Switzerland. Safer.

He pulled the digital recorder out of his pocket, unhooked the microphone, pulled the microphone wire out from under his lapel and curled it up. He rewound the recorder and hit 'play'. He felt his chest constrict, his arms tense. *Nothing.* He rewound some more, then again. He felt a bolt of shock. There was nothing on the recorder. He tried to stand, as if he could run from the fact, felt himself jam against the seatbelt and plopped down again. *Damn.* The Devon guys said it was possible to jam a digital recorder with sophisticated equipment, no way to assure it was failsafe. *Now what?*

His mind raced through the options he'd considered but dreaded having to pursue. Milner looked out the widow, starting to think it through, then his gaze settling on the other Gulfstream taxiing Richard toward a different runway, toward an uncertain future. He felt a stab of guilt, lowered his eyes.

#

New York City. After he landed in New York, Jack saw Sir Reginald was calling him on his cell phone. *What the hell does the old fart want now?* He answered it.

"I say, old boy, how was your trip?"

"Uneventful. You miss me so soon?"

"Are you familiar with the old expression, 'call off your dogs'?"

"Is there a point here?" Jack's antennae were up.

"Do you remember our two young friends we discussed recently?"

Where was this going? "They're at the top of my mind."

"There've been some developments. I can explain later. I urge you to stand down with your plans for them. It could result in some severe complications for all of us."

"I think I understand."

"I sincerely hope you do, old boy, or it could result in your taking an extended holiday by yourself."

Jeez. He'd have to make a stop in Canarsie before heading back into Manhattan.

#

"Thought for a while there you'd run out on me," Kathy said when Richard walked into their hotel room at the Waldorf, "maybe found a perkier girl." She stood in a tee-shirt and panties in the bedroom doorway, her hand on her hip. Her hair was a mess, eyes puffy from sleep.

All Richard could think was how beautiful she looked. Richard froze there just inside the door of the darkened room, watching the early morning light from the bedroom window play in her hair, on her skin.

"You gonna stand there all day, farm boy?" She smiled.

The smile he'd cross an ocean for. Richard walked over and kissed her. Her breath was musty, but she tasted great. She held onto him tighter than usual. "I have a lot to tell you," he said after a moment.

"Later," she said, pulling him toward the bedroom.

#

"You're clean, young man," Toto said. "I just talked to Jack. Have you seen the news?"

"Yeah," Richard said. He sat on the bed in a hotel bathrobe, Kathy just finishing dressing. He'd seen the announcements. François LeClaire was identified as Source X. He'd turned in ten other Wall Street legal and investment banking professionals, all of whom had been arrested by 10 a.m. that morning. British and French authorities had arrested another four GCG and Schoenfeld & Co. back-office personnel. Harold Milner, who Roman Croonquist, SEC Director, Division of Enforcement, called 'the central figure in this diabolical ring' was nowhere to be found. He was believed to have fled the country. Walker & Company was granted full immunity, was cooperating in the case, and was reported to have been instrumental in convincing Mr. LeClaire to turn himself in.

"Come over," Toto said. "Bring Kathy. Jack and Mickey are on the way. I'll take you all through it when you get here."

Jack and Mickey were already in Toto's office when her assistant ushered Kathy and Richard in. Toto was standing behind her desk, looking like she'd been mugged, but beaming. Richard watched Jack for any signs. He felt a prickly sensation in his spine, tension in his forehead.

Toto said, "Holden was like negotiating with the Russians. He had nothing in the end, though. LeClaire had insisted upon full immunity for all directors, officers, employees and shareholders of Walker, as well as the firm itself. He admitted he was acting on his own, at least at Walker, and in concert with the cast of characters you saw get arrested this morning. And of course, Milner."

"Did he say why he did it?" Jack said.

Richard held his gaze on Jack. *Nothing.*

"Never talked to him. I saw part of his plea bargain agreement, though. They're taking most of LeClaire's assets in escrow for the eventual fines."

"What about the potential for liability for Walker?" Steinberg said.

"I think you're clear. The SEC, the U.S. Attorney's Office, the Manhattan District Attorney's office, are all party to your immunity from criminal prosecution. There may be some civil lawsuits, but since LeClaire was acting on his own and the Feds have exonerated you, they shouldn't cost you too much."

Richard saw Jack shoot Mickey a look, then a theatrical exhale of relief.

Jack winked at Richard, and then Steinberg and he headed for the door. "Thanks again, Karen."

Richard and Kathy stood around until Jack and Steinberg got on the elevators, waited another half hour downstairs in Shearson & Stone's conference center, then left. Richard wondered what came next. Was he just supposed to sit around until Milner called? They decided to go back to the Waldorf.

#

After three days at the Waldorf, Richard knew something was wrong. He turned to Kathy and said, "Still no call from Milner. But that's Jack's second voicemail joking, 'Honeymoon's over, kids. Get back to the office.' Like nothing ever happened."

"When was the last time you tried Milner's cell?"

"This morning. Still no answer."

Kathy said, "I think something went wrong at Milner's end."

"I can't decide if I want that to be true or not."

She read his mind. "After everything you told me about him, he wouldn't double-cross you or run."

"Unless someone had something on him."

"Like what?"

"You saw the news that Mary Claire was missing."

"Yeah, I just figured they both ran after all."

Richard shook his head, thinking.

After a moment Kathy said, "You try Croonquist?"

"I don't have anything new to tell him. I told him last time I'd have this thing locked. And he hasn't called me."

Kathy looked at him for a long moment. She said, "Sounds like we could let it sit where it is. A stalemate with Sir Reginald and Delecroix." She paused. "And Jack and Mickey."

Richard shook his head. "Not with two dead bodies. And Sir Reginald, Delecroix, Jack and Mickey still out there. You know I'm gonna figure out a way to get these guys."

Kathy narrowed her eyes. "Maybe it's better to just leave it. You said yourself Milner and you had Sir Reginald and Delecroix boxed-in with the deal you cut in London, and you still have the data. Even if Milner ran, I can't see anything that would jeopardize the leverage you have on those guys."

"The data's not enough proof without them admitting it all on tape and you know it. And I don't have the tape."

Kathy's eyes were like hot coals. "Just leave it."

#

Richard and Kathy went back to work the next day. Two weeks later Jack transferred Richard into the new debt restructuring department he created at Walker to take advantage of all the bankruptcies from the global financial meltdown. A few days after that, Richard was making coffee for Kathy and he in the kitchen of his apartment before work. He pondered the phone call he'd just hung up from, how Kathy would react.

Kathy walked in, gloomy, dark.

Uh-oh. "Peace. I left my boxing gloves in the bedroom."

She didn't even try to smile. "Like I said last night, did you see the East and West Germans provoking each other in Berlin? They had a stalemate. The worst they did was stare at each other over the barbed-wire on top of the Berlin Wall. You didn't see them poking each other in the eye."

"I told you I'm not provoking anybody."

"Not yet, but if you keep on this crusade to get what you need to go to Croonquist, you risk it. And Jack & Co. are bad guys. If they want a fight, you're playing into their hands." She brushed past him, poured her coffee.

"I'm not playing into anyone's hands. I've been keeping my poise, waiting for an opportunity. And tonight's the night."

Kathy spun from the counter. "Milner finally called?"

"No, Jack. He wants me to join him this evening at his apartment to meet with LeClaire, of all people."

Kathy shot him a wary look.

Richard looked back, stood his ground, "Jack wants to hire LeClaire as a consultant to our new debt restructuring department, until LeClaire's done testifying at all the trials and gets sentenced. And he wants me to help convince LeClaire to do it."

"What are you, eight years old? It's some kind of setup. He'll probably try to kill you."

"In his apartment?"

"An accident on the way, or leaving."

His back stiffened and his neck went cold. "If he was gonna do that he'd have already tried. Whether you like it or not, I'm going to Jack's tonight." Richard pulled his Dictaphone out of his breast pocket. "Two weeks with no word from Milner. This is my shot to make it happen on my own. Maybe get Jack on tape gloating about beating the Feds."

"Oh, so you're *nine* years old. You're going in there with some dumb-ass Dictaphone? They jammed Milner's wire last time. You think Jack's that stupid?"

"I think he's that cock-sure he's untouchable. Besides, Milner's wire was digital, easy to jam with state-of-art equipment. This is a low-tech analog tape recorder. He couldn't jam it if he tried."

"Stop it!" she yelled.

"I'm going."

Kathy turned and stormed out of the apartment.

Kathy was still fuming, muttering to herself when she got downstairs. She walked stiff-legged around the plaza outside Richard's apartment building, the muscles in her legs tense. Her palms hurt where she dug her nails into them from balling her hands into fists. After a lap around the plaza she stopped. She felt a moan working its way up from her chest. Tears flushed into her eyes. Now she remembered another time on this plaza, after she'd retrieved Richard's clothes and the mole's data from his apartment, and then spotted the man from the U.S. Attorney's Office tailing her. A wave of that same panic hit her. Then she was scared for herself as well as Richard. Now her nerves were on fire, petrified for him.

Stubborn ass. But he was her man. She turned and strode back into the building.

Richard sat at the kitchen table, sipping his coffee, waiting for his emotions and his pulse to come down a few notches. *Dammit, she can be impossible.* Sure, it's risky, but what the hell else did she expect him to do? If he got what he needed tonight, he could take it to Croonquist, nail the bastards so Kathy and he could sleep easy for good.

His pulse was still thumping in his ears when Kathy burst through the door and walked into the kitchen, head lowered, looking all business.

Ding. Round two.

"Alright," she said, cruising up to him, her eyes fierce. She grabbed the Dictaphone from the table. "These tapes only have 30 minutes per side." He watched her rewind the tape, turn it over to the other side, reinsert it and hit the "record" button. A second later the Dictaphone emitted a high-pitched wail. "And they scream like a banshee to let you know when it's run out." She slapped the Dictaphone back down, leaned forward with her palms on the table and stared at him. "That'd kind of put a damper on your evening, babe." Her eyes softened then.

Richard smiled. "I'll be okay," he said. He stood up and started to move toward her.

She held up her hand, backed up. "Wait." She reached into her briefcase, fished for something and pulled out a watch. "My sports watch has a stopwatch that counts down. Set it for 30 minutes and keep an eye on it. It's better than nothing if you're going in there without a wingman."

Richard felt warmth in his chest. He took the watch, put it on. "Yeah, but you've got my back." He put his arms around her and kissed her. "Thanks, and don't worry."

Kathy didn't look convinced. "Be careful," she said, "Jack's nobody to mess with." Her eyes were urgent, moist. She took his arm, pulled it in front of her and pressed his hand to her breast. "Now put your hands on me," she breathed, "make love to me."

#

"You guys are friends, aren't you?" Jack said to Richard. Hearing it pissed Richard off. They were in Jack's apartment across from the Carlyle, waiting for LeClaire to show up. Richard was awkward with Jack, but figured that was nothing compared to how he'd feel once LeClaire showed up.

LeClaire arrived about fifteen minutes late at 6:45 p.m. "Sorry to be late. François LeClaire," he said, shaking Richard's hand. Richard's puzzled look must have made LeClaire remember himself and he showed warmth in his eyes. Richard thought to try to let his face go blank, then realized it had.

"Hello, Richard, how are you, my friend?"

"Good," Richard said. He felt that odd sensation of seeing the girlfriend he'd just broken up with on the street. Like he could reach out and touch her as intimately as he had a week earlier, but now he was wearing fireproof gloves.

"Hi, Jack," LeClaire called, waving, "sorry to be late." He walked over and shook hands.

Richard reached into his breast pocket and switched on the Dictaphone, then pressed the button to start the stopwatch countdown from 30 minutes.

Jack poured himself an Evian and Richard a red wine. LeClaire elected grapefruit juice. He settled into the sofa.

LeClaire wore tennis sneakers, khakis and a polo shirt. He took off sunglasses as he sat down. He'd lost about ten pounds, gotten suntanned. Richard wondered if LeClaire lost the weight from stress, realized he was thinking LeClaire deserved to. Jack looked at LeClaire as if to say, "Well . . ."

"I am sorry I was late," LeClaire said again, "but I had a small crisis to take care of back at home. The pump broke down on the artesian well and Elaine and the kids are there without water. I was trying to arrange for a plumber over the phone and it was not easy." He smiled. "The joys of living in a little developed area in Florida," he said.

"You bought a house down there, didn't you?" asked Jack.

"Yes, a small town called Melba Beach, north of Naples on the West Coast. We are in a beautiful spot right on the Gulf. We bought about ten of the last fifteen Gulf-front lots left."

"You own ten lots on the Gulf?" Richard asked. *Damn.* So much for getting skinned by the Feds.

"Yes," he said. "We wanted as much privacy as we could get. I took all the proceeds from the sale of my Walker stock and the New York townhouse and bought as much property as I could just before the government removed my cover."

Quite a setup. *Am I missing something?* It seemed like the Feds were making it too easy on LeClaire. Richard started trying to do the math in his head, but didn't know where to start.

LeClaire went on, "I had to invest as quickly as I could. In Florida they are not allowed to take your house. So even if my creditors get judgments against me that go beyond the five million dollars I deposited with the SEC with my fine, Elaine and the kids will still have a roof over their heads."

Five million. How much was from his insider trading?

"The five million is for settlement of my fine and on any civil judgments against me. The criminal charges, of course, are different." His voice grew hushed as he said 'criminal.' Until then he was the precise, objective investment banker LeClaire, talking about the transactions on his house, segregating assets from his creditors like he was outlining strategy for an M&A assignment. Now he seemed to deflate. Richard thought of Elaine for the first time, how she'd hugged him as Kathy and he were leaving after dinner at their townhouse the last time he saw them as a couple.

Richard glanced at his stopwatch: only 13:45 left. *Shit.* And he'd gotten nothing so far.

"I made one horrible mistake and that was it," LeClaire blurted out, his eyes focused off into space. He was again the awkward stranger at the door. "And that was it," he said. "And that was it." He held his arms outstretched. "It was just a question of a few young people making a lot of money too quickly." He breathed heavily, his voice strained. Richard realized that a knot had formed in his own throat some time earlier. LeClaire paused and looked at his glass for about a minute.

"I am merely trying to set up some kind of an arrangement to shelter Elaine and the kids, and to take care of my legal bills. I have been asked to do some consulting for others through my law firm to act as an offset to an hourly charge for my attorney's fees." He looked up at Jack, "And I really cannot anticipate beyond that how I am going to do anything to take care of Elaine and the kids while I am away. I am also not sure how long I will be away. I do not know what I am going to say to my five year old," he said and looked at the floor.

Richard said, "You can explain it to her when she's a little bit older. And by that time the whole thing will probably have blown over." He was angry at himself for being sympathetic. But it was hard to think about LeClaire's kids, watch LeClaire's anguish without reacting.

"I am not talking about when I get back, I am talking about when they put me away. What do I say to Cynthia about why I am going away for maybe a year or two?" Panic now in his eyes.

Richard looked away, not wanting to feel his throat burning.

"When are you gonna be sentenced, François?" Jack said.

"Not until the trials against the others in the ring are over. Until then, I am in a holding pattern."

"What about your contacts?" Jack asked. "Are they gonna be at all useful to you or to us?"

"No. Part of my cooperation is that I would not contact any of my former clients."

Jack had been swirling his glass the last minute or so. Richard could see he was thinking about something.

They all paused.

Jack said, "We'd like to work out how to have our new restructuring department use you as a consultant, François. How would we arrange things?"

"I would prefer that you pay my law firm directly, billed on an hourly basis for my services which they would directly offset against my legal fees."

"What do you think about that, Richard?" Jack asked.

"I don't like it. It might be perceived after the fact that the firm was trying to hide something," Richard said. "It would be better if it paid you directly."

"That would be acceptable to me. I was just thinking of you . . . and how it might look." They all fell silent again.

LeClaire slouched on the sofa now, sipping his grapefruit juice. He looked around, seemed to sense there wasn't anything else to discuss. He sighed. "Okay, thanks," he said. LeClaire stood to leave, picked up a plain manila envelope he'd brought.

"Nice briefcase," Richard said, trying to smile.

"Well, I am trying to stay relatively incognito," LeClaire said, holding his arms out and looking down at his khakis. "I figured that if I dress like a tennis pro instead of wearing a suit that no one will recognize me. It has not always worked. A banker-looking type came up to me in a restaurant in Florida the other day and asked me if I was François LeClaire. I told him yes because I could not think of what else to say. He shook my hand and complimented me for some of the things I had done professionally prior to my going down. It is nice to talk to somebody," he said looking at them from across the coffee table, like he was reluctant to step out from behind it and move toward the door. "I really do not get to talk to too many people anymore." They all shook hands and he put on his sunglasses again as he walked through the door to leave.

"Wow, what a mess," Richard said after LeClaire closed the door. Jack just looked at him, then turned to the bar.

"Don't be a sap," Jack said with his back turned.

"What do you mean?" Richard stepped closer, butterflies now in his stomach. He checked his stopwatch: 7:35 left.

"Don't feel too sorry for him. He's got great bullshit, and he's playing it up to his eyeballs. Although it's obvious he's not pretending to be a complete wreck; that part is sure as hell real. But 'one mistake'? Ridiculous. One mistake, my ass." He paused and turned to face Richard again. "Don't let yourself get sucked in. Sir Reginald and Delecroix paid him well for what he did. He'll have a stash the Feds and creditors won't know about waiting for him in France when he gets out."

"You and Mickey were in on the whole thing, weren't you?"

Jack didn't respond but the corners of his mouth showed a hint of that golden boy smirk. Then his face got hard.

"In on it? We dreamed it up years ago, and pitched it to Sir Reginald and Delecroix when they invested in Walker. With their capital we made it into Walker's biggest profit center."

Strung me and everybody else along the whole time. Richard wanted to tell Jack what he thought of him, but didn't want to interrupt him if he was gonna keep talking. He felt his blood pumping in his temples.

"Remember me telling you about skiing? None of us knew the route or how it would turn out. We just saw far enough ahead to react to each gate one at a time. And don't look so scandalized. We aren't plotting, methodical crooks, just guys with college tuitions to pay, cars to buy and wives who like nice stuff. We're no different than anybody else. Everybody cuts corners; we're just playing with more chips."

Now Richard felt an odd knot in his stomach. His face felt brittle, tense. He said, "That's not how everybody operates."

"Don't give me that self-righteous, wounded puppy look. You're a big boy now. I heard from Sir Reginald you were a tough infighter teamed with Milner over there in London, cutting your deal to negotiate your way out of the trading scam. You're one of us, whether you like it or not, and you're good at it. There's nothing to be ashamed about that you've got the balls to fight bare-knuckles when you have to. And you know what, you're right about LeClaire, we can't use him. He's shot." He clinked an ice cube into his glass, as if to underscore his words.

Richard turned to the windows and stood looking out over Madison Avenue, down at the Carlyle. He reflected on the past months, on Jack, Steinberg, Cole, LeClaire, Sir Reginald and Delecroix, spending his career among guys like them. Some masters of high finance; they couldn't see beyond their next deal and didn't give a damn what they had to do to get it done. No wonder the whole financial system had almost melted down. And high tolerance for ambiguity or not, they were a rotten bunch. He glanced at his stopwatch: 5:16. *Push him.* He turned to Jack and said, "What did you guys do to Milner?"

Jack said, "Milner's a cagey bastard, but don't count on him. We blew his scam. The wire he was wearing lit up Sir Reginald's sniffer equipment the instant you guys walked into their office. His tech boys jammed it."

Richard felt his face flush, his jaw tense. So that's why he hadn't heard from Milner.

He turned to the window again. He checked his pocket for the Dictaphone, felt the vibration of it still running. Then out the window he noticed LeClaire walk along 76th Street, cross and then head up Madison. Richard's throat ached and his eyes got moist. He felt like something irretrievable of his own was vanishing with LeClaire as he continued up Madison.

Richard caught himself, remembering the tape. *Shit.* He turned from the window to Jack, who was looking at Richard as if he expected him to respond to their last exchange. *Get on with it,* he thought, and moved closer to Jack.

Jack smirked. "Don't wait for Milner; he's staying lost in Europe. No tape, no deal with the Feds. You're safe as long as you hang onto your data. But don't forget where you hid it, or you might wind up like Chuck White or Ken Stern."

Rage surged in Richard's veins; he got ready to lunge at Jack. Jack sensed it, stepped back.

"You killed them, didn't you?"

Jack smirked more broadly and leaned in toward Richard. "Yeah, we did what we had to do. Just don't lose your cool. Keep the balance of power. A standoff. And get used to it. That's how it works on Wall Street. Allies on one deal, enemies the next. I got something on you, you got something on me. Like the Cold War Russians and the U.S. military: mutually assured destruction."

Richard was resisting the urge to come at Jack and punch him. He knew he was almost out of tape, anticipated the squeal of the Dictaphone, but he wanted to get more, so he leaned in closer to Jack, sneering.

Jack said, "Oh, yeah, Mr. Tough Guy. You fuck with me and I'll fuck you up, big time. Wonder why Milner folded? No doubt you saw that Mary Claire disappeared. Yeah, she's with Milner now, but not initially. We disappeared her. She was our ultimate leverage over the big guy to keep him quiet. He agreed in a heartbeat once we told him we had her. And now he knows we can get to her anytime we want. He gets cute and turns us in, we take out Mary Claire. See? Mutually assured destruction."

Richard didn't want to answer. *Keep him talking.* He felt perspiration on his upper lip.

"Keep Kathy close, Tiger. And keep quiet. Then nobody gets . . ."

The Dictaphone screamed as the tape ran out. Richard felt a blast of adrenaline. He saw Jack's head rear back in surprise, then his eyes narrow and a scowl form on his lips.

"You little punk," he said and lunged at Richard.

Richard dodged him, but Jack spun and landed a punch on Richard's temple. Richard saw black things like insects swimming in his vision and went down, felt Jack clawing at his pocket for the Dictaphone. He scrambled to his feet and leaned backward to avoid a wild right and left from Jack, then stepped into him and landed a right uppercut square on Jack's chin. His hand exploded in pain like he'd punched a block of granite, but he saw Jack collapse over an ottoman. Now he saw him moving, shaking his head as if trying to clear it. Richard turned and ran for the door. He dashed down the stairs, panting, feeling his chest heaving. At the last flight he started to feel a swell of victory. *Almost there.*

As he burst through the door into the lobby he ran into four men in suits. He tried to rush past when one of them said, "That's Blum," and two others grabbed Richard's arms. Anger, then desperation washed through him. The men pulled his hands behind his back and Richard felt cold steel on his wrists, knew they were handcuffing him. They spun him around.

"U.S. Attorney's office, and just shut it, Blum," the first guy said as Richard opened his mouth to speak. "I don't want to hear it." He pulled out his cell phone, punched some keys and pointed toward the lobby door. The two men who cuffed him moved Richard toward the door. "We got Blum," Richard heard the guy say. "We're going up for Grass now." Richard could feel the weight of the Dictaphone in his pocket. His thoughts raced. He had enough on tape to nail Jack and the others. Then he felt a flash of panic. But what did these guys have on him?

#

In the interrogation room downtown at 75 Centre Street, Croonquist waited for his cell phone to ring a second time.

"Okay, we got Grass," Johnson said to him.

"All right," Croonquist said. "See you shortly." He hung up and turned to the big man seated on the other side of the table. "They're bringing them both in," Croonquist said to him.

Milner nodded back.

#

The agents brought Richard downtown in an unmarked Lincoln Town Car. They walked him into 75 Centre Street and up to the fifth floor. He felt his stomach tighten as he saw Charles Holden standing in the hallway smiling at him. They walked Richard into a room. A surge of surprise hit him: Milner sat there with Roman Croonquist.

Croonquist stood and nodded to someone behind Richard, who uncuffed him. "Sorry about that, but the field agents have their procedures," Croonquist said.

Richard was too stunned to answer. He saw Milner wink at him. "I don't understand," Richard said.

Milner said, "Sorry I didn't call, but they said this was a better way. I agreed."

Croonquist said, "Harold came in to talk, with no promises." He looked over at Milner, then back at Richard. "But it all checked out. So we set it up and waited until we got what we needed. We figured we could count on you."

Richard's mind was catching up. He felt for the Dictaphone in his pocket, pulled it out. Croonquist shook his head and stood up. "Follow me," he said. He led Richard and Milner down the hall to another room where Jack sat across the table from Holden. Holden shook his head at Croonquist. Richard studied Jack's face: sneering like Jimmy Cagney.

Croonquist said, "Mr. Grass, here's what you're up against. We were across the street from your apartment with a laser mike. We got your entire conversation with Richard on tape."

Richard continued to observe Jack. Now no hint of a sneer.

Croonquist said, "Harold Milner is prepared to testify against you, as I assume is . . ."

Richard said, "I am, too, and I got my own tape, in case their wiretap doesn't hold up," and he held up his Dictaphone, "and I did some research. It's my personal conversation, which I can record anytime, anywhere I want. Perfectly legally, with no wiretap authorization required." He was still watching Jack's face, now frozen like a death mask.

Croonquist said, "We don't need your cooperation in our prosecution of Reginald Schoenfeld, Philippe Delecroix and Mickey Steinberg, so don't bother to offer it." He sat down next to Holden and looked Jack in the eye across the table. "Now about the threats you made against Mary Claire Milner and Karina Cella. Mutually assured destruction. Not a bad term for the situation," Croonquist said. "You and your cronies will all go away for securities violations, and eventually, I presume, you'll get out. But there's no statute of limitations on murder, or kidnapping, and we've got enough to convict you all. We'll hold those charges over you indefinitely. You try anything, we'll charge you in federal court, which has the death penalty. Even if you don't get the chair, you'll never get out of jail. I assume you aren't stupid enough to risk that."

Richard couldn't help smiling as he watched Jack, whose upper lip and forehead now showed beads of perspiration. His eyes were wide. *A cornered animal.* No, caged like he belonged. "I need to call Kathy," Richard said and stepped out.

#

London, England. Milner rode the elevator at Schoenfeld & Co.'s offices in St. James Square with the two guys who escorted him there. A single U.S. Attorney's Office agent sat in the car outside. Holden insisted on the chaperone from his office, even though he saw little flight risk, given the $225 million Milner had put into escrow for the $25 million fine he'd agreed to, plus disgorgement of the $200 million the Walker ring paid him.

Once upstairs, Milner entered the dining room, where Schoenfeld and Delecroix, looking annoyed, were seated at a table set for three. Milner said, "I hope you don't mind I brought a couple of friends." The two guys walked past Milner toward Schoenfeld and Delecroix.

"Scotland Yard," one of them said. They cuffed them both. Milner watched Schoenfeld's and Delecroix's faces. He smiled at the surprise, then the anger in their eyes, thinking of Chuck White. His next thought was about getting home to New York in time for dinner with Mary Claire. This thing was over with; he didn't care about the money, the two years of community service, or the slashing he was taking in the press. Because even if the Feds or the public didn't accept the concept, Mary Claire believed in redemption.

#

New York City. Richard unpacked his boxes in his new office on his first day of work for Milner. His office was on the east side of the main floor, directly across from where Milner's stereo was set up: Chuck's White's old office. Stephanie had placed a vase of lilies with a note from Milner on his credenza; the fragrance was one he knew he would always associate with this day. He also didn't think it was an accident that Mozart's Clarinet Concerto in A was playing on the stereo when Richard arrived. It was supposed to be like this.

The phone rang: Kathy. He knew that morning she planned to walk into George Cole's office to resign. She was considering her next move; she'd already interviewed for a job at Morgan Stanley, but was also talking to some HBS classmates about starting a satire magazine.

"How are you settling in, babe?"

"Great."

"I'm free for dinner at a normal hour if you're not working late. Either way I'm looking forward to kicking your ass at squash tonight." She laughed. "I love you."

Milner knocked and walked in just as they hung up. "Welcome aboard." He crossed the room and shook with Richard, enveloping his hand in that meaty paw.

"Thanks, Harold." Richard remembered meeting Milner for the first time in Walker's reception area, how awed he'd been by him. Richard couldn't get over thinking how much more impressive Milner was after getting to know him, especially in the last weeks. He was going to learn a lot from this man.

"I've got a deal I'd like you to look at," Milner said, and handed him a one-page spreadsheet. "When I get off my conference call, you can tell me what you think of it. You'll love it. It's a high-and stereo equipment company. Tiny, but it's got great growth potential."

Richard watched Milner turn and leave, then took in the expanse of midtown Manhattan through the clear glass that formed the entire north wall of Milner's offices. He looked uptown at the skyscrapers extending into the distance up Park Avenue and smiled.

The End

VACCINE NATION

A THRILLER BY

DAVID LENDER

CHAPTER 1

Dani North walked down West End Avenue toward the Mercer School, her son Gabe at her side. The air was cold and fresh. Minutes earlier, crossing Broadway, she'd seen the tulips on the median just beginning to bloom, and the leaves on the trees ready to pop. Now, scents of spring—wet earth and hyacinths in window boxes—were apparent. She yawned, bone tired from the hectic weeks of the Tribeca Film Festival wearing her down on top of work and the daily routine of single-parenting a pre-teen. Tired or not, she was on a high and Gabe walked close enough that she thought to take his hand. *That is, if he'd let me.* She reminded herself it was perfectly normal for a nine-year-old not to want his mom to hold his hand anymore. *Normal.* What would those morons at Division of Youth and Family Services in New Jersey say about that? Probably still call him ADHD and drug him up. She'd love to run DYFS into the ground, along with their partners in crime, the pharmaceutical industry. Legalized drug pushers.

Leave it, she told herself. Channel the anger into something productive. That made her smile. She had, and well. It was starting to feel real that *The Drugging of Our Children*, her latest film, had won best documentary at Tribeca last night. That channeled anger was doing some good, getting the word out. Educating parents about their choices, ones she hadn't been aware of for Gabe. Who knew? If she had, she might never have lost that three-year nightmare of lawsuits with DYFS in Hackensack. It forced her to accept mandatory drugging of Gabe, because otherwise the court would have taken him from her.

She looked over at Gabe now. Chin high, proud of how he looked in his Ralph Lauren blue blazer, grey pants and white oxford button-down, school tie snugged up against his neck. Only his black Vans betrayed his age. *Yes, normal.* Thanks in part to Dr. O.

Gabe caught her looking at him. "Now that you won, you gonna get a bonus and turn the electric back on?"

"You mean 'going to' and 'electricity'." She thought about the last two weeks of burning candles at night instead of the lights. She'd put off the electric bill in order to scrape up Gabe's tuition for this semester at Mercer. "Besides, we were camping, remember?"

"C'mon, mom, that worked on me when I was five years old. I'm not a kid anymore."

"Yes you are."

Gabe thought for a second. "All right, but I'm not stupid."

"No, I'm not getting a bonus," Dani said, running a hand over Gabe's hair, "but I get paid today and we'll be back to normal. Lights and TV."

"Next time I'm telling Nanny. She'll pay it."

"Do that and you can forget about TV until you're eighteen."

They reached the corner diagonally across West End from the entrance to Mercer. "Leave me here," Gabe said, looking away from her.

Dani didn't respond, just grabbed his shirt sleeve between her fingers and started across the street. He pulled out of her grasp and increased his pace. Dani saw Damien Richardson on the opposite corner as they approached. He stood looking at the half dozen kids grouped around the entrance to Mercer, tentative. She knew the bigger boys picked on Damien. "Morning, Damien," she called.

Damien turned to them. His face brightened and he smiled. "Morning, Mrs. North. What's up Gabe?"

"Come on, Damien," Dani whispered when she reached him. "I'll walk you in."

Ten minutes later she crossed 79th Street toward Broadway, her mind buzzing with last night's triumph and her upcoming day. She pulled her BlackBerry out of her pocket, checked the screen. *8:25.* Enough time to get through her voicemails and emails before Dr. Maguire, the researcher from Pharma International, showed up. Now she wondered again what his agenda was, why he was so anxious and secretive about the meeting. But it was something important—at least to Maguire. She'd been calling him for weeks, coaxing him into an interview for the new documentary on autism she was just beginning. She'd been referred to Maguire by his friend, John McCloskey, the KellerDorne Pharmaceutical technician who'd served as whistleblower on KellerDorne's painkiller, Myriad, after patients who took it started dropping dead from heart attacks. Dani's interview of McCloskey published in the Crusador was well after McCloskey went public, but somehow it managed to electrify the issue. As a result, the contributions had flowed into Dr. Orlovski to fund the documentaries he produced, including Dani's *The Drugging of Our Children.*

Maybe Maguire needed to get something off his chest, too. Dani picked up her pace. Her BlackBerry rang and her breath caught in her throat when she saw Mom's number on the screen. How could she forget? *Dad.*

"Hi, Mom. How are you doing?"

"Okay." She paused. "You know what day it is, don't you?"

Dani's mind automatically did the math. She'd been twenty-two. Seven years. "Of course." She stopped walking and leaned over the BlackBerry as if sheltering her words from passersby. She said, "Each year I think about him constantly during this day. Sometimes it seems like . . ." her voice trailed off.

"I miss him more each year, too," Mom said. Her voice was steady, like she'd steeled herself to get through the day.

"When's his Mass?"

"One o'clock."

Dani didn't respond right away. "I can't make it this year."

"I know, sweetie. I just wanted to hear your voice. I knew you weren't coming. You had a big day yesterday. I'm sure lots of people want to talk to you."

"It's not that. I'm just jammed with the usual stuff. Will you light a candle for me?"

"Sure. I'll speak to you later. Gabe okay?"

"He's great. Maybe we'll get out this weekend. How's Jack?"

"The same." Dani felt her hand muscles tense around the BlackBerry.

"Anything going on?"

"The usual. He was out most of the night, couldn't get up for work."

"I'll get out there this weekend," Dani said, feeling guilty. They signed off.

Dani reached the entrance to Dr. Yuri Orlovski's office at 79th and Broadway. A half-dozen patients already sat in Dr. O's waiting room when she stepped through the door. She paused to wave at Carla behind the reception desk, who mouthed "congratulations." Dani nodded and smiled, then headed up the steep, 20 steps to her office. By the time she reached the top, she reflected as she usually did, "What would I do without Dr. O?" It was the best job she'd ever had, even aside from him rescuing Gabe a year ago from Child Protective Services, New York's equivalent of New Jersey's DYFS. Dr. O's homeopathic remedies and detoxification had purged Gabe's body of the mercury and other poisons that Dr. O maintained were largely caused by vaccines. And his certification as an M.D. that Gabe's ADHD was "cured" got Gabe off Child Protective Services' list and off mandatory ADHD medications to attend public school. This year she'd scrounged up enough to afford to get him into Mercer.

And now she ran the non-medical practice side of Dr. O's mini-empire, as he jokingly called it. But it was no joke. It was a flourishing internet business of whole food based vitamins; health-related DVDs and books; and healthy lifestyle products like juicers and water filters. And a good portion of the profits funded Dr. O's real passion: documentaries on health issues, the thing—

except, of course for Gabe—that got Dani out of bed every morning.

Her colleagues, Richard Kaminsky, Ralph Waite and Roger Weinstein stood talking near the entrance to Dr. O's Vitamin Shop when Dani got to the top of the steps. Richard started applauding and the others joined in. She stood, cringing inside from embarrassment, yet secretly relishing the recognition, as they walked over and greeted her with hugs.

"I knew you'd do it," Richard said.

"Absolutely," Ralph said.

They were joined by a half-dozen others, including Nancy Drake, her editor. Dani allowed herself to enjoy it, but was gradually overcome by an odd sensation of discomfort as she recalled how she'd wilted under the spotlight when asked to say a few words while accepting her award last night. It made her feel as if her colleagues would think she was unworthy of their praise if they'd seen her frozen with panic, unable to utter more than "Thank you," in front of 2,000 people.

It took Dani another ten minutes to reach her desk. She booted up her computer and started going through her voicemails. One was from James, at first congratulating her, next a little pathetic and finally lecturing her about not throwing away five years. As she neared the end of her voicemails she heard his voice again, and feeling nothing at all—rather than angry or impatient— deleted the message without listening to it. That one probably hammered at James' constant theme: commitment. After she finished reviewing her emails she checked the time—8:58—then sat back in her chair to wait for Dr. Maguire.

#

Stevens waited while his partner, Turnbull, double-parked their police black-and-white in front of the doc's office.

"Don't be long, Alice," Turnbull said.

"How come I gotta listen to your shit every time I go to buy my vitamins?"

"And don't catch a wittle cold while you're there, girlie-man."

Stevens opened the door. "I need five minutes, asshole."

"Five more minutes for the crooks to prey on our harmless citizens."

Stevens stepped out of the car, looked back at Turnbull and said, "Less time than it takes you to feed greasy fries and cholesterol to your fat ass at Burger Heaven." He slammed the car door and headed toward Dr. Orlovski's. At the top of the steep stairway he turned right and got in line behind three other customers at the Dutch door, open at the top, that served as the sales window for the Vitamin Shop.

#

Hunter Stark sat behind the wheel of a Ford Taurus across the street from Dr. Orlovski's office, a spot he'd staked out at 6:30 a.m. to make sure he was positioned properly. He rubbed his hands, admiring his custom-made nappa lambskin gloves. They were an essential element of his professional toolkit, as important as his Ruger; form-fitting and almost like wearing nothing at all. At $1,000 a pair from Dominic Pierotucci's shop in Genoa, they were a bargain.

Stark's gaze scanned the street in front of Dr. Orlovski's office. He was tense. These jobs were tough enough in a low-risk environment, but this last-minute bullshit didn't allow for any planning, choice of site or operational subtlety. But figuring out things like this and taking the risk were why he got paid the big bucks.

The girl had entered about 8:30, and now he checked his watch again—just before nine—as he saw a cop car pull up. One of the uniforms got out and walked through Orlovski's front door. *Not good.* It would be a complication if Maguire showed up with the cop in there.

He felt one of those odd pains he got behind his eyes when things were about to go wrong, because less than a minute after the cop went in, he saw a guy that matched Maguire's description on the corner of 79th Street. Stark glanced down at the picture he held in his lap. Maguire, no question about it. Shit, they told him the man was big, but he must be 6'5", shoulders like an ox. A guy who looked like he could take right lead from Muhammad Ali and keep coming. Maguire walked with his head tilted down at the sidewalk, hands in his pockets, real purpose in his stride, moving fast.

Stark felt adrenaline surge through him. *Off your ass. Double-time. Move, move, move.* He threw open the car door and headed across the street, matching Maguire's pace, then faster. He unzipped his jacket as he passed the police cruiser, slipped his right hand inside and grabbed the handle of his knife, just underneath his Ruger in its chest holster. By the time Maguire reached the door Stark was only a few strides behind him. Stark now felt the familiar thud of his pulse in his ears, dryness in his mouth, his jaw clenching involuntarily.

When Stark got inside Maguire was on the third step, his feet pounding like he was Frankenstein. Stark glanced up to the top of the steps just as he reached Maguire. *Nobody there.* He swung out the knife and plunged in a clean stab all the way to the hilt in Maguire's kidney.

Maguire let out a howl like a bull mastiff and grabbed his back. Stark pulled the knife out for another stab, saw blood on the blade and felt the rush. Maguire then spun to face Stark, just as they always did, so Stark could go for the kill gore just below the solar plexus. But the guy was big and strong. Too late, Stark saw the left hook coming toward his head. The knife hit bone just as Maguire's fist caught Stark on the chin. The lights went out for what must've been only a fraction of a second because Stark found himself grabbing the banister, his back against the wall but still on his feet as Maguire thundered up the steps again. Stark righted himself and started after him, shoving the knife back in its holster, grabbing the Ruger with its silencer attached and sliding it out of his jacket. By the time Maguire got to the top of the stairs and turned left Stark was only about six steps below him.

Stevens heard someone crashing up the steps like a buffalo, a yell like a wounded animal, then some scuffling and what must've been a couple of guys running up the stairs. He turned and saw one guy get to the top, duck into the first office and lean against a woman standing there, then push her aside. Then another guy came up the stairs with—holy shit!—a Dirty Harry-sized piece with a silencer on it. On instinct, Stevens flipped open his holster and grabbed his service revolver. As he did, the guy with the gun reached up and—thunk—put a round square in the big guy's back, and the big guy went down like a tree right in front of the woman. Stevens now held his Smith & Wesson in both hands, crouched in firing position as the guy with the gun bent down and started reaching into the big guy's pocket.

No clear shot. The woman was in the way. "Freeze!" Stevens yelled.

The guy with the gun glanced back, flicked his wrist and pulled off a round without even seeming to move. Stevens felt his left hip explode in pain and found himself on his back, looking upside down at the guy, who now turned and pointed the piece at him. Stevens' arm was outstretched. He fired a crazy round over the guy's head and when the guy ducked Stevens rolled onto his stomach, aimed and squeezed the trigger one, two, three, four times as the guy dived down the stairway and out of sight. Stevens dropped his head to the floor and everything went black.

Stark skidded to a stop about a quarter of the way down the stairway, got up and bounded down the rest of the steps and out the door. He held the Ruger at his side as he turned down Broadway, seeing the other cop still sitting in his squad car. How the hell hadn't he heard the shots? *The guy must be deaf.* Stark turned to look into a store window to conceal his movements as he slid the Ruger back into its holster. Then he zipped up his jacket and started toward 79th Street again. He'd leave the Taurus across the street. Leaving Maguire's picture in it was dumb, but who cared? The cops would know it was a hit anyhow. Stark's heart was still thudding against his chest when he reached 72nd Street and hailed a cab. Inside, he pulled out a handkerchief and wiped Maguire's blood off his gloves. A clean kill on Maguire, no question. But the client would be pissed he hadn't been able to check Maguire's pockets, even see if Maguire had handed anything off to the girl. And she'd gotten a good look at him. He'd have to circle back on that. And the cop was unfortunate. If he lived he might be able to ID him, too. And if he didn't live, well, that was unnecessary heat that might send him underground and out of work for a while, at least in the States. Overall, messy. Not a good day's work.

#

Dani didn't think it was possible to choke on air, but that's how she felt. She gasped for breath and she knew air was flowing in, but somehow it seemed to be suffocating her. She stood in front of her desk. Her knees were weak and she slumped backward, supporting herself with her hands behind her on her desk. Her ears rang from those awful shots, and she felt sick to her stomach from the smells in the room—blood mixed with gunpowder. She stared down at the man lying at her feet. He must be Dr. Maguire; he'd arrived right at nine o'clock, their scheduled time. She looked across the hall and now saw two people bent over the cop, who wasn't moving. That must have snapped her out of it because now she knelt down and put two fingers on Maguire's neck to check his pulse. *Nothing.* As she did so she realized she clutched a USB memory stick in her palm, and now remembered Maguire had thrust it there before he shoved her away. She slipped it into her blazer pocket.

She heard sirens and a moment later a single uniformed cop ran up the stairs, glanced at Maguire, and then went in to tend to the other cop. By the time the paramedics arrived, Dani's stomach was beginning to settle. She wanted to go back behind her desk and sit down, but was still afraid to move. Just as the paramedics were taking the wounded cop away, two men in suits appeared at the top of the stairs. They spoke to the cop for a few moments, then came over to Dani's office. The short one bent over and started going through Maguire's pockets. The one who approached Dani was taller and skinnier, with watery eyes.

"I'm Agent Wilson. FBI." He flipped open a wallet-sized case and showed her a badge.

Dani felt her mouth move but no sound came out. She realized she was clutching the desk behind her as hard as she could with both hands.

"Tell us what happened," Wilson said.

Dani cleared her throat. "I was waiting in my office for my appointment with Dr. Maguire when I heard a commotion on the stairs and then he ran in. His face was white and he was bleeding. He grabbed me and then pushed me away just as—" Dani heard the tremor in her voice, realized she was spewing words and took a deep breath to slow herself down, "—another man came in with a gun and shot him in the back." Hearing herself say it made the horror of it come back to her. *My God.* She'd actually seen a man murdered right in front of her. She took a few more breaths.

Wilson didn't nod or show any reaction, just stood looking at her through those watery eyes.

Dani went on. "Then the man bent over and started poking around in Dr. Maguire's pockets. At that point someone yelled 'freeze' or something from across the hall, and I looked up to see a policeman with his gun outstretched, and then the policeman went down when the man shot him and I dove under my desk and heard three or four more shots. When I looked up the man with the gun was gone and the policeman was laying face down."

Wilson still didn't say anything. He seemed to be waiting for Dani to go on. After a moment when she didn't, he said, "You said Dr. Maguire. Do you know him?"

"No, but we had an appointment, and I've been talking to him on the phone for some time to set up a meeting."

"You sure it's him?"

Dani paused. Actually, she wasn't. "I assume it's him."

The man looked down at Dani's hands.

"How'd you get blood on you?" Dani looked down at her hands and noticed they were bloody. Her blazer, too. "I told you. The man grabbed me and almost fell over on me, then shoved me aside."

"You just called him 'the man', not 'Dr. Maguire'." Wilson said, still observing her with no expression, just those watery eyes.

"I already told you, I assume it was Dr. Maguire."

"Listen, we need you to cooperate."

Huh? Now Dani leaned forward toward the man, annoyed, felt her fingernails scraping the underside of the desk behind her. "What's that supposed to mean?"

The short man finished going through Maguire's pockets. He looked up at Wilson and shook his head. "He's got a knife wound in his back," the short man said.

Wilson nodded back at his partner, then looked at Dani. "You're not giving us anything," he said.

Dani just stared at him. Now she wasn't just getting annoyed, she was angry. Was this guy just dense, or was he fishing for something in particular?

Wilson said, "You expect us to believe this man, Maguire— Dr. Jonathan Maguire, a senior research biologist at Pharma— comes in here dying with a knife wound in his back to speak to you or give you something, and you don't know him?"

"I don't expect anything. You asked me what happened, and I'm telling you."

"Why did he come here?"

"I told you. I've been calling about an interview, and he wanted to meet me first."

"That's all?"

Now Dani decided she didn't want to tell Wilson she believed maybe there was something more on Maguire's mind than that. She shrugged.

Wilson said, "Who set up the meeting?"

"He did."

"Who introduced you? You obviously had a reason to talk to him, and you didn't call him out of the blue."

How the hell did this man know who called who, or anything?
"I was introduced through a friend of his. John McCloskey."

"That KellerDorne guy? The whistleblower?"

Now this was getting weird. It dawned on her that it was strange that the FBI was probing her about Dr. Maguire even before the homicide cops showed up. And this guy, Wilson, knew who John McCloskey was with no prompting. Not exactly a household name. And how did he refer to Maguire? A research analyst at Pharma. How would he know that? Something didn't add up.

Then Wilson said, "What did he give you?"

She leveled her eyes at him. No way she was telling. "Nothing."

At that moment two more men in suits appeared at the top of the stairs, followed by six or eight more, some with bulky cases, some uniformed cops. Wilson nodded to his partner, turned and said, "She's all yours fellas. We're done here." And they left.

The two suits who just arrived looked at each other like they were confused. Then they turned their backs to Dani and spoke to each other in hushed tones. They motioned the uniformed cop, the one who arrived first, over to them and spoke for a few moments. Yes, something really odd was going on. She got the idea that these cops had no clue who the FBI guys were, or why they were here. If they really were FBI.

She put her hand into her blazer pocket and felt the USB memory stick. It had to be why Maguire wanted to see her. And now she remembered that he said something to her. Something about "being on the right side." She eyed the men talking to each other in front of her and decided that until she figured out what was going on, she'd keep her mouth shut about it.

CPSIA information can be obtained at www.ICGtesting.com
Printed in the USA
241599LV00005BA/15/P